## Also by Natalie D. Richards

Six Months Later

Gone Too Far

## Praise for *Gone Too Far*

"Richards delivers a gripping whodunit with a challenging ethical dilemma at its center… Richards maintains a quick pace and creates enough red herrings to keep readers guessing."

—*Publishers Weekly*

"Plenty of drama, mystery…a thoughtful exploration of social justice in high school."

—*Booklist*

## Praise for *Six Months Later*

"An intriguing story line…readers will be drawn into the mystery of what happened to Chloe and will never guess the ending."

—*VOYA*

"The story is well paced and beautifully written, with fully developed characters teens can easily relate to. This romantic thriller will leave readers on the edge of their seats until the very last page."

—*School Library Journal*

"An intense psychological mystery… Richards constructs Chloe's fear, paranoia, and scheming with great care. Her novel has the feel of a high-stakes poker game in which every player has something to hide, and the cards are held until the very end."

—*Publishers Weekly*

# More praise for *Six Months Later*

"The pressure and angst of precollege life, perfect grades, and test scores take center stage in this debut thriller. Readers are thrown right into the mystery alongside Chloe, and as the plot is slowly uncovered, the suspense rises to a shocking crescendo of events. Chloe is an intriguing character with plenty of gumption, and she makes for a splendid amateur detective... With several twists and surprises, this is a well-plotted mystery, sure to keep readers guessing."

—*Booklist*

"Confusion and a desperate search for answers drive the action in this captivating thriller... As the mystery builds, so do the stakes and the romantic tension."

—*RT Book Reviews*, 4 stars

# MY SECRET TO TELL

### NATALIE D. RICHARDS

sourcebooks
fire

Published by Sourcebooks Fire, an imprint of Sourcebooks, Inc.
P.O. Box 4410, Naperville, Illinois 60567–4410
(630) 961–3900
Fax: (630) 961–2168
www.sourcebooks.com

Library of Congress Cataloging-in-Publication data is on file with the publisher.

Printed and bound in United States of America.
VP 10 9 8 7 6 5 4 3 2 1

*To Romily*
*Above and beyond doesn't even come close*

# PROLOGUE

• • • • • • • • • • • • • • • • • • • • • • • • • • •

Emmie?"

My name lands somewhere between a hiccup and a sob, and my feet stall out on the sidewalk in front of my house. I adjust my grip on the phone, hoping I misheard her tone. This doesn't sound like Chelsea. This voice is breathless. Frightened.

"I'm here," I say. "What's up? You don't sound right."

"I'm not." She takes a shuddery breath.

My shirt's sticking to my back and cicadas are click-buzzing the end of another blistering day, but I go cold. Something's wrong. Wrong, wrong, wrong.

"It's my dad, Emmie," she says. I can tell she's crying.

I grab my chest. It's too tight. Burning. "What happened?"

Her words all tumble out on top of one another, interrupted by shaky breaths. I try to pick out pieces that make sense. "He's hurt—bleeding—we're behind the ambulance and I can't—he's not—someone attacked him."

I start climbing the porch steps, because she'll need me. I'm her best friend, so I should be there. I need to change clothes and go. "You're on the way to the hospital, right? They'll help him there."

Another sharp breath. "I don't know if they can. He's so bad. *So* bad."

My heart clenches. "Where are you?"

"We're almost there. Joel's with me."

"Okay, good. I'm coming," I say, crossing my porch and hauling my front door open. "Let me just call Mom. I'll borrow the car."

Chelsea's still crying when I storm down the hallway toward my bedroom. "Emmie, I can't find Deacon…"

"Your brother never answers his phone," I say, pushing open my door. "I'll run by the docks first and—"

"No. No, he was there. He was at the house."

Chelsea makes a strangled sound, and I notice the liquid-thick heat in my bedroom. The kind of heat that tells me the air conditioner is broken. Or my window is open.

My gaze drags to my fluttering white curtains, to the dark smudge on the windowsill.

Chelsea's voice goes low and raspy. "He ran, Emmie. God, he was there with Dad. He was in the house, but he *ran*."

I swivel with an invisible fist lodged in my throat. My bathroom door is open, a red-black smudge beneath the knob.

My mouth goes dry, my pulse thumping slower than it should. Then I see the blood on the floor by my sink, and my heart tumbles end over end.

"We're here. I'll call soon," Chelsea says and hangs up.

I see him, his back to my tub and his dark head bowed on one bent knee. Oh God.

He's covered in blood. It's on his legs, his hands. Dripping onto my white tile floor. He looks up, and my heart goes strangely steady.

I take a breath that tastes like purpose.

"Deacon?"

# CHAPTER ONE

. . . . . . . . . . . . . . . . . . . . . . . . . . . .

Eight Hours Earlier

Where is my green pen? I check my inbox basket again, but it's not there. Everything is as it should be. Phone on the right corner. Laptop dead center. A single inbox on the left, and a phone message pad—a relic from some prehistoric time—in front of me. No green pen though.

I slide open the meticulously organized drawer, moving a pencil that's shifted. Everything's arranged like a box of chocolates. Rubber bands, paper clips, and extra staples in tidy heaps. My pens are lined up: blue, black, empty space, highlighter. I chew my lip and try to reach for the blue pen, because who really cares about ink color?

Me, that's who.

I stand up and sit right back down. Check under the desk, under my rolling chair.

Then I stand up again, hands sweaty. Joel's leather office chair creaks in the next room. He's leaning back. Probably trying to figure out why he extended this internship to a girl who's popping up and down like a jack-in-the-box. I plop down with a sigh.

Once upon a time, I was a normal person. I miss that.

"All right there?" Joel asks.

"Sure, I just…" Yeah, I just *what*? Lost my super special pen? Spiraled down the drain of a green ink fixation?

*As if that's my only fixation.*

I need to dial it back a notch. A lot of notches. Joel is *paying* me for this. More than that, he's giving me a recommendation letter for the dean of admissions at Duke. I can just imagine telling my parents this story. "Mom, Dad, I'm sorry I lost my job and might not ever go to law school, but I had no choice, because blue is for file notes. Black is for supply lists. Phone messages have to be green, see?"

They've already had one kid trash his future, so I grab the blue pen.

"Sorry, I'm good," I finally say. It's all breathy Southern charm, just like my mom. I button on a smile for good measure. "Lost a pen. It's nothing."

This would be easier if Joel would take advantage of the eleventy billion options cell phones and computers offer for relaying messages. Something I might say if he wasn't practically my best friend's uncle *and* the lawyer/manager/advisor of their family business.

My blue pen hovers over the paper, and I wince. Maybe one last check. Super quick. I crouch under my desk, patting around the floor under the drawers. Carpet, carpet, the paper clip I knew I was missing yesterday—

"You looking for this?"

I freeze, still on all fours, under the desk.

*That's not Joel.*

Dread rolls over me in a slow wave as I sit up, careful not to hit my head.

Yep, definitely not Joel. Too tan. Too sweaty. Too hot.

But every bit as familiar.

"Hey, Deacon," I say, taking the green pen from his fingers.

"Hey back."

I take a breath and look down, because I've learned it's best to avoid eye contact with my best friend's brother. For most girls, it's his looks—a hormonally lethal combo of Venezuelan coloring and boat-boy physique. He's eye candy for them, but he's something much more dangerous for me. Something a lot like gravity. Because being around him feels like falling. Every. Single. Time.

"Is everything okay?" I ask.

He nods. "One of the charter boats has a problem. It's no big deal, but we all know Dad can't tie his shoes unless he checks with Joel first." He pauses, his smile barely more than clenched teeth. "So here we are."

Holy family tension. Chelsea warned me it was ugly between them, but *wow*. Outside the window, his dad is waiting on the sidewalk, phone to his ear and the quiet residential street behind him. Deacon follows my gaze.

"Not getting along, huh?" I ask.

He smirks at me. "When do we ever get along?"

He leans over my desk. I catch a whiff and make an awful face.

Hot or not, this boy is fresh off the boat, and he smells like a dead fish wrapped in a sweaty T-shirt.

"That bad?" he asks, flashing Chelsea's smile at me.

"Worse." I glance briefly at his face where I can see a red-purple shadow down the side of his cheek. "Did you hit your head?"

He grins. "Took a corner too fast in Chelsea's car. Smacked my head into the door when I clipped the light pole. And before you even start, at least it wasn't my bike."

I drop the paper clip I'm still holding in the pile in my drawer, but I don't *start* anything. Why bother? Deacon's been creating his own personal version of *Fast & Furious* up and down the Carolina coast since he got his license two years ago. And he was a daredevil long before that. Ever since they lost their mom really. You've got to pick your battles with him.

"Hell, I do reek," he says.

"Reek might be too kind. I hope you're keeping the tourist girls at a distance." Not likely. "They'd probably dive off the boat if they got a whiff of you." Even less likely.

"I've got charms to make up for the stench," he says around one of those devil's grins he's famous for. "One of these days, you'll let me flirt with you long enough to find out."

"You're hysterical," I deadpan, ignoring the fire that's shooting up my neck. I uncap my green pen, focusing on the message for Joel.

*Call Mr. Trumbull about his overnight charter arrangement.*

I add a date and a time, though neither are necessary. It's a stall tactic so Deke doesn't see that I'm annoyed. I shouldn't be. He doesn't even know I'm into him. Still, we've been friends for forever. Seniority alone should exempt me from the flirty comments he tosses at a revolving door of dit-dotters (our local word for "tourist") from the Midwest. I'm not with him, but I'm not temporary either.

He plants his hand on my desk. He's going to leave fingerprints. "Hey, are you mad? I didn't mean to—"

"It's fine." I might have convinced him if I hadn't cut him off.

His hand slides forward, and I forget about the prints. My stomach wads up. Shrinks tight. The vanishing distance between our fingers pushes me closer to that invisible edge.

"Emmie." His tone is one I've never heard.

Joel's chair creaks, and Deacon's hand is gone. I let out a breath I didn't know I'd been holding. By the time I look up, Joel is beside me, shaking Deke's hand across my desk.

"Hey, Dink. Everything all right?"

He's Dink. I'm Eddie. Everyone who matters gets a Joel nickname. Deacon could have it worse. Chelsea is Chickadee, for God's sake. Their dad is *Daffy*.

They're talking about the boat now—something to do with a broken compartment, I think. It's all "storage" this and "hinges" that, but the only thing that interests me is the hateful look Deacon's shooting out the window. Mr. Westfield is still on the phone—probably a customer—but he looks worried. It's his business, so I get it, but Deacon's eyes might as well be slinging bullets.

Joel must notice too, because he catches Mr. Westfield's attention through the glass and gives him a wave and a smile. Then he points at Deacon and gives a thumbs-up, like Deke had the solution all figured out before he even walked inside. Which is probably the truth.

Joel puts a hand on Deacon's shoulder. "Before you know it, he's going to see what you're capable of, Dink."

He scoffs. "Doubtful. He's been unbelievable all morning. He's blaming this whole thing on Thorpe and Charlie. It's insane."

Joel laughs that makes-it-all-better laugh. It's a little too loud, but it works. "He just takes pride in the business. Let me get my keys and see if we can't smooth things over."

"I'll hang outside with the kraken." Deacon smirks and heads to the door, looking back at me before he leaves.

He and Chelsea have the kind of eyes that stop you in your tracks. Not green, not brown, but something way better than hazel. They make me think of old pennies and dark secrets. He doesn't speak, but he gives me a smile that curls like fire through my insides, and then he's gone.

He disappears on the porch stairs, but then I see him on the sidewalk with his dad. Joel bought one of the run-down cottages in the historic district for his office, so we don't have to deal with as much tourist traffic. There's no water to see, but it's quiet and convenient. We all live in this several block stretch, a section of old white houses with porch swings and well-tended flowerbeds. It's also as small-town as a place gets, so this fight the Westfields are having on the front sidewalk? Everyone will know about it by dinnertime.

Mr. Westfield adjusts his hat over graying blond hair and points at Deacon. The air conditioner is humming, so I can't hear what he says or how Deacon responds, but it's pretty obvious there are plenty of four-letter words involved. Deacon turns, face dark with rage, and then he's storming across the street.

"They're at it again," Joel says at the edge of my desk.

"Chelsea told me it's been bad." I grab Joel's arm. "Which reminds me, you're picking her up, right?"

"Oil change this evening. I've got it," he says, chuckling. "Aren't you headed to the shelter at two?"

"Yeah, but I can check the supply list first. Mr. Christopher's monthly weekend is coming up, and I want to make sure you have enough reels on board." I start wiping at a smudge on my desk. Deacon's doing, no doubt.

"Do it tomorrow," Joel says. "You're organizing this office to death, you know."

"Is it annoying?" I gnaw my lip and stop wiping. "It *is* annoying."

Joel's hand pats mine on the desk. "You're doing a lovely job, Eddie. But you can go easy." He glances outside with a sigh. "You kids all need to go a little easier."

"I wish Deke would go easy with his driving," I say, though Joel probably has more right to gripe about it. Being the lawyer, he's the one left to clean up the mess.

"That boy's got to let up on the throttle in more ways than one." He claps a hand on my shoulder and smiles. "But *you've* got to stop worrying."

"Oh, I know. No sense in worrying about things you can't change, right?" I add a smile, because this is my best lie. It's also the easiest, because it's the one I almost believe.

\* \* \*

"Seth and I were talking," Chelsea says midstride. "You came up."

She met me at the office to walk with me to the shelter. And now she's stirring the very tired pot of Seth drama, so she's obviously bored out of her mind.

"Are we really back on that? I stopped seeing him months ago."

"For no reason."

I scoff. "I had a reason."

"Uh-huh. And does that *reason* leave socks on my bathroom floor and a string of broken tourist hearts on the decks of our boats?"

Chelsea has a smile like bottled sunshine, but I shut it down with a glare. "It has nothing to do with Deke. Give me some credit."

"Okay, then why?"

The sun's beating hard enough to make my shoulders tight when I shrug. "He was getting attached, and I'm not ready for that."

"Oh sure. That'd be crazy. Future veterinarian. Honor roll. Great arms. Seth's *terrible* boyfriend material."

I step off the curb and smile at a mom with a double stroller before answering. "I'm not looking for boyfriend material, Chelsea. Why don't *you* date Seth?"

She ignores my barb and swirls her coffee, looking a little smug. "Your mom likes him, doesn't she?"

Good guess. I don't tell her she's right, but I don't need to. We fall in step again, and she turns with me toward the animal shelter, where practically a third of our high school volunteers.

Community service is required for graduation, and puppies beat out old people any day of the week.

It dies down over the summer, but Deacon, Seth, and I are still regulars. Community service with a heaping side of awkward. It was better when Chels was there too, but she quit the minute she met her required hours. Scooping poop isn't her thing.

Chelsea sighs. "Is that what it is with Deke? The fact that your mother would crack in half if anything happened between you two?"

"Doubtful. Mom was less crazy before my brother left, and I still had this…problem. Maybe I was dropped on my head as a small child."

She grins. "That would explain some things."

I laugh, but I'm thinking about Deacon being in the office. I can still see his fingers sliding forward on my desk. My whole body coiled up tight. Was it obvious? Did he notice?

"Hey, you haven't said anything to him, have you?" I ask. "Anything about me, I mean."

She wrinkles her nose. "No chance. I love my brother, but he doesn't deserve you. Aside from impromptu hookups with complete strangers—"

"Thanks for that."

"All I'm saying is Deke doesn't do relationships. Not really. Anything emotional and he just can't. Not since Mom."

"I know."

He can't do them, and Chelsea always wants one. Funny what the same grief can do to two different people.

13

She smacks my arm lightly. "Omigod, did I tell you? He wrecked my freaking car! I mean, it's not that bad, and I know it's a piece of crap, but it hasn't even been a week since his last ticket."

"I saw the bruise. He got a ticket at the wreck?"

"No, for speeding. Eighty-seven in a sixty-five. They might take his license."

We turn onto Queen Street, finally catching some shade. I bump her shoulder lightly. "A brother with no license is better than a brother wrapping your car around a tree."

"Or one who hits the highway one night because he can't take it anymore." Chelsea catches herself fast, grabbing my shoulder. "Oh God, I didn't—I wasn't thinking about—"

She wasn't thinking about Landon. *My* brother. The former prince of Beaufort who left for Duke with a golden cardiologist future only to crash and burn nine months into his freshman year. Good-bye, college. Hello, shattered parents.

"It's okay," I finally say, though it's not. Talk to my parents for two seconds if you want to see how not-okay Landon's "I need time to find myself" disappearing act is. They need to get over it, but it's not like they have much chance with him never being here.

"I can't believe I said that," Chelsea says, misreading my quiet for anger. "I'm so worried about Deke, I'm being stupid. I'm sorry."

I shrug. "You're just scared for your brother."

"Yeah," Chelsea says, slowing by the shelter. "I'm scared I'm going to lose him too."

Before her mom died, before Landon, maybe I would have told her that would never happen, but I know better now. Sometimes we do lose people. As bad as I want to reassure her, I know enough to keep my mouth shut and let her be afraid.

"You gotta get in there," she says. "Give my brother hell for that ticket."

"Call me tonight when you're done?"

Her slim brows pull together. "Done with what?"

"Oil change? Joel's picking you up at the repair shop at seven thirty."

"Oh crap, that's right."

"Chelsea, you have *got* to get more organized."

"What for? I have you for that." She sticks out her tongue and waves.

Deacon wasn't scheduled for this afternoon, but Chelsea was right about him being here. I spot his motorcycle in the back lot. Figures. He's always good for an extra shift when he's fighting with his dad. Or when a dit-dotter from the Midwest gets too clingy.

I step inside and straighten the volunteer time sheets before I write myself in. Deacon's the only volunteer I know who kept working after graduation, but it's no shock. He and I have always been animal people. When we were in preschool, we constantly set up a veterinarian station on the picnic table in my backyard. We never had Band-Aids at my house, because they were all on Chelsea's stuffed animals, especially the turtles. They've always been my favorite.

I pass through a tiled hallway with rows of cat cages and the smell of fresh litter heavy in the air. There's an "Adopted" sticker on Chester's empty cage. I smile and take his old heart-shaped name tag before I head into the prep room. Deke's not here either, which means he's in the dog zone.

I find him with Rocky, a ninety-pound Rottie mix miss-ing half an ear. He's a special-needs adoption, a deaf senior with that *scary-dog* look that keeps families walking. We keep him in the back on busy days, because too many squealing four-year-olds wear him out. Deacon's sitting on the floor, rubbing Rocky's shoulders—they get a little stiff sometimes and the massage seems to help. Rocky noses at the pockets of his faded jeans.

"Nothing left in my pockets, Rock," he says, switching to scratch his ears.

Nothing left, but I'm sure that dog's had a few smuggled shrimp from the boat today. Deacon always brings him something. And I always go soft at the edges when I see it.

"Twice in one day. Lucky me," Deacon says. He's got an uncanny knack for sensing people behind him. Made water balloon fights a real pain over the years.

"Did you hear the bad news?" he asks. "Dr. Atwood had to rescue a stray today."

"How is that bad?"

"Well, you didn't get to do it yourself." He turns to smirk at me, and my insides do annoying fluttery things. "You're one rescue away from a spandex outfit and a catchy name."

"Yeah, well, Chelsea thinks we're both going to get bitten and catch rabies."

"Her paranoia is dependable. Remember when you went up that tree for the cat?"

My breath stutters at the memory. "How could I forget?"

Deacon chuckles. "Chels was screeching like a banshee. She kept punching my arm, telling me to call the fire department."

He didn't though. He scolded her instead, telling her I was perfectly capable of climbing that tree. And then—the part I remember best—his hands touched my waist when I hopped down and stumbled. It was the briefest touch, just a graze to steady me on my feet, but I was a fourteen-year old with a crush, and that half second is burned into my memory like a tattoo.

"You still going to climb trees and save mongrels when you're a fat cat lawyer like Joel?"

I sigh. "You're really not going to let this go, are you?"

"I just never thought the law thing would stick. You've always been an animal lover. You were going to save sea turtles, remember? You'd walk around with that damn lunchbox full of gauze and tape, looking for injured crabs. What did you call that thing again?"

"The coastal critter kit." I grit my teeth, trying to bite back my irritation. "There are practically zero jobs in marine biology. It's not sensible."

"You could be a vet. There's money in that."

"There are already plenty of vets in Beaufort," I say. It's true, but it's not the real reason. But how do I explain that it's not about money? My mom's family is a sea of medical practices and law firms. It's a legacy thing, and since the disappointing child slot in my family is full, it's my job to fill the role.

"Hey, I didn't mean to rile you up." Deacon's voice is low and tender.

He doesn't mean to do a lot of things to me, but he does them all the same. I reach for paper towels and a subject change.

"I'm surprised you're here," I say. "Don't you have an issue on one of the boats?"

"I have an issue with my Dad riding the guys' asses like a jockey." Venom is injected in every word. "Figured I'd rather check on my favorite boy than deal with him anymore today." He leads Rocky back to his cage and latches the door with a reluctant sigh.

"He needs you, you know," I say. "You're talented with the mechanical stuff."

"According to Dad, my *talent* is looking pretty for girls who might buy tickets."

True, but he's being a mule. I should say something about the ticket and the constant fighting. About the way he's trashing his future a little harder every year. I chicken out and wipe down an empty cage that I already disinfected two days ago.

"You've got that look, Emmie." Out of nowhere, he's right behind my shoulder. His arm brushes mine. "You're biting your tongue, aren't you?"

I laugh softly. "So hard that blood's about to shoot out of my ears."

I turn to look at him. The air hums like power lines between us.

"Go on and say it," he says.

"Say what? What *can* I say?"

"Something," he says, voice softer, eyes cast down. "Hell, *anything*. You've known me forever, haven't you?"

Our sleeves are touching. People don't stand this close...I don't think. I don't know what this is. I've got a handful of cards, but I'm not sure what game we're playing.

I swallow hard. "I've known you long enough to remember

when you weren't so angry. When Chelsea and I didn't sit around worried sick about what crazy thing you'll do next."

He arches a brow. "Maybe you two need to get lives."

"Maybe you need to be a little more careful with *your* life."

His face twists into a scowl. "Like you, right, Emmie? Crossing every *T* and dotting every *I*."

My cheeks go hot. I don't know how this became a fight, but his face is red and my jaw is so tight, my teeth hurt.

He runs a hand over his hair and steps forward. Like he's going to reach for me. Touch me maybe. "Emmie, I'm sor—"

The door bangs open, sending all of the dogs into a barking frenzy. Deacon springs back in time for me to see cargo shorts, battered sneakers, and a stack of dog food bags coming through the door.

Seth French. Incoming senior like me. Half-assed sprinter on the track team and my not-quite-but-almost boyfriend last winter.

He drops the bags, and Deacon slinks away, palming his keys off a storage cabinet. The unspoken things hanging in this room make it hard to breathe, but Seth doesn't notice. He just adjusts his baseball hat over his dirty-blond hair and winks at me.

"Well, if I'd known you were going to be here, I'd have come earlier." His gaze shifts to Deacon. "Hey, man."

Deacon barely glances at him. "Hey."

Ah, our little awkward triangle of doom. I'm crazy about Deacon, Seth's crazy about me, and Deacon's just crazy.

Fantastic.

"So, Sunday night," Seth starts, flashing me his smile. It's not a bad smile. Charmed me once upon a time, as Mom constantly reminds me. "Let's go get burgers."

"Burgers?"

"Yeah, burgers. Maybe some fries. If we're feeling really wild, we could even commit to coffee at the Cru afterward. We used to do that. It wasn't so bad."

I grin. Seth brings that out in people. He's easy. Goofy. The kind of guy any girl should fall for. My mother fell for an easy, goofy guy. I flinch.

*And that worked out oh so well in the end, didn't it?*

"Have I convinced you?" Seth asks.

I like Seth. I don't want to not be friends because I don't see happily ever after every time he looks at me. Maybe dinner would be a good way to clear the air. Set things straight.

"Help me clean out the darn cages and we'll talk about it," I say. I'm about to clarify that this is not a date, but then I see Deacon waiting at the door.

He's checking his phone, but I know him. He doesn't care about his phone. He's watching this, and I don't like it. Maybe he thinks he has the right to know my business too, but he doesn't. I don't butt into his exploits on the boats, and he doesn't have an all-access pass to my universe either.

I shoot him a glare, and he heads out, the door clanging shut behind him.

"So I'll take it this Sunday won't be a date," Seth says with a meaningful look at the door Deacon just exited.

I've got to give him credit. He's not as oblivious as I figured.

I snatch another paper towel from a roll and fold it in half. Scrub at a perfectly clean spot on the counter. "I'm not dating Deacon, Seth."

"No, but you've got that weird *something* vibe going on. It's fine. I got the message when you cooled off last winter."

I quirk a brow at him. "Then why do you keep asking me out all the time?"

"I don't know. I like seeing you flustered? It's a small town?" I make a sound somewhere between bewildered and outraged, and Seth laughs. "I do like you, Emmie. Friends is fine. Really."

I soften. "Are you sure? If we go Sunday, it won't give you the wrong idea?"

"It's all good, I promise."

"Then Sunday it is."

Even after all day playing with dogs and mindlessly scrubbing cages, I'm still mad at Deacon on the walk home. The heat isn't helping. The sun is low in the sky, but the wind feels too heavy and moist. It's like walking through soup. I'm ready for air-conditioning. And a gallon of iced tea. My phone rings in my pocket, and I pull it out, grateful to see Chelsea's name.

Maybe she can explain why her brother is being a complete tool.

I bring the phone to my ear and say hello. I can tell by the way she takes a breath—ragged and shaky—that something isn't right.

# CHAPTER TWO

· · · · · · · · · · · · · · · · · · · · · · · · · · · · · ·

Present

I pocket my phone and crouch on my bathroom floor, careful because he's shaking. Shaking *so bad*. He's been crying too. Tear tracks on his cheeks make my fingers itch. Our earlier fight is gone. There's no irritation. Nothing but Deacon covered in blood and terrified into silence.

"Okay." I'm quiet and still. "I'm here."

I don't ask what happened. It's obvious he tried to help his dad—God, I can't even imagine what that did to him. How he even got here. Chelsea will know the details, and she'll fill me in later. For now, I have to get him back together. No one else really knows how bad he gets. Joel and his dad have noticed, but Chels and I are the ones who track him down. We clean up his scraped elbows and busted lips, and we have for years.

I feather a finger over the side of his hand, and he flinches.

"Hey," I say. "This isn't our first rodeo, right?"

He doesn't meet my eyes or respond. Just sits there, trembling on my once-white tile.

I spot a bobby pin on the floor, pick it up, and drop it on the side of the tub. It tinks against the ceramic—the only sound between us.

"I'm going to clean you up," I say. "Then we'll talk."

He looks at me with those eyes that steal my breath, even now, but he doesn't speak. I don't know what Deacon saw when he found his mom in the bathroom all those years ago, but this blood thing is one of the scars it left.

I grab the first aid kit and some makeup wipes. There's nothing but the drip of the bathtub and the sound of me breathing—fast, because Deacon's staring now. I'm always nervous when he's watching me.

I clean his hands first. Most of the blood is on his palms. Did he have to put pressure on a wound? It's…a lot. I clean from wrists to fingertips, using a makeup wipe to get the worst off. Everything's pink-brown-red, but it doesn't matter. It needs to be done.

Next, I move on to the sterile wipes inside the kit. He's mostly uninjured, but two of his knuckles are puffy and split, like he hit something. My stomach pulls tight looking at those knuckles. Did he fight back?

I'll ask when I'm done. I clean up his legs, his shoes, the floor. I'm careful not to miss a speck. His knuckles are the only injury I find, not counting the old bruise on his face.

I pull out the antibacterial cream and squirt some on a cotton swab before I take his hand. He looks away, and it's just like every other time I've done this.

It happened first six years ago. I was ten. He was eleven. Scraped his elbow in a bike wreck. It was six months after his mom died. Lots of kids freak over blood, but this was crazy. Back then, I didn't know how it all tied together with his mom. I just knew he needed help and he was scared.

He was really embarrassed, so Chels and I promised to keep his secret. It was just a quirk in our eyes. Chelsea's allergic to eggs. The color yellow gives me a headache. Deacon goes catatonic at the sight of blood.

Two Band-Aids later and the knuckles are good. I place all the trash in the can and cover it with toilet paper folded into a neat square. Then I spot brown-red splotches on his shirt.

I go to my room to find something else for him to wear. My hands are shaking as I flip through the T-shirts, finally settling on a Pirate Invasion freebie from two years ago. Back in the bathroom, he's still in the same position, but his eyes and fists are clenched tight. Neither of us has said a word since I started cleaning him up. That had to have been half an hour ago. The clock reads eight forty-five, and my stomach drops away.

*Mom.*

She'll be leaving work soon. I look around, a little frantic, grabbing wet wipes from my end table to clean the windowsill, the smear beneath the doorknob. Have I been careful enough? Because if Mom finds him here, if she sees this blood, she's going to assume Deacon did something awful.

I pause, taking a breath. Am I sure he didn't? Banged-up knuckles and bloody clothes don't look too goo—*Stop. You need to stop.* This is Deacon. He's a lot of things, but violent isn't on the list.

"Deke, we need to get rid of that," I say, pointing at his shirt.

I offer my replacement, and he just blinks. I'm not sure he heard me—I never know when he's like this—but then he tugs his shirt off in this easy, over-the-back-of-the-head motion.

I've seen him shirtless countless times but never in my bathroom. Deacon's worked on a boat after school and on weekends since he was a kid. Every inch of him is ultra-cut and ultra-tan, and screwed-up timing or not, I notice. I'd have to be blind to not notice. Still, I avert my eyes and fold his T-shirt neatly until it's the size of a napkin. I drop it in the trash on top of everything else and tie the bag. Trash day tomorrow, so there will be nothing for Mom to see.

But tying the bag brings my own questions. If Deacon cleaned up the blood—even if he tried—why isn't he at the hospital? Why is he here?

My mind flashes back to the argument outside Joel's office, the dark looks he shot his father. I take a step back, and pain blooms in Deacon's eyes. Not just pain. *Hurt.*

"I didn't do it, Emmie," he says, voice rough.

"I didn't say that."

"You didn't have to." His sigh is a shudder. "I *couldn't.* You know that."

I *do* know that, but I also know what I'm looking at. Something happened with him at that house. I just don't know details. Interrogation will have to wait though. He needs to get out of here and to the hospital with Chelsea. Right now.

"I have to go," he says.

"Good. Right. I'll find out what room your dad's in." I go for my phone to text Chelsea.

He roughs his dark hair up with his fingers. "I can't go to the hospital."

Fear moves in, cold and slithering in my belly, those bandages on his knuckles looking more sinister by the second. "You said you didn't do this."

"I didn't."

"Then you need to go. It's your *dad*. Chelsea's alone in there."

He shakes his head. "Joel's with her. He's better at this kind of thing."

"Joel isn't *you*, Deke. You're her brother."

He paces another lap in front of my sink, and every breath comes faster and sharper for both of us. Everything I've ever known about Deacon is weighing against everything I'm seeing. I'm not sure I like the way the scale is tipping.

Because he looks like he's guilty of something.

"Don't look at me like that," he says, voice as raw as I've ever heard it.

"Like what?"

"Like you're afraid of me. I can't stand seeing you afraid."

But I *am* afraid. Afraid of him? For him? I don't even know. Deke's the saver of spiders. Rescuer of cats stuck in porches. He doesn't hurt people. Not ever.

*So act like it!*

I force myself to touch his arm. It's like grazing a live wire. We both go still.

"Just tell me what happened," I say. "*Reader's Digest* version."

His face crumples up, and then I hear the unmistakable crunch of tires in the driveway.

*Mom.*

Deacon's face goes hard, and he eyes the door, the window, and then me. I've known him long enough to get the look in his eyes. He doesn't want her to find him here.

That makes two of us.

I flinch when Mom's engine shuts off. The car door wrenches open and then closed. She's on the back steps, and I still have so many questions he doesn't have time to answer.

Deacon moves to my bathroom window, and I help him with the old, fiddly locks. It scrapes and grunts. We get it halfway open before it thunks to a stop. There's almost but not quite enough space for him to get out.

He grips the frame. Pushes hard, but it's good and stuck.

The back door jangles—the owl wind chime I made in fifth grade singing out my mom's arrival.

"Emmie? Sugar?" Her voice is both faraway and right next to me.

I open my mouth and find a tone that isn't blatant terror. "Just a minute!"

I flush the toilet and turn on the water to buy some time. Then I take Deacon's hand and drag him into my bedroom. I trip over my slippers, and Deke tugs my curtains aside. He's halfway out, the glow from the streetlights catching across his face. Half angel and half demon. That's how he looks when he reaches for me.

I hold my breath, wondering if I should say something. Call for my mom. Turn him in. But, God, it's *Deacon*! There has to be an explanation for this.

"Please believe me, Emmie. Please."

I want to answer, but I don't. I brace my hands on my open window frame and watch him escape into the night.

\* \* \*

Hospitals have a smell that gives me the creeps. It's not just the industrial cleaners or the faint whiff of bodily fluids that can't be washed away. It's a scent that seems to drift up from the linoleum floors and out of the pale yellow walls.

A carefully coded message crackles through the intercom, and I grip my shopping bag from the drugstore a little tighter. Two new nail polishes and a stack of magazines. We bought them this morning before coming in. Mom held off opening her antiques store. Wednesdays bring a lot of midweek "we've had enough of the beach" tourists, so this is a major deal.

Mom hustles beside me, arm linked with mine as we head past the vested volunteers and easy listening music in the lobby.

"Are you sure you don't want to do flowers too?" Mom asks. "We could grab some from the gift shop."

"I don't think they can have flowers in ICU," I say. I'm not sure if it's still true, but we had an ICU nurse at the high school on career day. She said it's highly restricted. People in the ICU are on the edge of life and death, and every tiny thing can upset that balancing act.

With that in mind, I probably shouldn't be worried about flowers. I should be worried about how Deacon affects that balance. I didn't tell anyone he came to me. Not my mom or even Chelsea, though I tried to text her twice. God, I just hope that's the right choice.

Mom squeezes my arm. "Well, I love your ideas with the polish and magazines."

The elevator on the left gives a soft *bing* as we approach. A thin man with dark circles under his eyes and a pack of Winstons wheels an IV behind him as he heads for the lobby. Presumably for a smoke break he could probably do without.

Inside, I press the button for the fourth floor, and the doors swish closed. The elevator lifts, and my stomach drops away. Chelsea's dad is in the ICU, hooked up to machines, fighting for every breath. I think of my dad. Bristly beard and flannel shirts in the winter. What if my dad were in here?

I jerk when the doors open. We're right at the edge of the waiting room. I hear the soft warble of more announcements over the intercom, the tinny murmur of a television in the corner. A haggard woman sleeps fitfully in an uncomfortable-looking chair. My stomach bunches up. I want to leave.

But I need to stay.

We step off, and Mom touches my shoulder. "Emmie, you don't have to do this. You can wait downstairs, and I can take this to them."

"I need to be here for Chelsea." I smile at her. "That's the way you raised me, right?"

Mom lifts her chin, touches my cheek. We walk into the waiting room, and Mom speaks with the nurse at the information desk while I resist the urge to straighten a painting of flowers.

"They're visiting with him now, but I'll let them know you're here," the nurse says.

They? They meaning Chelsea and Deacon? A smile flutters across my lips. God, I hope so. If he's here, everything is okay.

Mom returns and repeats what I just heard. I nod, and we take a seat on two cushioned chairs. I try to ignore the woman who wakes up to take a call, where she tearfully relays information about failing kidneys and not much time.

I smooth the plastic bag and try to look around. There's not much to see. A coffee station. Boxes of tissues. Racks filled to bursting with untouched magazines. I tighten my grip on my own bag, suddenly feeling uncertain.

Maybe this is a terrible idea. Nail polish feels childish in here. My chest constricts. I should have done something better, something she might actually—

The heavy door that leads into the ICU opens, and I stand up. There's Joel, tall with his shock of white hair and the bluest eyes I've ever seen. Those eyes are sad today.

He's got his arm around Chelsea. She's still got a scab on her knee, and that cuts right through me. It happened last week when she tripped off a curb, texting. Her dad had laughed about it when we stopped by the dockside office. Last week, he was laughing, and today, he's in here, fighting for his life.

She lifts a tissue to her face, and Joel squeezes her in, kisses the top of her head, and says something I can't hear. It must be about me, because Chelsea looks up. I drop the bag and cross the room, and we wind up tangled in a hug somewhere between the chairs and the nurse's station.

Her sobs bring my own. It's been that way since forever.

"You came," she says into my hair.

"Of course I came. I wanted to come last night."

She leans away from me and wipes her swollen eyes. I find her a fresh tissue and push her hair back behind her shoulders.

She gives me a weak smile. "Always the mother hen."

"Can't help it."

"I'm glad you're here."

I look over to where Joel's nodding with my mom, filling her in on details, I'm sure. I don't see Deacon. I don't think he's here, or Chelsea would say something.

Everything that happened swings back at me like a sledgehammer. The blood on his hands. The fear in his eyes. What did I clean up in my bathroom?

I can't think about that now. My focus and my worry shift to Chelsea. Her lips are chapped, and she looks tired. Even her signature diamond studs—a sweet sixteen gift from Joel—lack their usual sparkle.

"Have you slept?" I ask.

"No."

"Eaten?"

She shrugs, and I take her arm gently. "Come on. Let me get you a little something."

She stalls, and Joel walks over. He winks at me and pulls a long arm around both of us. "I knew if someone could get you to eat, it'd be this one. We're real glad you're here, Eddie."

I can count on Joel for three things: smelling nice, wearing gray suits, and talking people into things in the nicest way possible. Lawyer trick, he always tells me.

"I'm going to stop by your office today," I say, feeling a swell of gratitude.

"Oh, you don't have to do that," he says.

"No, it's no problem at all. I'll pick up the mail and get all your messages. I'll bring them to you here so you don't have to worry about them. I'll even get the time sheets."

"I admit, that'd be wonderful. But…" He trails off, always worried to overwork me.

I put my hand on his sleeve. "Joel, there's so little I can do. I know you and Mr. Westfield are friends. You should be able to be here."

Chelsea needs an adult she can trust. She needs someone strong enough to handle this.

"If you're absolutely sure," he says.

I grin. "Positive."

After that, I take Chelsea downstairs to the cafeteria. She follows me through the line, glassy-eyed and stumbling as I load her tray with everything I think she might consider eating. We sit down at a quiet table away from the TVs, and after she takes a few bites, I decide it's safe to ask about Deacon.

"Has Deke been here? I tried to text you."

"Sorry, I had to turn off my phone in the room." She puts

down her spoon with a frown. "He hasn't. He was there when it happened, I think. I was still getting stuff out of the car. Joel went in first and found Dad. He saw Deacon leave. Said he looked panicked."

"He was. He came to my house. I helped him get cleaned up. It looked like…" I don't want to tell her what it looked like, because it will scare her. "I think he tried to help your dad."

She looks up, shock and fresh tears glimmering in her eyes. Then she swallows. Nods. "That's what I thought. Thank you for being there for him. Where is he?"

I sag. "He said he couldn't come. He seems totally flipped out—worse than I'd ever seen him—but it was a lot of blood. I figured you'd know what was going on."

"But I don't." She squeezes her hands together so hard I can see her knuckles go white. She's scared. "I know he freaked. You know how he—"

"I know."

Chelsea shakes her head. "I didn't see much because Joel tried to keep me out, but I saw a little. It was bad…" She trails off, lost in the ugly memory. "I get that he ran. I know how he is, but where is he? I need him here. It's our dad. Our *dad*! How can he not be here?"

"Chels." I cover her hand with mine, desperate to calm the pain. She's shaking. It feels like it's coming from the inside out. A dull ache wads up beneath my ribs. "What can I do for you? How can I help?"

"You're letting Joel stay. That helps." She pushes a spoon

through her yogurt, a furrow creasing the space between her brows. When she speaks, her voice is pipsqueak soft. "Do you think he did this too?"

She means Deacon. I don't have to ask to be sure. I blow out a slow sigh and straighten her napkin. Brush a stray crumb off the table.

"No," I finally say, and most of me believes it. But then I frown. "Why did you add the 'too'? Are people accusing him?"

"Lots of people, I think," she says. "Maybe even Joel."

"Everything in me says no," I say. "Deke is a lot of screwed-up things."

"But not *this* kind of thing. I know." Chelsea looks relieved. "He's never hurt anyone."

"He doesn't step on spiders," I add. Then I sigh. "But he's not helping his case by acting so weird."

She closes her gold-green eyes. "He shouldn't have run at all. Now he's probably worried sick that Joel thinks he's guilty, but who could blame him? It looks bad."

"Yeah, it does."

She bites her lip and sniffs. "He isn't answering his calls, Emmie. I'm…I want my brother. I want him here. I'm scared."

I squeeze her fingers and square my shoulders. "Then that's something I can do. I'll find him for you."

# CHAPTER THREE

. . . . . . . . . . . . . . . . . . . . . . . . . . . . .

I straighten Joel's stapler and step away from the desk, careful to stay in the one strip of plush beige carpet I haven't swept. Then I back my way out, vacuuming through the front office until I'm coiling the cord and putting everything back in the cleaning closet.

*Okay, what did I miss?*

Mail is opened and sorted. Messages are in my purse. Just need to go pick up time sheets from the docks and I'm good. I breathe in the smell of lemony wood polish. Better. Clean is always better.

On my way out, the phone rings. I frown at my pretty vacuum stripes, but the trilling of the ringer bugs me like lint on a sweater, so I make my way across them as carefully as I can.

It's the second line blinking, so it's a Westfield Charters call. "Westfield Charters, this is Emmie speaking."

"Yes, I need to speak with Joel."

"I'm sorry, he's out of the office right now."

"Well, that's a real pity."

I don't know his voice, but he sounds rich. Joel arranges the charters for the high-profile Westfield clients, and they've all got the same decadent-as-velvet voice. Like even the words they use cost twice as much as mine.

"This is Mr. Trumbull," he continues.

"Yes, of course. Is there anything I can help you with?"

"You can get me in touch with Joel," he says. "I have arrangements for later this week, and I'm sure old Joel wouldn't want to lose my business to someone more *available*."

I cringe at the sugary edge to his threat but force a smile into my voice. "I know we have you in the books, and I'm sure Joel will be happy to speak with you. He's in a bad reception area, but I'll see him this evening. Will that work?"

His pause is long enough to make it clear it won't work. But before I can change my offer, he's back, crisp and polite. "By tonight then. I have your word, Emmie?"

"Absolutely."

The sunshine outside thaws me from the frosty call. I take the long way to the waterfront, heading past the maritime museum. July is tourist season, so the boardwalk is thick with sticky-looking families and well-dressed yacht folks with shopping bags looped up their arms. I spot a couple of Mom's bags, which is good. Money seems tight lately.

Past the shops, the docks stretch along Taylor's Creek. I can see the tall grass on Carrot Island and past that the sound. The Atlantic is somewhere beyond all that—always hard to tell where the sound ends and the sea begins.

The harbor is crowded today, sprawling white yachts nudged in close to skiffs and slim sailboats. The pedestrian traffic isn't much better. I spot the line of tourists waiting at Westfield Charters, most of them fanning themselves with the color brochures. In the tiny dockside office, I find Charlie, a weathered redhead with a scruffy beard.

"Hey, Charlie, can you hand me the time sheets? I'm taking them to Joel."

"Sure thing, sweet pea," he says. He hands them over with a smile and moves on to the next customer quickly. Too busy for chitchat, so they must have a boat leaving soon.

I scan the time sheets for Deacon's name while I walk around the opposite side of the office, hoping for a break from the crowd. A black line is crossed through the week by Deacon's name. So he marked himself off? Quit? Or did somebody just get sloppy with a pen?

I bump past someone and look up to find friendly eyes, a neat moustache, and a badge.

"I'm so sorry," I say, holding up my hands.

"No problem, miss."

The police officer—P. Nelson, according to the name tag I practically rubbed off his shirt—moves past me, the radio on his belt chirping. He's got a partner in tow, blond and older. Both are pleasant but forgettable by most standards, but a pang stabs at my gut. They're walking toward the Westfield office. They're here about what happened to Chelsea's dad.

I swallow hard against the lump swelling in my throat as they disappear. Seconds later, they're back with Charlie, who whistles with two fingers in his mouth, waving someone in from the boat.

The guy who joins them would make my mother cross to the opposite side of the street. He's large, tattooed, sweating heavily enough to leave dark stains down the gray sides of his Westfield Charters T-shirt.

A shiver rides up my spine. Maybe I should tell someone this is going on. It could affect business, create rumors. They don't need that. *Someone* should know.

I'm halfway through dialing Joel's number when I hear them talking. My fingers hesitate and my ears strain. A group of kids passes between us, and I will them to move faster. I probably shouldn't be trying to listen. Okay, I definitely shouldn't be listening. But I want to know. If they arrest this scary guy, then Deke can breathe easy. I can bring him to the hospital, and Chelsea will be able to get some rest.

I can tell right away Nelson is fishing for something. He gestures at the bigger guy's hands. Even from here, I can see the right one is discolored. Bruised maybe. My heart squeezes out an extra beat seeing that. I can't be sure, but it looks much worse than Deacon's hands.

"Looks like you're a little busted up," Officer Nelson says. "Care to tell me how that happened?"

"Fishing's a rough business."

Nelson doesn't look convinced. "Is it now? Where were both of you last night?"

"On the boats until eight," the big one says. "Look, we ain't what you're looking for here. Westfield's got a line of enemies up and down this little stretch of coast."

I miss something Charlie says, but then he scratches the back of his neck. "He pays my check, so I don't ask questions, you know?"

Officer Blond and Boring takes notes without emotion, but the smile underneath Nelson's moustache tells me he smells a lie. "I'll be checking with your boss. Seven o'clock, you said?"

"Eight." This from the big one.

"Mr. Thorpe, Mr. Jones." Nelson offers their names as a farewell and heads out, his partner a pale shadow behind him.

I take a deep breath and look down at the time sheets in my lap. It's easy enough to find them both. My finger touches each of their clock-out times. 1700. Which is five o'clock, not eight o'clock.

My vision shrinks down to those four digits on the page—the ones that prove they lied through their teeth.

I look up, but the officers have disappeared. Thorpe is still there though, eyes scanning the boardwalk, that bruised hand rolling into a loose fist at his side.

Okay, stop jumping to conclusions. They didn't say they were working, just that they were on the boats. Maybe they were just relaxing. Maybe there was an off-the-clock meeting.

*Or maybe they attacked Mr. Westfield.*

My hands prickle with sweat. If they're involved, they wouldn't stay in town. Why aren't they running? And why am I still here, holding time sheets the police probably need to see.

I glance at the boardwalk again, but I don't see either officer. Not surprising. Everyone in North Carolina is down here. I'm not sure I could find an elephant dancing the samba. God, I hate days like this.

I'll call Joel. This is way outside my job description. Across from me, Thorpe trudges down the dock back to the boat. They're loading passengers, and my shoulders hunch when I catch sight of his hand. He definitely looks like he's been in a fight.

Even if they had nothing to do with Mr. Westfield, I don't want that guy seeing me with the time sheets. I don't want him seeing me—period.

When I'm sure they're distracted enough with the boat to not notice, I walk quickly to the opposite side of the next stretch of shops, an outdoor strip mall with archways beckoning visitors from both the boardwalk and the street. I stop beside the Whaler Inn, time sheets still trapped between my clammy fingers. I fold it and tuck it into my bag so I can call Joel.

He picks up on the second ring, and relief rolls over me. "Joel, thank God. I'm freaking out a little here."

"Well, whatever it is, freaking out won't help."

"I think it's warranted this time. I was just picking up the time sheets, and there were police officers interviewing Charlie and Thorpe on the docks. I think they lied to them."

"You think the police officers *lied*?"

"No, no. Thorpe and Charlie. The police were asking them about last night, about Mr. Westfield. They said they were on the boats until eight."

"Sounds about right."

"But I have the time sheets right here, and they say five o'clock. I didn't know if I should run after the police or call you or what. I could bring them in right now."

"The time sheets? I don't need them. Those two do contract

work down in Morehead City. Cleaning and such. I'd have to check the logs there, but I think that's where they were."

"But, Joel, Thorpe had really busted-up knuckles too. Like he's been hitting someone. What if he attacked Mr. Westfield? What should I do?" I take a sharp breath, a new thought jarring me. "What if they run? I mean, they could steal a boat, right? Maybe even take hostages."

Joel gives a soft, short laugh. "Neither of those boys is taking anyone hostage."

"How can you be sure?"

"Because those gentlemen are on parole. I'm pretty sure Charlie's on GPS monitoring, and Thorpe's desperate to hold this job. He's had a hard time finding one."

A sunburned woman in a purple dress brushes past me, so I drop my voice to a whisper. "They're ex-*convicts*?"

"Now you know Mr. Westfield is passionate about giving people a chance to start over," he says, but then he pauses. "You say Thorpe's knuckles were bruised?"

"Yes!"

"Hm. Maybe I'd better head down to the police station. I'll check with some of the other guys to see if anybody knows what happened to his hand."

"Thanks," I say. "I'll feel better if someone looks into it. Shoot, speaking of things I have to make you do, Mr. Trumbull called. He wants a call as soon as possible, but I swear his charter supplies are all ordered, and I prepared the receipt for him just yesterday."

Joel sighs. "That man always wants something, doesn't he? I'll take care of it. When are you stopping back by the hospital?"

"Tomorrow morning if you don't need the time sheets. It's getting late, and I still have an errand to run after dinner." The lie goes sour in my mouth. Finding Deacon isn't exactly an errand, but I promised Chelsea. I need to at least *try* to find him.

I hear muffled voices in the background. Joel tells someone he'll be right there. Then he's back. "Emmie, I've got to get in there. The doctors are making rounds. Thanks for calling about this. I'll see you tomorrow?"

"Yes. See you soon."

Sooner than tomorrow if I can find Deacon.

* * *

I find Dad at our kitchen table when I get home. He's drinking out of his favorite coffee cup and reading the paper. It's almost like he still lives here. Almost.

Mom and Dad share custody of me and our Newfoundland, Ralph, now. They're not divorced, just separated. Which means we do holidays and school events and sometimes dinner like everything's the same as it's always been. Until you mention Landon. Mom and Dad have two speeds when it comes to my brother—fight about his bad choices or pretend he doesn't exist.

Dad grabs a dishtowel from the counter to get what looks like calzones out of the oven.

"Tim, you know where I keep the potholders," Mom says, but she pulls out a stack of plates for him nonetheless.

"Haven't used a potholder in thirty-nine years, Mary. Not going to start now." He pushes a calzone onto a plate. "How's James doing?"

Mom sighs, leaning back against our kitchen island. "They're concerned about some swelling in his brain, but they're relieving pressure—"

"Relieving pressure?"

Mom gives him a look that she still thinks I can't interpret. She's wrong. That look means *We'll discuss it later when our daughter can't hear*, but they really don't need to bother. "That probably means they're drilling holes in his skull," I say, because I've watched enough medical shows to guess. Mom blanches, so I must've been right.

I scratch Ralph's ears and take the plate Dad offers because it will make them happy. Actually eating it is another matter. I can't eat right now with Joel maybe talking to the police and Deacon God knows where and not answering his texts. He needs to go see Chelsea so we can get this stupid mess straightened out.

I square the calzone on my plate and fold a napkin in half, wishing I had a pen to make a list. I need to stop by their house. Feed the cat. Pick up a sweatshirt for Chelsea, because she's probably staying at the hospital. She'll need a toothbrush and—

"You all right, Emmie?"

I jerk my gaze up to my dad. "Sorry. Fine."

"It's such a shame," Dad says. "Plenty of murmurs around the docks today about it."

I perk at that. Mom glances at my calzone, so I saw off a corner. "What kind of murmurs?" I ask.

"Nothing you should worry about," Mom says.

"She's not a baby," Dad argues, turning to me. "People are guessing who might have done it. Westfield wasn't exactly well liked, so there's a long list."

"He wasn't?" I pull back, trying to imagine it. He's gruff, quiet. But disliked? "He always gives back to Beaufort, doesn't he?"

"Sure, but he reaches deep into the pockets of the town first. Makes some people angry."

"Now, hush, Tim. You're going to worry her sick." Mom brushes an imaginary strand of blond hair behind her ear. "You're just saying that because you lost *that* contract with him."

"What contract?" I ask.

"Engine maintenance on the boats," he says, but then he leans in and winks. "It wasn't *that* big of a contract."

"Eight boats between here and Morehead City," Mom says softly, washing off the calzone pan. "I'll bet it was nothing to sneeze at."

The air turns a little frosty, so I force a big bite and make yummy noises as I chew. Steam burns my tongue, and a wad of cheese lodges in my throat. I try to swallow, but the cheese is determined to choke me. I'm coughing like crazy, eyes streaming while the kitchen erupts into activity. Mom is so frantic, it's like there are four of her, pouring me water, patting my back, asking Dad to *do something*.

I hold up a hand, still coughing, because I know how scared she gets. They watch me while I recover, Mom's hands shaking and her eyes so wide. Finally, I can talk, so I laugh.

"Don't I feel stupid?" I say.

"No, sugar, don't," Mom says.

I push out from the chair and try to get my plate, but Mom takes it too fast. Dad offers me water. My chest feels tight. They're watching me like I'm a soap bubble, like if any little thing goes wrong, I will pop. I wipe at the table with my napkin until I can't take it anymore.

"Well, on that note, would you mind if I excuse myself?" I ask.

Mom glances at my barely touched calzone, and I flinch. "Sorry. This has been a lot, you know? I feel like I'm just sitting here. I need to do something to help Chelsea."

"Nothing to do but wait. A prayer or two might not hurt," Dad says.

"I know, but I want to call her. I could pick up a change of clothes for her and bring it up to the hospital. Somebody else from school might want to check in, or I could borrow the car if you guys don't mind."

"All this running around," Mom says, touching my arm. "I wish you'd settle down. You need to just…"

"Now, Mary, our Emmie's a fixer. That's her safe spot."

"My what?" I ask.

"Fixing things. That's your safe place when things are all in an upheaval," Dad says. "Remember when Landon—"

"Don't," Mom says, voice thin. "Please."

Tears well in her eyes, and Dad quiets. I fold her into a hug and make all the right noises to calm her down. It feels like a lie. I can't afford to let Mom down the way Landon did. I have to be the kid who is careful and safe. The kid she can count on.

If I tell her the truth about my running around—that yes, I'm going to get some things for Chelsea but that I'm going to try to find Deacon while I'm at it—she'll be terrified. It will make her think she could lose me too.

# CHAPTER FOUR

· · · · · · · · · · · · · · · · · · · · · · · · · · · ·

I take Turner up to Ann Street and turn right, grateful for the shade provided by the tall trees that flank the sides of the road. I pass Mrs. Gillespie's place with her prize azaleas and the house with a Great Dane who spends his afternoons dozing on the porch.

This is the Beaufort that brings the tourists back year after year. It usually feels charming and safe. Not today though. The wind hisses a little too hard and it's still oppressively hot, though the daylight is fading, leaving glowing windows to watch me pass.

I see the low wall with the iron fence and the white church at the corner. The Old Burying Ground sits behind it. I step inside the gates and take a deep breath that takes me right back to another summer day, when Deacon hid with bloody elbows and I cleaned him up with a wad of napkins from my back pocket.

He's not by the wall today, so I walk under the sprawling live oaks that stretch gnarled arms to the sky. Long leaves spread from the withered limbs, whispering to one another. The heat loses its grip in the burying ground, a place lost to shadows and tombstones and the sweet, fecund smell of old earth.

I find him leaving a flower for the Rum Baby, and just like that, I'm back six years to that first time. We were coming home from getting ice cream, and he'd hit the curb on his bike. I saw him fly headfirst over the handlebars and heard his body scrape across the pavement before he came to a full stop. It was awful.

He got up, bleeding like a stuck pig and sprinting full out for the cemetery. Chelsea ran home, but I ran after Deacon. I knew right then this was more than a kid who doesn't like blood. This was different. He wasn't just scared; he wasn't there at all. So I crouched there in the dirt, my own scabbed knees scraping on an exposed root, and used a wad of napkins from the Fudge Factory to clean him up.

Clean might be a stretch, but I did my best, talking a mile a minute to fill the silence.

*"I had a scrape like this last year. All the way up my arm. Hurt so bad, I refused to take a bath. I got it jumping off the pier, so I probably smelled like a goat in a crab-shell bikini."*

*On and on I talked, and he just stared into space. Ten minutes later, we were walking home, looking for Chelsea and their dad, and he laughed out of nowhere.*

*"A crab-shell bikini?" It was the first thing he'd said since the accident.*

*"I didn't think you were listening," I said.*

*"I heard every crazy word." His smile cut me off, bright and unexpected. I'd seen him smile a million times, but it had never sent fire up my neck before that moment.*

*"You always hang out in the cemetery when you're hurt?" I asked, rubbing my hot cheeks.*

*"I like it there."*

*"You go there a lot?"*

*He'd looked me right in the eye. No smile then. "Don't tell, Emmie. Please."*

*The way he looked at me stole my voice and opened doors to feelings I hadn't had much use for at ten. But they unfurled in that moment, young and greedy and rooting as deep as the trees watching over us.*

A dove coos, bringing me back to the present. I press my hands to the sides of my neck, remembering the heat I'd felt six years ago. Deacon watches me quietly, looking every inch the sweet boy I've always known.

Whatever happened in that house with his dad can't be what everyone's thinking.

I dig through my own pockets, finding Chester's old tag and setting it on a stone ledge. I don't know how it started or why, but tourists and townies alike always leave the Rum Baby a little something, stuffed animals or plastic beaded necklaces. Maybe it's just too sad thinking that a baby died and the only thing we know about her is that she was buried in a rum barrel.

"Playing hide-and-seek?" I finally ask.

"Did I leave a trail of breadcrumbs?"

The jokes fall flat because neither of us can manage a smile.

"Your dad's stable," I tell him. "Joel's with your sister. I couldn't see him, but they said he's all cleaned up. If you want to visit him, there won't be any blood. You'll be safe now."

He shakes his head and laughs a strange, distant laugh.

"Deke, you need to go to Chelsea. She's scared and she's hurting and she wants her brother. Plus the police will need to talk to you. Joel's already talking to them today."

"What about? Did he hear something?"

I nod. "Two of the guys who work on the boats who are lying about when they clocked out yesterday."

His brow furrows. "Who?"

"Thorpe and Charlie. They said they were on the boats until eight, but they clocked out at five. Joel thinks it's legit, but Thorpe's hand was messed up."

He deflates, shakes his head. "It's probably not them. I know about Thorpe's hand. Charlie told me he mashed it good on a run this week. Plus, Charlie's got a tracking cuff and they do a lot of flat-rate work after hours. Cleaning and charter drop-offs."

I frown. "So you don't think they could have done it?"

"Hell, Emmie, a lot of people *could* have done of it. Most of the guys who work for him, half the boat owners from here down to Morehead City. He's not exactly adored."

"So I keep hearing." I steel myself, because it's time to push for answers. "You seem to have plenty of problems with him."

"I didn't beat him to a pulp." He steps away from me, clenching and releasing his fists over and over, his jaw working through words he won't let out.

What isn't he telling me?

"Okay, you've got to help me out," I say. "Why are you still hiding? Because frankly, you sneaking around a cemetery avoiding everyone is suspicious as all get-out. I get why some people think you did this, Deke. Heck, if you don't start talking, *I'm* going to start thinking it."

He doesn't respond, and I watch him closely. Tense might not be the right word for him. Terrified feels closer. If he did this, he'd be worried about getting caught. But then why is he still in town? If he's guilty, he'd take off. Or fess up. He's never been one to hide his screwups, a fact that annoyed Chelsea to no end when he was still in school with us.

"What are you afraid of?" I ask, though I'm not sure I want the answer. "I get why you *were* afraid. I get why you ran. I don't get why you're *still* running."

"I'm not—" He cuts himself off and gives me a hard look. He's still wearing the pirate shirt from yesterday, so he hasn't been home. Has he been here since then?

I cock my head, making sure he can see my "I mean business" eyes. They usually don't hold much weight with him, but today, he sighs.

"Joel thinks I did it," he says.

"Joel's talking to the police about employees, so he's obviously not sure of anything yet."

"I saw it in his eyes, Emmie, and he cares about me. The rest of them?" He shakes his head. "I know how it looks. If I go in and they haven't found anyone, I'll get arrested. Whoever did this to Dad will get away with it. Case closed."

"Okay, then tell me what happened to your dad. Tell me what you saw."

"I don't know. Not all of it anyway." He takes a breath. "I ran home after I saw you at the shelter. Dad and I had been at each other's throats since that morning."

"I remember. I saw it."

"Well, it got worse when I got home. I took off, but I didn't want to leave it like that, so I went back to talk. It couldn't have been more than forty-five minutes."

"Okay."

Deacon's face reminds me of Chelsea's in the hospital cafeteria. Everything alive in him withers. "When I got there, the back door was open. I went inside and Dad was still in the office, but he was on the ground. He was…"

"Hurt." My stomach loops like a shoestring. Pulls tight. "That's when you ran? When you saw him?"

I can tell he's fighting for the words, choking on them. "No. Not until Joel came. I tried—hell, I didn't know what to do, but I tried to help. To wake him up. Joel and Chelsea pulled around back, and Joel's headlights lit up the room. Before then, I couldn't see the blood. I mean, I *knew*. It was everywhere, and Dad's face was wet when I touched it. But I couldn't see it well, and once I did, I lost it."

"So you ran to me." I let out a relieved breath. "Deke, Chelsea and I both know about the blood thing. We'll explain the truth, and that will be that. They're probably already closing in on a real suspect. Trust me, this will be okay. But we have to talk to the police."

Deacon closes the space between us so fast that I don't have time to prepare. But then there he is, rough hands on my bare shoulders and eyes so sharp they cut into me.

"Emmie, I know you want to help. But words aren't going to get me out of this. I need to figure out who would do this. Dad has a lot of enemies. I have to be careful, but I know a few people who might know something. Might have heard something."

"Let the police do that!"

He laughs at that. "These aren't the kind of people who talk to the police. Half the people working the docks have a record or are hiding something. But they might know things, and then I can give that information to the authorities."

I throw up my hands. "Do you realize how crazy this is? You are *not* Sherlock Holmes! You're eighteen years old. Tell Joel so he can help you. He knows the law, and he's helped you guys a zillion times. Think of the whole marina mess!"

"Joel's not an option. He told me he wouldn't get me out of this. When he walked in and saw me, that's what he said. He's not going to help, because he thinks I'm guilty."

"He *will* come around. Probably when you stop acting like a cornered dog. You need to cool off and come talk to everyone, Deke. This is ridiculous."

"I think it'd be better if I just lay low until something else comes out or I find something. I'm the token troubled teen around here." He sighs, shoulders slumping. "Ever since my mom died, this whole town's been waiting for me to snap. Now it looks like I did."

"It *does* look like that, which is why you have to go in. If you don't, I'm going to go to the police myself, and I believe you're innocent. We all do. Chelsea and Joel too."

"Not Joel. You weren't there, Emmie. I can't even think about the way he looked at me. And it's not like the police are going to be chomping at the bit for my side of the story. Sheriff Perry has had it in for me ever since the marina incident."

The marina incident being Deacon slamming his dad's boat into one of the docks. A couple thousand in damage. It might not have been so bad if he hadn't waited two days to confess. From what Chelsea said, Sheriff Perry was ready to combust.

I press my fingers to my temples and try to focus. "Okay, let's just start with calling Chelsea," I say. "The rest will sort itself out. Just call Chelsea."

His face softens, a smirk curling one side of his mouth. "Bossy."

"Logical," I argue. "Where's your phone?"

"In my room at the house."

"Then use mine." I punch in Chelsea's number before he can argue, but after a couple of rings, it moves to voice mail. "She's not answering. She has to turn it off in the room. Why don't we just go in?"

The leaves rustle overhead, and I watch long shadows pass over his face. Then his jaw sets in a way that tells me he's relenting. "Tomorrow."

"Tomorrow?"

"Yeah, tomorrow I'll do all the things you want. Talk to Chelsea, go to the hospital, maybe even to the police. Whatever. Tonight, I'm going to find some of those guys."

"Deacon—"

"Look, I'm meeting you halfway, Emmie. I'll come with you. I just want a few hours to try to find answers."

I huff. "Fine. Where are you going to sleep? Are you going home?"

"Hell no," he says. "I'll be fine. I've got resources."

I'm sure he does, but I'm also sure I can't sit by while he blatantly uses some starstruck dit-dotter for her hotel room. "Deke, listen, I'm not trying to judge, but I really hope you aren't planning on shacking up with some poor tourist in the middle of this mess."

"Seriously? You think I'm going to hook up with some girl for a place to crash?"

"How should I know? I've seen you kiss waitresses for an extra side of fries!"

He flushes now, not embarrassed—angry. "That's different. That's a game."

I cross my arms. "Yeah, well some of those girls probably aren't playing."

"Are you serious with this? And what about you? In there with Seth at the shelter, agreeing to another date when you know damn well he is never going to be *it* for you."

"That isn't your business!" Heat flashes up my neck. "And I told him that I was not interested. I was *completely* honest with Seth."

"So you *honestly* think he's just going to get over his years-long crush?"

"I don't know! I don't—" I stop, throwing up my hands. "Why are we even talking about this right now? What does this have to do with anything?"

He opens his mouth, looking fit to spit fire. He sighs instead, and it sucks all the anger out of both of us. "I don't know. Hell, my head's all over the place. I'm sorry."

I step closer, my flip-flops scuffing on the dirt. "It's okay."

"It's okay to piss off the one person who hasn't written me off as a criminal?" His smirk tugs at my stomach, but I push it down into the place where I bury all things Deacon-related.

"Nobody has written you off," I say. At the look he gives me, I relent. "Okay, some people maybe. But it's going to come clear soon. Just keep your word about tomorrow and you'll see."

"Tomorrow," he says. "You'll be here?"

"Do I ever let you down?" I ask with a halfhearted laugh.

Deacon doesn't laugh. His expression turns so grave, I can't laugh either.

"No," he says. "No, you never do."

# CHAPTER FIVE

· · · · · · · · · · · · · · · · · · · · · · · · · · · · · · · · · ·

I read back over the list Chelsea texted last night and smile, remembering our phone call.

*"Deacon's really coming tomorrow?"*

*"I think so. If he tries to back out, I swear I will hog-tie him and strap him to the roof of my mom's car."*

Chelsea's laugh made me ache for happier times. It hurt to hear her so tired.

*"How are you?" I asked. "Really."*

*"Not great. Joel reserved a room for me at the Ann Street Inn tomorrow. So I can rest."*

*"I think it's a good idea. Send me a list, and I'll pack for you. Because I am dying to do something to help you, and you know how I get."*

*"Yes, Twitchy, I do." I could hear the smile in her voice. "Thank you, Emmie. So much."*

Of course, Chelsea's list sucked. She asked for her earbuds, a book, and some clothes, but she sleeps like crap without her favorite pillow, and she's probably dying to change out of the rubber flip-flops I saw her wearing.

So I have my own list. See, if the apocalypse comes, I won't be the one hunting in the woods or guarding the perimeter. I'll be the one passing out step-by-step instructions on water collection and tent placement. Chelsea says I should work mission control for NASA. Deacon says I should learn to unclench.

They're both probably right.

I stroll up to the white cottage where the Westfields live. I stop on the front porch, because I'm a little shaky. My mind keeps dredging up the idea of someone in this house. Someone dangerous.

*List. Think of your list.*

> Plug in Deacon's phone.
> Pack bags for Chelsea and Deacon (hair ties for Chelsea).
> Feed Hushpuppy (check litter).
> Grab Deacon's phone and charger on the way out.

Okay, enough standing around imagining boogeymen in the bushes. I grab the mail from the box on the house and pull one of the too-small galoshes off of the boot rack where they leave wet or muddy shoes. I flip it over, and the spare key slides into my hand. Bingo.

Inside, I freeze on the welcome mat as Hushpuppy patters toward me with a happy meow. She does figure eights around my legs while I take a breath and try to get my bearings. Everything looks normal. The front door leads into the living room, and behind that I can see the bright kitchen. My eyes stray to the planked oak table that sits in the attached dining room. Mr. Westfield's office is on the other side of that table.

A hearty complaint at my feet reminds me to feed the cat. I grab a can from the pantry and check her water and then her litter. My gaze drifts to the dining room over and over. I can see salt and pepper on the table and the bottle of guasacaca sauce Chelsea puts on practically everything, but I can't see the office. Unnecessary, since my mind supplies a slideshow of possible images. Open desk drawers. Broken furniture. Bloodstains on the carpet.

Coming here was a terrible idea.

With Hushpuppy fed, I climb the stairs to the bedrooms. Rather than a hallway upstairs like my house, there's a large open space with five doors. Bathroom, three bedrooms, and the walk-up attic. I turn away from Chelsea's bedroom, the only open door, and toward Deacon's.

I pause with my hand on the doorknob. It looks like Chelsea's door but feels entirely different. I've never been inside. There's never been a reason. I've seen his dresser and the edge of his bed from the door a few times, but going in feels wrong.

I do it anyway, taking in the sailboat posters over his bed and the overflowing hamper by the closet. It smells like him, a distinctive blend of citrus and salt water. I take a breath through my mouth because I need to focus. Phone. Clothes. Relevant things.

His phone's on the nightstand next to his keys. I plug it into the charger and watch the screen bloom to life. Battery at 15 percent. Could be worse. The real question—what else to pack? I'm not sure how he'd feel about me rooting through his dresser.

Then again, it's not like he second-guessed breaking into *my* bedroom.

I find his backpack from last year and grab some basics—T-shirt, boxers, socks. Who knows what toiletries he'll need, but a tooth-brush and deodorant go in the bag before I head to Chelsea's room. I find tanks and shorts easily enough, along with her little overnight toiletries bag. It takes forever to locate her Blue Devils sweatshirt—she's planning on Duke too, Latino and Spanish studies and a zillion dollars in loans, she always says—but it's her favorite, so I dig through the closet until I find it. I'm just zipping her bag shut—a lime-green duffel we picked up in Virginia Beach—when I hear it.

*Thump thump. Thump thump.*

Footsteps? The sound comes again and I frown, moving for the door. Someone's on the porch. I force my shoulders down. It's fine. It's probably neighbors with food or flowers.

The door creaks open, and my vision narrows to a pinpoint on Chelsea's wall. One step and then another, closer now. *They're inside.* Someone's *in* the house. It can't be Joel or Chelsea, because they're both at the hospital. And Deacon said he wouldn't come home.

Who else?

Mrs. Stuart from next door? No. She's five-foot-one if she's an inch, and she probably weighs all of ninety-eight pounds. This person sounds bigger.

Scarier.

I press my back to Chelsea's doorframe and listen, but the steps are muffled by the blood rushing behind my ears. Where are they? My ears strain, trying to place the ambling steps. The living room, I think. I hear a throat clearing, unquestionably male. Hushpuppy meows, and the heavy tread moves closer to the stairs.

The footsteps stutter at the stairwell, shuffling like maybe someone's bending over. Something rustles. Jingles. The spare key. I left it on that table at the bottom of the steps. My face goes marble cold. Am I in danger?

I eye the window and the tree outside, even though I know it's too far away. Chelsea and I calculated the odds of escaping her room using that tree on more than one sleepover. We always chickened out, sure we'd fall. Today I might have to take my chances.

A foot hits the creaky bottom stair, and I stumble back, bumping the dresser into the wall.

Shit!

"Eddie?"

Joel's familiar voice brings a rush of relief in its wake, and I sag against Chelsea's dresser, feeling like a Grade A lunatic.

"I'm in Chelsea's room," I holler. I walk to the top of the stairs and look down at him with a sheepish grin. "You scared half of my lives away. How'd you know it was me?"

"No one else knows about the spare key." Joel smiles, but he looks tired. His eyes are red-rimmed, and his white hair, usually perfectly in place, looks a bit flat on one side. He's still wearing his diamond pinkie ring—Chelsea and I tease him mercilessly about his man-bling—but otherwise, he lacks his usual polish.

I walk down the stairs and hold out the green duffel, glad I left Deacon's bag upstairs and out of view. "I got her some clothes."

"Chelsea mentioned it. I should have figured you'd check the mail and feed the cat. I wasn't thinking."

I smile. "Well you're exhausted. The inn is a great idea. Chelsea's always wanted to stay there, and she loves Donna. Here, I have those time sheets with me. I added up all the hours last night."

He takes it with a nod. "Thank you. I paid a visit to Sheriff Perry. Thorpe and Charlie *were* detailing in Morehead City. And Thorpe hurt his hand on a tour."

I shudder. "Hard to believe he's innocent. He's kind of terrifying."

"Well, the sheriff said he'd keep an eye on it, but he mentioned he's got another lead that looks quite promising."

My gut tenses. "What kind of lead?"

"He didn't elaborate," Joel says, but the look he's wearing has Deacon's name written all over. "I appreciate you packing this up for her."

"No problem."

"Say, Emmie, have you seen Dink?"

Does he want to know so he can tell the sheriff? Does he really think Deacon did this?

My throat closes up so fast, it's a miracle I don't make choking sounds. I shake my head before I can think about it. I don't know if I'm doing it too fast or too slow, but it feels off.

Joel doesn't notice. His wide shoulders drop, and he leans against the wall. "He isn't answering my calls, and Chelsea's worried sick."

"Do you think he's doing something with the boats? You

know how some people focus on work." This is awful. I'm stacking up so many lies, I wonder if I'd recognize the truth.

Joel rubs his forehead. "The boats are all in. I closed everything down early today to sort out schedules."

He looks as worn through as an old T-shirt. I chew my lip and feel myself cave. "Joel?"

"Hm?"

"I've seen Deacon."

"I figured." He smiles, sits down on the steps. "The three of you are thick as thieves. I knew you'd want to find him for Chickadee."

"He's afraid to come to the hospital. Says you think he's guilty."

Joel nods. "Running from what you're afraid of doesn't fix it though."

My heat drops. "Do you really think he could have done this? Even with him being so paranoid around blood?"

"I think he's an angry boy who was hovering over my best friend's beaten body. And I know when people are angry, they can do unspeakable things." He takes a breath and looks past me, his gaze going blank. "Emmie, when I lost my girls—my wife and my daughter—when I lost them in Katrina, I went crazy. Blamed everyone I could find and made a long list of enemies. I filed so many lawsuits, called the media with wild claims. I used my particular talents for bad purposes. That's what anger did to me."

"I'm so sorry," I say, aching for him.

"So am I. I had to shut down my practice. I lost everything. That's how I ended up here." His smile is sad when he looks back to me. "I love Dink, but that boy's had a hard life. I hope he didn't do this, but we're all capable of bad things if we're hurting enough."

"I still don't think he's capable of this," I say. "He might come to the hospital today."

Joel perks up. "You don't say? When?"

I chew my lip, worried that I'll have to talk him into it again. I don't want Joel to give up if it takes longer than I planned. "I'm not sure, but he promised me he'd come. He will."

I feel the threat of tears coming on, so I tamp them down, swallow hard.

Joel isn't fooled. He chucks me gently on the shoulder. "Don't be too grim, Eddie. Sheriff Perry thinks he's closing in on answers, so we won't be in the dark much longer."

I force a smile, but my heart pumps out an extra beat. And then another. Perry hates Deacon. If he gets it in his head that Deke did this, it's going to be big trouble.

"Well, I need coffee," Joel says. "You need a ride home? I could run you by the Cru first. It'd be my treat."

My mind throbs with an image of Deacon's phone upstairs, his bag still propped by Chelsea's door. He needs that phone—at the very least.

"If it's okay, I was going to tidy Chelsea's room a little. Thought I could make her bed and leave her a note or something."

"You and your cleaning. My office is spotless."

"Chelsea loves it when I clean. She always says she'll return the favor when the frog grows hair, whatever that means."

Joel laughs. "It means it'll never happen. Daffy says it too. I think their mother used to say that. Hey, I talked to the admissions dean at Duke last week. We're trying to set up a round of golf, so we talked about you. He's really looking forward to reviewing your application."

My application. To Duke. Mental images of the chapel and long stretches of velvety grass flip through my head. It's been my dream to go to Duke since the campus tour with Landon. Back then, I wanted to be a marine biologist, but back then, Mom was fine with that.

She had my brother.

The legacy she gave up at eighteen—when she wound up pregnant with my very blue-collar father's baby—was all turning right. I remember her slim arm tucked through my brother's on that tour, her eyes bright as she said, *"Mama thought there'd be no doctors and lawyers from my branch of the family tree, but she didn't see you coming, Landon."*

Probably a good thing Grandma didn't see. She had a way of rubbing things in until they left a mark.

"You look lost in space." Joel chuckles. "Don't let it scare you. It's a good thing."

"It's incredible. I just thought you were doing a reference letter. I never expected you to talk to the dean."

"Well, Emmie, I've known you long enough to know that you're cut out to go all the way at Duke if that's what you choose, though it's not a bad idea to change schools either. We can talk about it later, but for now, you'll have someone keeping an eye out for you."

Hope floats into my chest, bubble light. "Really? Joel, you're amazing."

"Well, it's no guarantee. You'll still be in the application process, but greasing the wheel a little never hurt, right?"

Joel picks up his keys and Chelsea's bag. He tells me he'll drop the bag by Ann Street Inn, but I can't do anything but smile.

"I'm going to head out. Don't clean all day, you hear me?"

"I do."

He lumbers to his feet but seems to hesitate before heading to the door. "Emmie?"

"Yeah?"

Joel looks down, knocking his knuckles softly into the doorframe like he's not sure how to phrase this. When he looks up, his eyes are too bright. "If you see Dink, tell him I'm sorry. I said some things—" He trails off, shaking his head. "Just tell him I'm sorry. I do want to hear his side of this, and I'll do whatever I can to help with this situation."

"I'll tell him."

My smile is in place, but I'm cold all over again. If Joel thinks he needs to offer his help, then I might be wrong about things working out. Deacon might end up arrested.

\* \* \*

He's not by the Rum Baby. Tourists have descended on the cemetery. I have to step around a couple dressed in store-creased T-shirts from one of the beach shops across the bridge. Next, I smile at a pair of women with their hands full of papers from the Beaufort Historical Society. As much as I wish Deacon would show, the wait is probably a good thing. I feel like a pot that's boiling too hard, so I probably need the time to settle.

I also need answers in case he tries to weasel out of coming with me today. I can't hide him forever, because no matter how much I believe him, I don't *know* that he's innocent. My shoulders tense. I want to do what's right, but what does that mean? Going to the police sounds right. But standing by a friend in trouble sounds right too, doesn't it? Especially when you know that friend has always, *always* stood by you.

I close my eyes, flashing back to the animal shelter when Deacon got me in with Dr. Atwood. I was too young, and he stood right with me outside the office door. Three Labradors were bouncing and barking like the world loudest pinball machine, and my nerves were rattled.

*"Maybe I should wait," I said. "The application says fifteen. And the hours won't count for high school until senior year."*

*Deacon snorted. "That's crap. You don't care about the hours. You told me you want this more than anything."*

*"I do."*

*"No one's going to be better at this job than you. Now get in there and fight for it."*

He stood beside me at Dr. Atwood's desk, singing my praises until she agreed to take me on. He was there for me. I'm trying to be there for him too, but he's running out of chances.

"Emmie."

Deacon's voice startles a group of birds in one of the live oaks. They rise in a thunder of pale wings and birdsong, and we both look up to watch them fly away. Once they're gone, he moves closer, but I lift up a hand to stop him.

"Wait," I say. "Did you have any part in what happened to your dad? Did you hurt him?"

Pain flashes across his features. "Not like you think."

"That's not an answer. I want to know everything. Joel wants me to tell you he's sorry and that he'll try to help, and I'm afraid he's saying that because he thinks you'll be arrested. Sheriff Perry is looking for someone. We both know that someone is probably you. Does Perry have a reason to be looking, Deke?"

His laugh is sharp enough to use as a weapon. "When does Perry *not* have a reason to look for me?"

"Don't start with that. I'm asking you to tell me the truth."

"I told you what I know," he says. "It's a shit show. And I'm sorry you got mixed up in it. As for Perry, yeah, I'm sure he's looking for me."

He turns away. Is he going to run forever? Would he do that to Chelsea, leaving her like Landon left me? And what will I do about it? Am I going to call the police? Maybe. Either way, I promised Chelsea I would bring him to the hospital, and that's what I'm going to do first.

But I need to make sure I still believe him.

I walk closer. "Look me in the eyes and tell me if you put your dad in the hospital."

His gaze doesn't waver. "I didn't."

"Then we can fix it. We'll fix this."

"Always the solutions girl." His voice is light and easy, but his eyes are a tempest. "God, Emmie, there's just so much you don't know."

"Yeah, I got that memo. How about you fill in the blanks for me? Because you look guilty as sin, and I feel like I should have called the police when you showed up in my bathroom and a dozen times since then, so level with me. You didn't put him in the hospital, but you did something, didn't you?"

Something in his expression breaks. Underneath, he's so raw. "I hit him."

My breath puffs out, and my cheeks go cold.

"I can't tell you everything," he says. "But I promise you I hit him *once*. One time. Hard enough to hurt my hand, hard enough to hate myself for it, and definitely hard enough to make me look guilty, but that was it. I might have left a bruise, but I didn't…" He trails off.

I square my shoulders, willing myself to stay strong. To ask the hard questions. "Have you ever hit him before?"

"No." He squirms like something is hurting. "I need you to understand he gave me a hell of a reason, Emmie. I wish to God I could explain better, but Chelsea made me promise not to say anything to you about this."

That stops me cold. My best friend is keeping secrets from me? I mean, sure, we've all got skeletons in our closet, but Chels and I have been close forever. She knows all the dirt I've got. I know Chelsea doesn't air dirty laundry, but I never dreamed she'd put on a show for me.

Deacon must see the hurt on my face, because he sighs. "Please don't be hurt, Emmie. It's not really about her. It's about Dad. She doesn't want you to think badly of him."

"Because of his reputation?" I ask. "Because he fired my dad?"

"He fired Tim?" Deke looks gobsmacked and then irritated. "Of course he did. Why not piss off every-damn-body."

"Look, it doesn't matter right now. Let's just go to the police. You can tell them everything you saw that day and all the people you think might have been behind this. What did you hear at the docks?"

"Mostly that everybody's pointing the finger at me." He nudges a root with his foot. "No one's heard a thing. I'm probably going to go down for this."

I don't know what to say. With anyone else, I'd offer a hug, but we don't do that. So I stand there looking like an idiot, arms crossing over my middle, while some small part of me wonders how I can save him.

Another part of me can't stop thinking how much Mom would want me to stay away from this. But who else does he have? Chelsea is lost. Joel is suspicious. His mom is…gone. I know what it's like when the person you need isn't there. When my parents decided they needed a *break*, my brother was a thousand miles away, with a string of disconnected phone numbers and bad email addresses. If I didn't have Chelsea and Deacon then, I'd have lost my mind.

I owe him this. I owe it to both of them.

"I'm not okay with this secrets crap," I say. "I deserve better. I deserve the truth."

"You do."

"But you said you'd go to the hospital and that you'd talk to Chelsea. You gave me your word about that."

"Would you come with me?"

"To the hospital?"

"We can take my bike."

My hands and feet tingle. He says bike, but he means motorcycle. I can already picture my mom's lips going thin, her head shaking before the *no* is even out. Still, I don't have a car. Don't usually need one since the historic district is walkable and a bicycle will get you anywhere else. The hospital, however, is a town over.

He shrugs. "It's okay. Maybe it's a bad idea."

No maybes about it—it's a terrible idea. A motorcycle ride with Deacon? There will be leg-to-leg, arms-around-waist touching involved. On a vehicle that terrifies my mother.

"Of course I'll go."

# CHAPTER SIX

· · · · · · · · · · · · · · · · · · · · · · · · · · · · ·

I hand Deacon the keys I scooped up with his phone. He doesn't say anything when we walk up his driveway, but I can tell he doesn't want to go inside. He doesn't even look at the house.

He finds an extra helmet in the detached garage and hands it to me, mounting the bike while I stand there with my knees knocking and my teeth chattering from nerves.

"Okay, do you see the silver thing here?" He's pointing at small pegs on each side of the bike, and I just zone out. I'm about to get on a motorcycle. A motorcycle. I swipe my hands down the sides of my shorts. Check the strap on my helmet. Check it again.

Three days ago, I would have killed for this opportunity. I could fill notebooks with a variety of daydreams that featured this motorcycle. But now that it's here, scaring me… I check my strap again.

"Hey." His fingers brush my elbow.

"Don't go fast," I say, feeling myself go crimson inside the helmet. And now I'm twelve. Maybe nine. A nine-year-old girl who's terrified of the big, scary motorcycle.

"I won't," he says.

Three days ago, he would have teased me.

But three days ago, Mr. Westfield wasn't hurt. Deacon wasn't a suspect. I wasn't needed like this.

Everything was different.

Deacon puts on his helmet, settles into the seat, and looks up at me with his too-pretty eyes. I'm sliding, just like always. Like it's gravity. This part is never going to change, is it?

I check my strap again, and he bites back a smile.

Deacon's saying something, but I can't make it out. I can't really hear anything beyond the humming in my head and the engine. I still manage to nod and scrape together enough common sense to figure out that it's time for me to get on.

I hesitate because there's no way around it. I'm going to have to touch him. Just planting one hand on his shoulder feels like crossing a line. Lots of lines actually. And when I'm settled in the seat, with about an nth of an inch between us, I'm thinking I've crossed continents.

With the way my heart's pounding now, I'll probably go into cardiac arrest when I actually have to hold on. It's ridiculous.

He inches the bike forward, and I feel like I might get sick.

"You're going to need to hold on," he says, voice strange and muffled through the helmet.

"Okay."

"Before I take off here."

"Okay."

"I won't scare you, Emmie."

"Okay," I say because my entire vocabulary has been reduced to *okay*.

I gingerly reach for his waist, but he says something I can't hear. It might be "need to hold on tighter." It must be something like that, because he takes my wrists and pulls my arms around him.

Now we're *really* close.

I shut my eyes and sort of expect him to take off like a bat out of hell, laughing his ass off while I whisper endless prayers and hold on for dear life. It's not like that at all though. He eases us out of the driveway and down the road. I feel every crack in the pavement, because I'm desperately focusing on the ride instead of the abs-of-steel guy in front of me.

Deacon picks up speed on Highway 70 to keep up with traffic. All I can hear is wind and engine. The rest of it fades away, and it's not exhilarating or scary like I thought. It's like floating on a tube in Taylor's Creek, all easy, mindless escape. I close my eyes and let the sensation take everything else away.

Guilt swarms me at the first lane change, so swift and sharp it's like choking on a knife. Chelsea's dad is lying in that hospital half-dead. I'm here for my best friend. Not to float away in dreamland or to think about Deacon's abs. I loosen my grip a smidge. The rest of the trip, I keep my eyes wide open.

The hospital must have just gone through a shift change, because when I usher Deacon toward the elevators, half a dozen nurses head our way with limp hair and mascara-smudged eyes. A couple of them still offer us smiles as we pass them.

We wind up on an elevator with a patient and two people I assume are visitors. They're chatting and oblivious to both of us, so they don't notice Deacon's face going ashy, but I do. I edge a little closer, until my shoulder bumps his arm.

I want to ask if he's okay, but everyone would hear me. People might look. It's the opposite of what he'd want, so I just stand there, willing strength into him.

The doors open, and I expect him to pause, but he surprises me, walking straight into the waiting area. I follow, running a hand through the snags in my hair from the ride over. Chelsea is sitting at a table with a cup of coffee that looks untouched.

She looks up and sees me first and then Deacon. The smile that breaks over her face makes it totally worth every ounce of hell I'll receive if Mom catches wind of the motorcycle situation. Their embrace fills all the spaces their silence leaves.

"She found you," Chelsea finally says.

I sit down and admire them together. They could be twins. Same thick hair and kaleidoscope eyes. Same sharp cheekbones and smiles that crook up just a little on the left.

"You're here," she finally says.

"I'm here."

"Joel's on his way too. They're trying to take Dad off the ventilator right now, so he'll be able to talk soon."

"Then he's awake," Deacon says, looking relieved.

Chelsea nods. "He's in and out, but he can't talk because of the ventilator. I haven't said much because we're not sure what he remembers."

Deacon frowns. "Is the ventilator because of the—"

Chelsea inhales sharply, cutting him off with a glare. I can't see the look that passes between them, but Deacon sighs. I'm pretty sure whatever he was going to ask has something to do with what Chelsea doesn't want me to know.

A nurse opens the door to the waiting room and sticks her head inside. She spots Chelsea and smiles. "He's all ready for you."

"I think it's time," Chels says, and then she takes Deacon's hand.

They're almost at the door when Chelsea stops and runs back to me. Her arms are around my neck, and she squeezes me tight. All my worries about her secrets vanish in that moment. We'll talk when she's through this. When life is normal again.

"I'll never be able to thank you enough," she says.

"You'll never have to."

Then they're inside. I slump down in my chair with a happy sigh. A game show is chattering on the TV in the corner, and there's a flower arrangement at my table, so maybe I was wrong about the flowers. I pull the basket closer and look it over. Roses, irises, lilies.

I finger the white edge of a calla lily, the first one I've touched since their mother's funeral. I wore a navy-blue skirt and an itchy sweater. I'd never been to a funeral before. Couldn't quite get my head around the idea that Chelsea's mom was in that strange box. Chelsea sat on her dad's lap, sobbing softly into his lapel. Deacon stood like he was carved from stone.

After the service, everyone gathered back at their little family sailboat—no big business then—and they tossed flower after flower on the deck of the boat. Once we were done, everyone headed up the block to the house to make small talk and eat casseroles. I'd wandered back down the road to the water. Deacon was there, picking out the lilies and throwing them overboard.

I'm guessing his mom didn't like lilies.

I climbed aboard to help, and he let me. It felt like it took hours. By the time we were done, the water around us was black and stars were blinking their own memorial. But there was not one damn lily in sight—and that felt good.

"Eddie." Joel's voice yanks me from the memory. He's standing by the table when I look up, hair still damp from a shower and tie only half-done. "Is Chickadee in with Daffy?"

"She's in with him right now," I say, and then I smile. "I think he can talk now. Oh, and I found Deacon. He's in there too."

The shock on his face makes me laugh. Almost anything would make me laugh right now. I'm just so relieved.

"Well, I'll be," Joel finally manages.

"Never underestimate my powers."

"I never would." He winks. "I can take Dink home if you want. They'll have lots to discuss."

I hesitate, not sure what I should do, but I don't think I should leave him. Joel must see as much in my expression.

"Emmie." Joel presses his lips together, like he's choosing every word carefully. "We still don't know Deacon's role in all this."

"I'd bet my life he didn't do it."

"Don't bet that," Joel says softly. "Never bet that."

"Do you really think he *could* do something like this?"

"I shouldn't talk to you about what I think at all."

"Because I'm under eighteen?"

"No, because I'm the attorney for the Westfield family, and there is a strict client confidentiality law that protects them and me. Something you'd do well to read up on, because I can tell you there's a good bit of work on that subject on the North Carolina Bar Exam."

"Which I have about thirty-six years to prepare for."

The door slams open, and I jerk back in my chair, surprised when Deacon storms out, barely looking at Joel on his way to the elevator. I lurch out of my chair, and he gives me a look that breaks my heart.

"What happened?" I ask.

"You can add Chelsea to the list of people who think I did this."

\* \* \*

I follow him down out of instinct alone. Three nurses join us on the elevator before I can ask him a single thing. We ride down in silence while they chatter about the jewelry one of them is selling. I watch Deke out of the corner of my eye, my body tensing as he clenches his fists.

The doors whoosh open, and Deacon waits until the nurses file out. Then he bursts from the elevator, and I'm right on his heels.

"Wait a minute," I say. "What's happening? What went wrong?"

"I'm leaving," he says. "You can stay or go."

"Just hold on a second!" I smack my toe into one of the chairs in the main lobby and cry out. Deke turns, not exactly sympathetic but not exactly ignoring me either.

"Are you all right?"

"Never mind me—what happened up there? Talk to me."

The other elevator doors open, and Chelsea and Joel slip out. Chelsea charges at Deacon the second she spots him.

"I'm going," Deacon says.

"How could you?" Chelsea snarls. "How could you hit him?"

Oh. *Oh.* He told her.

My insides snag on the pain in her voice or maybe at the unsteadiness of Deacon's breathing. They're both hurting, and hell if I know who to help or how. Deacon tries to back away until Chelsea scoffs, face purpling with rage.

"You're going to just run away," she says. "Watch me *not* be shocked."

The elderly volunteers at the front desk are casting worried glances in our direction. Deacon edges closer to me and his sister.

"You're the one who told me to get out."

I step right, toward Chelsea, and then back, hesitating. I don't get this. Any of it. All she wanted was for him to come. And now *this*? I know he messed up, but this rage isn't like her.

"Do you have any idea what it was like for me to see that?" Deacon says to her.

"Don't you dare! I don't care what it was like for you. *You* aren't lying in the hospital right now!"

The woman at the desk picks up a phone, but Joel lifts a hand, walking briskly across the lobby to talk them down. The three of us watch warily, clustering a little closer. I can't hear what Joel says, but he must smooth things over, because he's back with us fast, and the woman is no longer holding the phone.

"Chickadee, Dink, let's just all calm down here. We're scaring these poor ladies to death."

"I'm sorry," Chels says, voice much lower, head ducked.

"Sorry for scaring them but not for accusing me."

Deacon's laugh sends chills up my spine. I've played referee for plenty of their sibling fights—but this? I don't even know where to start.

I touch Chelsea's arm to ground myself. "You're both stressed," I say. "So stressed." I give her a squeeze, and she shrugs me off hard.

"Don't. You have no idea what's going on here."

My breath lodges like a knife between my ribs. "I'm trying to help, Chels."

Her expression gives me frostbite. "You *can't* help. Don't you get that? You can't do *anything*, Emmie!"

"Hey! Don't turn this on her," Deacon says.

"Oh, *now* you notice her? After how many years?"

My spine goes iron-stiff at her words, embarrassment knotting every muscle.

"Chelsea." Joel's voice coupled with her real name is a rare warning, but she's too far gone. Her eyes are dark with rage, and I'm still stunned by her words.

"You're unbelievable," Deacon says.

"What you *did* is unbelievable. That's the last thing Dad remembers, Deke. You hitting him."

Deacon's red now, and I can see a muscle in his jaw twitching, but he doesn't say anything. Just looks at the door.

"Just go," Chelsea says. "You've got your precious freedom now, and hey, you've got Emmie too, trailing around behind you like a puppy."

The words hit like a hard slap. I reel back, too shocked to respond.

"You're done," Deke tells her, and this time he steps in front of me. I feel the heat rolling off his back and the lingering sting of Chelsea's words.

"I agree," Joel says. "That's too far. Eddie didn't do a thing to you."

I close my eyes, fighting tears. How could she? *How could she?* She knows I didn't want him to know. Not ever, because I knew it was stupid and it would make everything weird. And now she does it here? In the middle of all this?

I'm out of my depth and sinking fast. No time for maydays or lifeboats, just a quick spiraling descent to nowhere.

Joel touches Chelsea's arm, and *he* doesn't get shrugged off. That stings. It shouldn't, but it does.

"Chickadee, let's you and me run Emmie home."

"*No*," Deacon says. "I'll take her."

Chelsea's laugh is the cruelest sound I've ever heard her make. "Of course you will."

I inch closer to Deacon, barely suppressing a shudder. I don't know this person. It's like a stranger wearing Chelsea's skin. Is this what grief does? Does it strip away every good and sweet thing until there's nothing left but darkness?

I take a tremulous breath but lift my chin. I don't know whose courage I borrow to meet Chelsea's eyes, because mine's used up.

"I can't imagine how you're feeling," I say softly. "I know I can't. But that was crap, and you know it."

"I'm sorry," she says, and the words are strangled on the edge of a sob. It breaks things in me to see her like that, but I need time. I need to breathe.

I feel warm, rough fingers on my arm, and then Deacon's looking at me. The apology is written all over his face. "I'll take you home."

The last thing I see is Chelsea's tear-rimmed eyes. They wring me out and leave me hollow as I follow Deacon outside.

# CHAPTER SEVEN

Outside, the humiliation hits me like a truck. My face is so hot I'm surprised I don't smell smoke. He knows. I've hidden this secret for years, and *boom*, just like that, it's out.

What should I say? What *can* I say? Deacon's not talking, so maybe I should follow his lead.

He hands me my helmet and puts his own on too. I check that damn strap and climb on the bike. The pain quickly wins out over the humiliation, and I hold on tight without being asked. I'll have to deal with the awkward fallout later if it comes, and after everything Chelsea said, it probably will. For now, being close to him helps.

Deacon stops at the Hess station, and I check my phone while he pumps the gas. Six o'clock. I have no idea where the day went. It's a miracle my phone didn't blow up with all the texts my mom sent. Will I be home for dinner? Where am I? Is everything all right? Will I please check in?

I fire back a quick response heavy with apologies.

I'm so sorry. Was with Chelsea at the hospital. With a friend now. Be home by ten.

Mom's reply flashes back fast.

I'd like some details. Are you back in town? Who drove you? Battery low. On way back to town.

I turn off my phone and put it away with a wince. I'll pay for ignoring that later, but it's going to be bad enough explaining this. Doing it over text is just too much.

Deacon puts the cap back on the gas tank and heads inside. A couple of girls in a convertible follow him with their eyes, but he doesn't even notice. Now I *know* he's upset.

When he returns, he slips me a pack of Big Red gum and a bottle of Dr. Pepper. My favorites. I can't even thank him though, because he's being just as weird as I am. I guess we're both embarrassed.

I'm grateful when he climbs on the bike and those helmets are back in place, keeping us apart. But at the first light, he flips up his visor and turns so that I can see the scar on his chin in the waning sunlight.

"Are you in a hurry to get home?" he asks, voice rough.

"No."

"Can we just ride a bit?"

I bury my head between his shoulder blades and tighten my grip. It's all the answer he needs. He takes us west from the city, deep into the Croatan forest. Spindly pines line the road as far as I can see, and the sun dips fast below the trees, leaving the air cool. My arms prickle with goose bumps, and my lower back is aching, but I don't let myself care. I press my palm against Deacon's ribs and feel his heartbeat instead, strong and steady.

It's almost dark when he takes us back into Beaufort. He doesn't turn on my street, thank God. Just drives us down to the farthest edge of the waterfront, where there are new stretching boards for joggers and a freestanding climbing wall.

The engine stops, but my ears are still buzzy with the noise. When I lumber off the bike, my legs feel weak and spongey. I'm still shaking out my hair when Deacon crosses the grassy yard, headed straight for the climbing wall.

"You don't have a harness," I say, trudging more slowly behind him.

It's obvious he's not going to stop. He's burning adrenaline. Burning all the darkness from that encounter in the hospital. He reaches the top in less than a minute, and I heave a breath, glad it's halfway over. Now it's just the descent.

Except it isn't. Deacon tilts his head. I've seen that look before. It's like the whole world is a dare and he'll be damned if he's backing down.

"Deke, don't." It's barely a whisper, lost instantly on the soft breeze.

He pulls himself higher, until he's clinging like a monkey to four pegs at the very top of the wall. I know what he's planning before he starts to rise. My vision swims as he slowly straightens, one foot on one top-row peg, one foot on another.

He starts to stand up, and the wind gusts. My stomach churns so much it might as well be me on top of that wall. I stand at the bottom for what feels like hours. Days maybe. Finally, he starts clambering back down. He's breathing hard when he hits the ground but looking more relaxed than he has since the hospital.

We fall into step without discussion, heading down the board-walk toward the center of town.

"I'm sorry about Chelsea," he says finally.

"Forget that for now. Tell me about your dad."

"He's weak. Confused. He hasn't been able to talk because of the ventilator, and he doesn't remember much." He jerks his gaze away, takes a shuddery breath. "We tried to see what he knew. Tried to fill him in on bits and pieces. He just…asked me why I hit him and left. Over and over, he asked me."

"Does he remember anyone else being there?"

"Nope. Just me hitting him." He shakes his head. "Maybe it'll come back, but Chels didn't take well to the punching news."

"Of course she didn't," I say. "Do you blame her?"

"No, I really don't. I feel like shit about it. I never should have—" He stops himself, looking disgusted with himself. I sigh, because the feeling's a bit mutual.

"Yeah, you *definitely* never should have," I say. "You know how protective she is."

"Daddy's little girl," Deacon says. "She always has been."

He's right. And it got twice as bad after their mom died. Knowing her own brother hurt their dad? I'm sure it made Chelsea crazy.

But that doesn't change the bruised feeling in my chest when I think about the things she said to me. I didn't hit *anyone*. And I sure as hell didn't deserve that.

"Hell, I did hit him," he says. "Maybe I earned this."

"Earned the possibility of a few *years* in jail?" I shake my head. "I don't know, Deke. It's screwed up and wrong, but I can't imagine your dad would really want you to go to jail over *one* punch. I don't think Chelsea would want that either. You're her brother."

"I'm also the guy they found standing over Dad. The same guy who's been fighting with him for days." His expression goes hard. "Chelsea made sure to point that out."

A sailboat slides by on smooth water. We're near the dockside office for Westfield Charters now. Deacon unlocks the door and slips inside. He returns carrying a zip-up sweatshirt for me, something folded—a map maybe?—and a backpack slung over one shoulder.

I slip on the sweatshirt, smelling a mix of unpleasant things with a hint of Deacon.

"I don't know what to say," I admit.

"What, they don't make a *Cosmo* quiz for this situation?" His humor is a thin cover for the sadness in his gaze. "You shouldn't even be dealing with this mess. You should be home or out doing something that isn't...this."

"This isn't some noble sacrifice for a stranger," I say. "You're my friend."

He tilts his head. "Still."

"Still nothing. Like you'd walk away if it was me."

A couple strolls down one of the piers closer to town. The woman's high heels are dangling from one hand.

Deacon locks up the office again and stuffs the folded paper into his back pocket. Something about that makes my shoulders heavy. Pieces fall together, snapping me out of my fog. The snacks. The backpack.

"Are you going somewhere, Deacon?"

He smirks at me. "Why? You worried I have a hot date waiting?"

Chelsea's words come back to me, and I feel myself go red, my fists clenched. Deke scuffs the ground with his shoe.

"That was shitty. I shouldn't have said that after—" He stops with a sigh. "Hell, I'm not good at this. I don't know what to say. But you being here? It helps."

I don't say anything. I have no idea where to start. I feel like we're cresting the hill of a roller coaster, but I'm not ready for the drop.

I turn away, pushing my hair behind my ears. "How long will your dad be in there?"

Deacon takes my hint at a subject change. "He'll need to go to a care facility for a while."

"Like a nursing home?"

His gaze seems to go hazy then, eyes drifting to the water. "Something like that."

"Maybe he'll start to put together the pieces and then this will all be a bad memory."

Deacon doesn't look convinced. "Maybe. Maybe not."

My insides shrivel. Go cold. I look over, wind whipping my hair into my eyes.

What if Deacon *did* snap? No matter what I feel, I have to acknowledge the possibility. He could have just closed his eyes and punched and punched and...

Deacon exhales, and I hold my breath.

"You're starting to wonder if I did it too," he says.

I don't deny it. Maybe Joel is right. We're all capable of darkness. Isn't Landon proof of that?

He slumps onto a bench, and I take the other end. I hear him shift, and then his fingers graze mine. It's too much, the rough feel of his fingers feathering over my palm, tracing the line of my thumb. Makes it hard to think.

"Emmie, I'm sorry you're mixed up in this." His arm curls around my back, tugging me against him. The sudden heat and closeness make me dizzy. "But I'm glad you're on my side. You're about all I've got right now."

My throat tightens. I *am* all he's got, and I'm smart enough to know that he could be using that. Using the way I feel about him.

Chelsea wouldn't push her own brother away for no reason. Joel wouldn't be worried for nothing. Am I so desperate to see good in Deacon that I can't see what everyone else is seeing?

No, I *have* seen it. The anger. The fighting. The blood on his hands.

He really might have done this.

A chill runs up the back of my neck, and I push myself out of his embrace. It feels like peeling off bits of my own skin.

I try not to see the hurt in his eyes. Surprise too.

I've never denied Deacon a thing. If he asked me for the moon, I'd have figured out a way to rope the damn thing down. But there are too many questions and not enough answers. I have to trust my head, not my heart.

Deacon nods. Just once. His face shutters, and his mouth goes tight. "I get it. I do."

"Deke, please. Talk to someone. Go to the police. Or Joel."

He smiles thinly. "You've been good to me, Emmie. You always are. I promise I'll leave you out of it from here."

I hear a smattering of laughter from somewhere down on the boardwalk. Tourists probably. I can't answer him, so I stare at my feet and silently curse the tears blurring my vision.

"You should go home," Deacon says. "Chelsea will come around. Dad should be out of the ICU in the morning, and she'll probably apologize all over herself."

He sounds far away. When I look up, I see him walking backward. He's leaving, and I need to let him go. I close my eyes so I don't have to watch him disappear.

"Emmie, is that you?"

I turn at the sound of my name. It's Seth, I think, standing just past the Dockhouse on the far side of the street. Yup, Seth. The yellow zip-up hoodie is a dead giveaway. He's with a couple of other guys I can't make out—Caleb and Liam if I had to guess—and they're probably heading home from the Cru. In a town this small, we run the same circuit over and over.

We exchange a wave, and he says something to the guys with him. Great. He's coming over. Probably to see if he can walk with me. I swipe my damp cheeks and slap on a wide grin as he crosses the street.

Down the boardwalk, I hear a familiar motorcycle start. *Deacon.* The engine roars, and I can almost feel the bike moving underneath me. But I'm still right here, exactly where I'm supposed to be. Far away from him.

* * *

When Seth offers to walk me home, I have no choice but to accept. Mom would throw a fit if I turned down a perfectly polite offer like that. It'd be bad manners.

I'm pretty sure my mom has a crush on Seth *for* me. He mowed our lawn all last summer and even carried in her groceries if he was around after a shopping trip.

*He's a good Southern boy*, she always says. Being Georgia born, she has a slower drawl, thicker than mine. She's from a long line of debutantes, so it makes sense that she'd pick a boy like Seth for me. Her family rode horses and held tea parties and married long lines of Southern doctors and lawyers. Old money. That was Mom's legacy—until she got pregnant.

Grandma snipped her neatly out of the family line then. My brother was supposed to change all of that, live the kind of life Mom was meant for. Now I'm up to bat. Every single time Mom looks at me, I know some part of her sees me as the last shot. Her final chance to get things right.

"Sure is a nice night," Seth says, reminding me that I'm not alone and should probably be saying something.

"I'm so sorry. I'm beat."

"It's all right. Quiet is fine."

We turn away from the shops and restaurants along Front Street, and quiet is exactly what we get. We're in the world of front porches and tidy flower boxes. Postcard perfect, even under moonlight.

Seth bumps into my shoulder. "Hey, Caleb's trying to arrange a shack party after the Pirate Invasion. Pretty sure he just wants a shot with Twyla, but it could be fun."

"Could be," I echo. "You guys are going to make sure no one brings those big lanterns though, right? It's turtle nesting season."

"You and those turtles. They've got plenty of beach, you know."

I tilt my head and frown. "But they're drawn to light. Those lanterns might look like the moon, and then they won't make it to the water."

He laughs. "Wow, I feel like some sort of turtle terrorist now."

I shake myself, force a chuckle. "Sorry, I'm off my soapbox. I promise I won't try to get you to join PETA on Sunday."

He bounces a little with each step. "You'll be too busy swooning to try."

My argument with Deacon comes back to me. I stop midstride and turn to Seth. "I really like you, but it's not like that. You know that, right?"

"I really do. It's not like that for me either anymore." He suddenly puts a hand on the back of his neck like he's blushing. "Thing is, I was wondering if you might give me some advice on…Chelsea."

My laugh is automatic, almost enough to make me forget about the incident at the hospital. But soon enough, her cruel words are echoing in my ears, and my smile falls flat.

"How is she?" he asks. "How is her dad? Do you know anything?"

"Yeah, I was at the hospital earlier," I say, careful to walk around a bit of gum on the sidewalk. "Things are looking better. He has a long road ahead of him, but I think he's going to pull through."

"Scary stuff." Seth nods at me. "Must be hard on you too."

Chelsea screaming at me? Joel suspecting Deacon? Walking

away from a boy I can barely remember not loving? Yeah, *hard* is one word for it. But it doesn't hold a candle to what they're dealing with.

"I don't know," I finally manage. "Mostly I'm worried about them."

"Me too. But I don't think we're worried about the same thing."

I glance over, crossing my arms. "What are you worried about?"

His lips thin, like he's not sure he should say. "I think Deacon might try to take advantage of you in all this. I know you're friends, but that guy is kind of a loose cannon. My dad says a bunch of people in town are talking. Mom says he hasn't been to the hospital."

Seth's mom is a nurse, true, but I doubt she's watching the hospital security monitors. I lift my chin. "Actually, he was there today."

"Well, good. That's good. But be careful with that guy, okay?"

"Deacon wouldn't hurt me." It isn't wishful thinking. No matter what else I might question, I'd bet my life on that.

"Okay, I give," he says. I stop on the corner, and Seth shrugs. "Love is blind, right?"

"I don't…" I can't say I don't love him, so I just trail into nothing, letting the crickets fill the silence.

"You still cool with going Sunday? It *is* possible to just hang out. No agendas, I swear."

"Sure, I need to get out of the house." I stop, looking up at my street sign, knowing his house is a block the other direction. "Thanks for walking me."

"Anytime. Sunday at seven then. No plans, so you'll just have to deal with it," he says.

I laugh and wave him off. Down the street, I spot the yellow glow of the windows in my house. Ralph is probably sprawled inside the door, waiting for me. Mom's waiting too, I'm sure. Time to face the music.

I quicken my pace, practically jogging up the steps. Inside, I smell apples and old wood—like usual.

"I'm home," I call out. I peel off Deacon's sweatshirt and hang it up in the closet, trying not to think about my arms around his waist or his look when I pulled away from him. Even if I push those memories out, there are a hundred more to take their place.

Mom's right where I expected, gold reading glasses perched on the bridge of her nose and e-reader in hand. She looks up, and her hair, which she's worn in a neat blond bob since her fortieth birthday, is long enough to hang in her eyes a little. Very unlike her.

"Figured you'd rather wait to do this in person?" she asks.

"I'm really sorry. My battery was low." True. "I turned it off just in case some emergency sprung up." Not so true.

She doesn't look as angry as I suspected though, so I drop a kiss on the top of her head and sit down on the other end of the couch.

"Well, you still made curfew. You are dependable." She smiles, but I can see something else in her eyes. I can read her like a book, so I know where this is going.

She knows I've been to the hospital. I'm not sure she's clear that I went with Deacon, and since the talk didn't start with "You're grounded forever," she definitely doesn't know we took his motorcycle. But she *will* know soon enough. Because part of me walking away from Deacon means coming clean about what I've done.

"I went to the hospital with Deacon, and before you ask, yes, we took his motorcycle, and yes, I know you're adamantly opposed to motorcycles and Deacon in general, and yes, I wore a helmet, and yes, I know I'm probably grounded until I'm thirty."

A slim brow arches above her reading glasses. "Well, my work here is almost done."

I press my lips together. "I'm not going to see him again until this is all settled, if that's what you're worried about."

She lays her tablet facedown on the coffee table, and Ralph drops his giant head on my lap. I scratch his chin while Mom clears her throat.

"I already knew about the motorcycle and Deacon. Joel called to give me an update and to see if I could take care of Hushpuppy tonight. He told me to go easy on you, because he knows you did it for Chelsea."

Chelsea. My mind goes back to her red face and cruel words.

"He also mentioned she was a bit unfair to you," Mom says.

"Understatement."

"She got upset with you?"

"Also an understatement."

"Well, this is tough, sugar. She's probably feeling pretty lost." I pull my feet up on the couch, and she pats my ankle. "Joel's applying for emergency temporary custody so he can help out while Mr. Westfield is healing up, but they've got that aunt in

Charleston. Jane, I think. Bless her heart, she means well, but she's a bit of a meddler."

Now that I'm here in front of Mom, my guilt swells. "For the record, I'm sorry. I wasn't setting out to scare you today. I just…"

She scoots to the edge of the couch. "You got caught up in a situation you were trying to make better."

"Something like that."

She nods. "You do this. Your dad's right, you do try to fix things. Ever since…"

"Mom, I'm sorry." My voice is soft, because I *am* sorry. The last thing I'd ever want is to remind her of the whole Landon situation. It's too hard for her.

Mom pauses a beat, and her smile is watery. "All right then. You're off the hook this time. But I want you to steer clear of Deacon. I trust you, Emmie, but when it comes to that boy, your judgment is often…compromised."

"Okay," I say. I want to tell her that I didn't compromise my judgment tonight, because I did walk away. But all I can think of is Deacon's face when I pushed away from him. I shake my head to clear the image.

"Did Deacon walk you home?"

"Actually, I ran into Seth in town," I say before I think better of it. "He walked with me."

"Seth French?" She leans back and beams. "I sure do like that boy. A true Southern beau."

"Mom, one of these days, you're going to realize we're in a whole different century."

"And one of these days, you'll see there's nothing wrong with enjoying the benefits of being the fairer sex. My mama could have taught you a thing or too, Emmie."

Maybe. But her mama didn't really like to think about me or Landon, let alone teach us things. We both look too much like our dad to please her upper-crust taste.

"Well, don't get too excited when I tell you I'm going out with him this Sunday. It's not a date. I really don't see him as anything more than a friend."

"Friends is a good place to start." She stands up and touches the crown of my head. "You always make the best choices. Always."

This is why I make those choices. To see her shoulders relax and her brow smooth. I know in this moment she doesn't feel like the girl who got pregnant too young or the mother who failed to raise her son right. She's at peace. I'm not sure I can put a price on something like that.

Mom steps over Ralph and heads for the kitchen. "I'll fix you some tea. It'll make you sleepy."

"I'm really not grounded?"

Her voice trails out of the kitchen. "Consider this your single 'get out of jail free' card for the summer."

I can hear the familiar clatter of dishes in the kitchen. Ralph twists closer to me and drools on my shorts.

"You need a towel, big guy," I say, but my shorts are probably filthy by now, so I stroke his ears and let my head drop to the back of the couch.

My eyes feel heavier than they have in ages. I let them drift shut. When I open them again, I'm stretched out on the couch. There's a pillow under my head and an afghan draped over my shoulders. Mom's doing, I'm sure.

I roll over, turning my face away from the bright early-morning light streaming in through the windows. The floor is still bathed in shadow. There's our rug. Frayed. A gigantic lump of black. Ralph. Two ratty sneakers lined up beside the table. Mine.

Ralph hears something before I do, his head emerging from the mountain of fur to tilt in interest. Mailman maybe? He usually comes later in the morning on Friday though. The doorbell rings while I'm folding the afghan. My heart stutters.

*Chelsea.*

It has to be. She'd never leave things like this with us.

I rush through the living room, but my smile withers before it can bloom. It isn't Chelsea on my front porch, or Deacon, or even Seth. It's the sheriff.

# CHAPTER EIGHT

· · · · · · · · · · · · · · · · · · · · · · · · · · ·

Sheriff Perry has a smile that could sell insurance and
the worst mop of mouse-brown hair I've ever seen. It's like a
bad toupee, except that it's tragically attached. He sits back on our
big, comfy couch, with his icky smile in place and his legs crossed
in that guy way—one foot propped on the opposite knee. My
gaze tries to stay on his face, but it pulls continuously to the gun
at his side. He's got a Batman-worthy belt of tricks—gun, cuffs,
mace, something else, another set of cuffs. Wow. Overkill much?

Thank God Mom was already up and dressed—if she'd left for
work, I'd be doing this alone. She bustles around the coffee table,
bringing in some banana-nut muffins and coffee. I swipe one and
peel off the yellow paper wrapper.

"I sure appreciate the coffee, Mary. Did you hear it hit ninety-
six yesterday?"

"Ninety-six?" Mom asks. "Well, that's something."

"Yes, indeed." He takes another sip, and I stare at his straw-
like hair and faded uniform shirt. Even the Timex strapped to
his wrist is dishwater dull. Perry sets the cup carefully on one
of the lilac-embossed coasters. The radio on his belt crackles.
Another excuse for me to look at the gun and for my stomach
to do a barrel roll.

"Well, ladies, as much as I hate to visit on official business, I'm afraid I'm here to ask a few questions."

"Questions?" Mom asks.

The sheriff puts away his "be your best friend" smile and looks right at me. I feel like there's a red laser target dot on my forehead.

"Questions for me." I don't bother posing it as a question.

"Mr. Carmichael said that you arrived at the hospital yesterday with Deacon Westfield."

"Yes, sir." I force myself to bite off a hunk of muffin so I don't look as nervous as I feel.

"Did Deacon drive you home?"

"Yes. He wouldn't leave me there without a ride."

Mom tucks hair behind one ear. "Sheriff Perry, what's this about? Is Deacon in some sort of trouble?"

It sounds like she's expecting a yes. Maybe even wanting one.

"We're just trying to get some answers." The sheriff abandons his coffee and scoots forward on the couch. "Now, Emmie, I know you want to find out what happened with Mr. Westfield as badly as the rest of us."

"Of course I do."

"So you understand we're trying to get to the bottom of things."

"Do you think Deacon is at the bottom of this?" I ask. His self-satisfied smirk is all the confirmation I need. My throat goes dry.

"That boy's had his share of trouble," Perry says.

"But for speeding tickets. Traffic things, right?" My voice sounds weak, even to me.

"Charles Manson started by rearranging furniture. Did you know that?"

He's comparing Deacon to an infamous psychopath? My worry ratchets into real fear. Deke's guilt is a possibility. I know that. But it looks like a cold, hard fact for Perry.

"I know how this probably seems to you, but I hope you're considering his history," I say. I hesitate. Maybe Deacon's fears aren't mine to share, but if it could save him... I shake my head, mind made up. "You might not know, but he actually can't stand the sight of blood. It shuts him down. I don't think he *could* do this. Ask Chelsea or Joel or even his dad. We've all seen it."

The sheriff hooks his thumbs in his belt. "I've had a lot of people tell me that someone just *couldn't* do something. But everyone is capable of doing bad things, Emmie. Nasty, terrible things."

Now he's talking to me like I'm very slow. Or very young. I bite my lip and adjust on the couch so I don't say nasty, terrible things in response.

"What possible motive would he have?" I ask because I've been wondering the same thing all night. Throwing a wild punch would be one thing, but what happened to Mr. Westfield? That took time. Persistence.

"I'm not going to discuss an ongoing investigation with you, Emmie, but that boy has a well-documented problem with authority."

"That doesn't mean he'd hurt his own father." I flinch because I shouldn't be arguing. I shouldn't be involved in this at all, but the sheriff seems *so* determined.

"You mean he wouldn't *hit him*, Emmie? He'd never ever do something like that?" His questions are greased fishhooks, and I can feel them pricking into my skin, trying to catch me.

I don't want to lie, so I look down at our smooth wood floor. Mom takes a breath that sounds shivery.

"My word, Martin, you mean to tell me that boy struck his father?"

"I believe he did, but my larger concern is the way he's steering clear of the hospital, steering clear of the people who need answers. See, after the attack, Deacon didn't go where you might expect a boy to go."

My insides sink like rocks in a pond. Mom takes the bait. "You know where he went?"

"Emmie, would you care to fill your mama in?"

His words sling themselves bone deep. Someone told him. Not just any someone either. Chelsea did this. She sold Deacon out and didn't warn either of us. Anger and hurt jockey for position in my head.

"Emmie?" Fear wins out when Mom says my name. I can see it written all over her face. She thinks it's starting all over again. Her second child, her last hope. I'm about to fail her too.

I don't dare look at her. I keep my eyes on Sheriff Perry's horrible hair and command my heart to slow down. Right this instant.

The sheriff bends down until I can see the red veins spidering across the whites of his eyes. "Emmie, you're a good girl. I know when your friend showed up needing help, you only wanted to do the right thing."

I nod automatically, wanting to look agreeable. But I'm only half focused. My mind is flipping through images of Deacon in my bathroom. The bloody T-shirt and stained wipes. I double-bagged them and put them in the outside trash, but I wasn't worried about the police then. I only worried about my mom. But now…oh God, could I get in trouble?

Am I an accomplice?

The sheriff leans back like he's got all the time in the world. "Now, this boy came to your house. Bloody. Looking for help. What kind of help could he need from you with his daddy laid up in the hospital?"

I can tell by his tone he doesn't really want an answer. It all feels scripted. I'm the good girl. Deacon's the bad boy. And none of this is about finding the truth. It's about building a case.

I swallow hard and start. "Deacon came to my window. He tried to help his dad but panicked. Like I said, Deacon can't handle blood—he completely shuts down. It has something to do with when his mom died. He came to get help cleaning up."

"Emmie!" The shock and horror in Mom's voice sting.

"You helped this boy clean up from a crime scene," Perry says. "Do you realize that, young lady?"

"I do now." I straighten the corner of the folded afghan. It's curled up, so I smooth it flat. Over and over again. "I told him to go to the hospital, but he was scared people would think he's guilty."

"When you're guilty, people often do."

I frown and adjust the afghan again. My hands are slick with sweat and shaky, but I clear my throat. "Sheriff Perry, Deacon said that his dad isn't too popular with a lot of folks around here. I noticed Mr. Thorpe down at the docks had bruises on his knuckles like he hit someone."

"Mr. Thorpe has an alibi, so why don't we turn this conversation back to Deacon? Where is he now, Emmie?"

My breath comes in sharp as a knife. "I don't know. I met him at the cemetery earlier, and then I saw him last night at the hospital—but not since."

The sheriff heaves a sigh, obviously not happy. And obviously not interested in the possibility of another suspect. Deacon's his guy. I squirm in my chair. Pick at the afghan again.

"Sheriff Perry, are you positive that none of the men who work for Mr. Westfield are behind this? Several of them are ex-convicts."

"Are you questioning my ability to do my job, Miss May?"

"No, sir," I say, ducking my head. "I'm sorry if it seemed that way. Some of them just had a rough look about them."

"Being ugly doesn't make a man guilty any more than being handsome makes a man innocent. Something to think on, Emmie."

Mom's cell phone rings on the charger in the kitchen. She looks over and then back at us, worry pinching her face.

"Mary, go on and get that," the sheriff says. "We're about done, and I'm sure Emmie can walk me out."

"Of course," I say, adding a big smile to hide my shaking.

Mom shuffles to the kitchen with a muttered apology, and I head for the door with the sheriff, who leaves his cup without another sip.

He pauses on the mat, adjusting his belt with its gun and handcuffs. I force myself to stay calm, because I'm pretty sure all his posturing is custom-tailored just for me.

"You know, your mom and dad went through a lot when Landon…" He trails off with a parody of a frown. "Well, it'd be a real shame to watch them deal with another child making poor choices."

I don't know how to reply, so I stay quiet, schooling my expression to a blank slate. He studies me, turning his hat around in his hands while I stare at the sweat stains on the liner.

Finally, he settles it on his head. "We'll talk soon, Emmie. Real soon."

"Thanks for coming by, Sheriff Perry," I say, feeling frostbite crawling up my arms.

"Sure thing." The sheriff grins, and I don't think of salesmen now—I think of wolves. "And, Emmie? If you see Deacon again, you be sure to give me a call, you hear?"

My smile is the biggest lie I've ever told. "Absolutely."

* * *

After two days on total lockdown, I feel like I'm about to come out of my skin. Mom didn't just ground me; she practically cuffed me to her side—from the mandatory tagalongs to the antiques shop all the way down to tense dinners and early nights. It's been miserable. My paranoia is in full swing when I head downstairs Sunday morning. Chelsea hasn't returned my calls or texts, and Mom's hovered way too close to risk a text to Deke.

I collect a stack of letters and stamped postcards on the kitchen counter. Sale notices for some of Mom's regular customers. I could definitely stand to do something nice for her.

"Want me to drop these by the post office?" I shout.

Mom comes out of the laundry room, basket under one arm and cheeks pink. "Are you headed out?"

"I need to run by the shelter."

"You're on schedule?"

"Just for an hour to feed and walk the dogs. Then I want to stop by Joel's to see if he needs anything. I could drop these in the mailbox at the post office if you want."

She presses her lips together. I can tell she wants to talk about the sheriff's visit, or maybe she just doesn't believe me. Confrontation isn't Mom's specialty though. She's good at social hour and condolences and making complete strangers feel like friends.

In the end, I help her out. "Mom, I'm sorry about Deacon. I really am. I know you've got your reservations about him, but he's my friend, and he was scared. I just wanted to help."

Her brow puckers, but I know she's torn. She's raised me to be a helper, to do the right thing. "Well, so long as you've learned your lesson, we can put this behind us." She flashes a bright smile, ready for a subject change. "Are you coming back here before your big date?"

"Not a date, Mom. We're just friends."

"You're coming back to get ready though? Need me to press anything out for you?"

"No, I'm meeting him there. And, *press something out*?" I laugh.

"We've really got to get you out of the shop. The antiques are starting to rub off."

She ignores the barb to frown at my outfit. Eh, she might have a point. I've got on a white tank and a pair of cutoffs. Pretty underwhelming for a night on the town. Even our town.

Thing is, this is Chelsea's forte. I'm not great with finding the right pair of earrings or knowing which shoes work with which skirts. But I want to try to make things better with Mom.

"All right, what would you prefer?" I ask.

Her relief shows with a big breath. "A nice dress. Maybe some pumps?"

"We're going to Clawson's. I'm not sure pumps are required."

Mom's face falls a little. She tries hard to respect my "girls are not pretty *things*" stance, but she's also a former homecoming queen, raised in the land of Southern belles. I spent an insane amount of my childhood zipped into a variety of pink, frothy dresses. They all itched something fierce.

"I suppose I'm old-fashioned," Mom says. "We used to really do it up for an evening out, but I guess that's just silly these days."

I soften with a smile. "No, maybe you're right. How about we split the difference?"

Her face lights up. "A skirt?"

"I'll even throw on some lip gloss, but my sandals stay. I'm walking all over town, so heels of any sort are out of the question."

"Well, you've got lovely feet, so I see nothing wrong with that."

I bite back the urge to tell her that there'd be nothing wrong with it if my feet *weren't* lovely. Right now, I'm just glad we're okay again.

I head to my room and switch to a gauzy shirt and a shorter khaki skirt. I even throw on a necklace. When I return, my mom is beaming.

"Please don't get too excited," I say. "I like Seth—"

"Oh, I like him too!"

Wow. Is this the part where she tells me she dreams of a spring wedding and grandbabies with Seth's nose?

"—but we're just friends," I finish. "Really."

If Mom's disappointed, she doesn't show it. Just pushes some hair behind my shoulder and smiles. "Be sure to powder your nose before you meet him. You'll get shiny in all this heat."

I smile. She gets a free pass on all the crazy comments right now. As long as she's happy again.

After dropping Mom's stuff at the post office, I stop by the shelter. It's closed on Sundays, but we still have staff for basic care.

I take out the dogs in groups, giving them a quick stroll and fresh water with their food. I save Rocky for last, rubbing his shoulders and letting him wander the dog room after the walk. He looks around with sad brown eyes, and I cringe like I'm personally responsible for Deacon's absence.

I give him a couple of treats and lock him back in his cage before heading to the sick bay to visit any recuperating critters. Dr. Atwood's vet tech, Joann, is here taking notes on the sleeping toy poodle across the room. She crosses to a German shepherd mix with cockeyed ears and a freshly sewn gash down his neck.

"Is this the one Dr. Atwood rescued?"

"Found him in an alley like that. The gash was probably six

inches long." Joann shakes her head and checks his food. "He still needs a name."

Deke does most of the naming around here. If it were left to the rest of us, we'd just start picking from the phone book after a while, but he always comes up with something clever. The dog rests his chin on his paws and looks up at me with weary eyes, one ear flopped over. *I feel you, buddy.*

"So what do you think?" Joann asks. "Punky? Floppy?"

I think there's a reason Dr. Atwood leaves the naming to Deke. But instead of saying that, I reach through the wire bars and gently rub the bridge of the dog's nose. He closes his eyes but still seems tense.

"Sarge. Let's call him Sarge," I say.

She chuckles and measures some antibiotics into a syringe. "When Dr. Atwood rolled this one into surgery, I wasn't so sure. He's got that mean look about him. Like he's up to no good. Some dogs just look that way, I guess."

Some people too.

Joann looks at me out of the corner of her eye, and I know where this is going. She's got gossip. And I have a feeling I'm not going to like the topic today.

"You look fit to burst, Joann," I say, knowing she'll tell me one way or the other.

"Oh, I am. I *am*. It's about the situation with the Westfields."

I pick up a few stray paper towels and spray down one of the stainless steel counters. "I don't know much. He's doing better. They're moving him to a physical therapy facility soon."

"No, no, *everybody* knows that." She waves me off, hanging her clipboard on a hook. She comes close to me, her nose wrinkling. "I'm talking about the rumors about Deacon."

My heart punches out a hard beat. "What about him?"

"Dr. Atwood told me Wednesday that Deacon was taking time off, and then the sheriff turned up yesterday, right in the middle of the adoption rush. He was asking all kinds of questions." She drops her used needle in the sharps container.

"Questions about Deacon." My voice is a dead thing, but my heart's running rabbit-wild.

"Yeah. He didn't say anything, of course, but it sure looks like Deacon had a hand in it. The sheriff kept hinting around that we should all keep our eyes open and be careful."

I scrub the counter harder, gritting my teeth. The sheriff isn't just building a case—he's lighting torches and handing out pitchforks. Deacon was right. He's going to go down for this.

If I was sure he did it, that would be okay, but I'm still not convinced.

"Deacon's a lot of things, but I can't imagine him violent," I say. "Can you?"

Joann steps back, nods too quickly for me to believe her. "Oh, sure, but you never really know a person, do you?"

"I guess not."

Sarge yelps in his cage, and I rush over, making soft noises as I push his water closer. "You pulled those stitches, didn't you, buddy?"

He laps the water, then gently bumps into my hand, and I laugh, scratching his ears.

"You have a way with him," Joann says. "That one can be a real turkey."

"He's just hurting is all."

Joann refills a tub of cotton swabs with a laugh. "That's why I keep saying you should think about veterinary school."

"My mom's pretty set on doctor or lawyer. It's a family thing," I say with a smile.

"A veterinarian is a doctor," Joann points out.

"My mom doesn't see it as the same. She's got tunnel vision," I say with a rueful laugh.

"Mamas always do."

Maybe, but probably not like mine. Still, even if she did support me again in marine biology or veterinary medicine or whatever, I'm not sure I'd take it. Beaufort has plenty of vets, so there's a good chance I'd have to move. Who would Mom have left then? No one, that's who.

When I head out, the heat's stickier. It lingers in the grass and turns liquid thick in my lungs. I'm tempted to duck into the Cru for an iced mocha or maybe head home and stand over an air-conditioning vent. But I can't shake the conversation with Sheriff Perry out of my head.

He's so focused on Deacon, he could miss something. The injustice of it picks at me all the way down the block. If they don't investigate this properly, someone could end up getting away with it. Deacon's an easy suspect, but is he actually guilty?

Would Perry notice either way?

I find my way to the Westfield Charters dockside office again.

I'm not sure what I'm thinking. Is there going to be some clue lying on the deck of one of the boats? It's ridiculous.

The boats are up and running with tour times on the dry-erase board, but there's no one in the office. A sign on the window informs customers the ticket booth will reopen at one o'clock. I check my phone.

Twenty minutes from now.

Would there be anything in the office? Any sort of proof? I doubt someone's going to leave a pair of blood-spattered boots behind, but maybe there's a note on a time sheet or some sort of disciplinary charge that might give someone motive.

God, it's *such* a long shot. But it's better than no shot at all. If something assault-related jumps out at me, I'll call Joel so he can report it. If not...no harm, no foul, right?

Heat rushes into my cheeks at the idea of snooping, but I have a key for tidying up and checking supplies. It's hardly breaking and entering. I'll pop in, see if they're low on batteries or tape. Maybe sweep the floor if the broom hasn't ended up on one of the boats.

Cold sweat trickles down my back as I unlock the door. I close it behind me, letting my eyes adjust to the dim light. It's a tiny, dark box of a building, no bigger than a bathroom. The heat seems to push the walls closer, and a potent mix of fish and brine taints the air. A row of yellow slickers hangs on the far wall, and a few thermoses and lunch bags litter the bench beneath that.

There's a counter with a locked register that they usually prop on a tall stool in the open doorway. I don't blame them. I couldn't imagine sitting in this sweatbox taking money through the small dirty window beside the register.

Standing around isn't comfortable, so I straighten the time sheets right away and then pick up stray pens while my heart beats twelve million times a second. This was a bad idea.

*Okay, calm down and stick with the plan.*

There's no broom to sweep with and no cleaner for the counter, so I inventory supplies. Pens look fine, and there are no busted batteries for the handheld radios on the bigger boats. I crouch down to check the box under the register. I see plenty of tape and two stacks of tickets. It's official. There's nothing left for me to do.

I shove the box back, but something snags and catches on the shelf—paper, I think. A receipt?

I slide my hand over the bottom of the box, finding a partially crumpled Post-it note. There's a heavily inked square around a series of handwritten numbers.

*11 46'01.91—64 24'29.24—Call EM*

I squint at it closer. That's my initials. Emerson May. It could be a lot of initials, I guess, but it still gives me the creeps.

I draw my finger across the numbers, trying to figure out what they are. The format looks familiar. International phone number? Account number? No, wait—I know this.

It's coordinates. Longitude and latitude.

So, what, a good fishing spot? Maybe. I don't remember much about longitude and latitude, but I could swear Beaufort's latitude is roughly thirty-four. So what the heck is this for? Because

I doubt anyone's taking a charter boat through twenty-three latitude lines on a four-hour fishing trip. Either way, I doubt anyone's missing it.

I tuck the paper into my back pocket and stand up just as the door thumps open and shuts behind me. A shadow closes off the little light in the room, and my breath lodges in my lungs like glue.

I smell him before I see him. Tobacco. Fish. Sweat. My stomach sloshes as I turn, a large silhouette filling the room. My gaze darts from the red-brown chest to the mouth full of silver-capped teeth, lingering on a column of blue-black tattoos on a leathery arm.

"You lost, little girl?"

# CHAPTER NINE

. . . . . . . . . . . . . . . . . . . . . . . . . . .

I take a step back. Hit a wall. There's nothing around me but walls.

Don't panic.

Don't. Panic.

I force myself to look him in the eye. "I'm not lost. I'm checking supplies."

"You're Joel's girl, ain't ya?" Thorpe asks me.

I don't respond, because it's pretty obvious I'm not applying for a job to swab decks. But he's stalling, letting the silence stretch. He wants me uncomfortable. I can see it in his eyes.

I glance at the edge of the door behind him. I can't get there, but I could scream. There's got to be a thousand people on the waterfront right now. Someone would hear me. Still, sweat slides down my back and between my breasts.

"Didn't mean to scare you." His laugh is an oil stain in the putrid air. "I seen you around here with Chelsea. Looking for Deacon, I bet."

I force my shoulders back. "Nope, I'm checking supplies. And I'm all done." I move for the door, and he dodges to block the few inches available to me, jiggling his keys in his left hand. Adrenaline surges, burning behind my ribs.

"You sure you don't want me to leave the pretty boy a message?" he asks, putting his keys back and tapping his fingers on the register. They don't look bruised anymore.

He stops, left hand reaching for the pen on the clipboard to sign himself out. The look he gives me feels filthier than the business end of the boat mops. I tug at the edges of my skirt.

It hits me when he's scrawling out his time. Thorpe is left-handed. And his left hand isn't bruised. It was his *right* hand.

My heart sinks. I think I'm looking at the alibi Sheriff Perry was talking about. Even if he somehow lied about being down in Morehead City, he probably wouldn't have beaten someone half to death with his nondominant hand.

"Cat got your tongue?"

The hair on the back of my neck prickles. Maybe he didn't hurt Mr. Westfield, but this man is a walking bad intention. I need to get out of here.

"Excuse me. Please." The Southern manners polish is gone from my tone now. My voice is firm. I keep that purposeful eye contact too, the kind that promises I won't be an easy target. I will fight.

"I could help you check those supplies," he says, gaze dragging down to my skirt. "I could help you in a lot of ways."

My hands clench into fists.

And the door to the office swings wide.

"Mr. Thorpe?" Joel's voice booms into the room like divine intervention. "Step outside this minute."

My whole body unclenches. Thorpe disappears from the doorway as commanded, and light and freedom pour in. I bolt

116

outside on rubbery legs, passing both men as I gulp in one deep breath after another. I find a free bench by a nearby parking lot and sink onto it, my vision going gray at the edges.

Am I going to pass out? *No.* That's absolutely not happening. I concentrate on the boats in the harbor and the heat of the sun on my shoulders. I'm fine. Safe. I say it over and over in my head until my breathing starts to slow.

While I'm remembering how to move air like a normal person, Joel speaks to Thorpe outside the office. I can't make out what either of them is saying, but Thorpe loses several notches on the formidable scale getting dressed down like this. My stomach squirms seeing him nodding over and over. Three minutes ago, he was sniffing around me like a hungry coyote. Now he's a kicked puppy? Maybe he *is* desperate to hold this job.

Eventually, Joel heads inside the office—I'm guessing for the previous day's receipts. With the sun behind me, I must be camouflaged, because Joel wanders right past me. I call his name, and he turns back with a smile, walking over to join me on the bench.

"I'm so sorry, Eddie. I generally don't dismiss employees without Daffy's permission, but I'd be more than happy to make an exception."

"It's fine. He didn't actually do anything. Just tried to intimidate me."

Joel sighs, watching Thorpe climb on board the boat where Charlie is mopping. "Men like Kevin Thorpe weren't given many tools in their lives. They tend to use a machete when a pair of tweezers would do. Probably exactly how he ended up in trouble in the first place."

"What was he in jail for?" I give him a look when he hesitates. "Joel, you and I both know criminal records are public. I could get it online if I wanted."

Joel hesitates for a moment before relenting. "Assault. He served three years in the state penitentiary after a bar fight. He's got a temper when he's drinking, but he's in AA now. We haven't had trouble with him until today. What exactly did he do?"

I shake my head. "Just your typical 'whatcha gonna do, little girl' crap. It was creepy."

He frowns. "When Daffy gets to feeling a bit better, I'm going to discuss this with him. I hired him for his son CJ really. But I don't want him hassling anyone."

"Does he run tours alone?"

"Never. Everyone goes with a partner. It's safer that way."

I look at Thorpe now, scrubbing hard in the blazing sun. My stomach is still sour from our encounter, but in the light of day, I wonder how bad it was. Would he have actually done anything? I was scared out of my mind—I could have blown the whole thing out of proportion.

"How old is his son?" I ask.

"Nine," Joel says, sounding distracted. "I need to ask you—did he make any threats or touch you in any way? If he did, it's my responsibility to report that to his parole officer."

And then his parole officer will send him back to jail. For what? Leering? What he did was gross and *vaguely* threatening. But I don't know if I can send him to jail for being icky. Not with him spraying out coolers that reek of dead fish while I spend most of my paid working hours answering phones at a mahogany desk.

"He just spooked me," I say, rubbing my arms with both hands. "I shouldn't have been in there anyway. I was just trying to keep an eye on supplies."

"You're a kind girl." He pauses to arch a brow at me. "But I'll be talking to Daffy about that gentleman all the same. We need to keep a much closer eye on things."

"Please don't bring it up until Mr. Westfield is well," I say. "How is he anyway?"

Joel brightens. "Much better. He still doesn't remember too many details, but perhaps that's for the best." His smile tightens, and I can practically feel the Deacon-shaped elephant between us. "He'll be moving to a rehabilitation facility up in New Bern tomorrow."

"Oh, that soon?"

"Yes, and I'll be honest, I'm feeling a bit guilty about not being able to be there."

"Why? What's up?"

Joel frowns. "Mr. Trumbull."

I turn sideways on the bench to face him, pushing my wind-blown hair out of my eyes. "Everything is set up for him. I double-checked his supplies, and we've got an order for food and water to stock in the coolers, mostly nonperishable. What else could he want?"

"You did beautifully, but this isn't about those arrangements.

He has other business interests here. He and his wife live in the mountains near Asheville. I'm supposed to leave today to come up for a conversation."

"Must be *some* business. You don't strike me as a hiking kind of a guy, Joel."

"You've got that right." His smile goes a little devilish, and my heart twinges. It's so much like Deacon. "Can you keep a secret? A business secret?"

"Of course."

He tugs at the cuffs on his shirt. "Even from Chelsea. This is all still up in the air, and I don't want her worrying or getting excited if nothing comes of it."

I slap the bench between us with a laugh. "Joel, tell me already!"

His eyes twinkle as he leans in. "Mr. Trumbull isn't just a renter. He might be an investor. One that could put Westfield Charters into the black for good."

"What do you mean?"

"Trumbull's a real angler. Sport fishing. Being a business man, he started to add up the potential dollars of all those tourist runs. We got to talking about Westfield Charters, and soon enough, I'd reeled in my own catch. He's interested in an expansion."

"Wow," I say. "Expansion. But where? You've kind of tapped Beaufort and Morehead, right?"

"Up the coast, in the Duck, Corolla area."

I suck in a breath. "Big money up that way."

His smile goes wide. "Real big. Daffy has been so worried about college, about the future. I don't want to breathe a word, because these things can fall through easily, but if it comes together…"

"Wow," I say again. "And here I thought you came to Beaufort for the quiet life."

It's Joel's turn to laugh. "Oh, I love the quiet life, but I'm a lawyer. I like money too." Out on the water, Charlie and Thorpe are still spit-polishing that boat. "You know, Dink won't even consider college. He thinks the business can't afford to be without him. And Chickadee is planning on loans. This could change that, give them a little padding. Maybe even give Dink the push he needs when it's all sorted. So if Trumbull calls, be discreet and treat him well."

My heart swells a little, pricking my eyes with tears. Maybe he's not so convinced Deacon's guilty either. If he was, he wouldn't talk like this about the future, would he?

Joel's ears go pink, and he rubs his head, looking like he's not sure he should have said anything. "You've really got to keep that one close to the vest, Eddie."

"I will. I promise."

"If I head to Asheville tonight, will you be able to hold down the fort? Maybe check the messages once or twice? Things are slow with Daffy out—but just in case something comes up."

"Of course. You should definitely go."

"I'm not sure what reception will be like in the mountains."

I wave that off. "It's no trouble at all."

Joel rolls his shoulders back with a sigh. "There's one more thing. I should warn you that Chickadee spoke with Sheriff Perry. She mentioned you in connection with Dink."

My spine stiffens. Mentioned? Sold me down the river might be more accurate.

"The sheriff was already by on Friday," I say, turning back to look over the water. "He seems pretty convinced Deacon is behind this."

"Maybe, maybe not. Beaufort has a fine police department. The truth will come out."

I want to ask him what his version of Deacon's guilt is, but I bite my tongue. Maybe Joel's right. The truth will come out.

"Chelsea was too hard on you," Joel says. "I hope you can forgive her for that. She promised to spend the entire day at the inn. I'm hoping a little rest will get her back to normal."

"We can hope."

Joel pats my hand. "So how is Dink? Have you seen him since the hospital?"

"I haven't." I sigh, watching an older couple walk past with bags from the Fudge Factory. "The sheriff asked too, but I honestly don't have a clue where he is."

Joel nods. "I wish I could just talk to him. Do you have any idea where he might go?"

I'm grateful I don't have to wrestle with telling him. It's easier not knowing. "He *was* at the cemetery, but I don't think he'll keep going there. I'll call you if I run into him though."

"I'll be waiting for that call." He stands up, squeezes my shoulder lightly. "I'll do what I can to help him. Make sure you tell him I said so when you see him."

"I might *not* see him, Joel."

"You will. You always do." Joel takes his time striding away.

I take a deep breath, letting the sun soak in. Out on the water, a golden retriever is pacing back and forth on the bow of a fishing boat. His owner tosses a tennis ball, and he leaps into the water. I grin, watching him paddle back and forth.

Thorpe and Charlie stop mopping on their boat, their gazes following Joel down the boardwalk. I stiffen, reminding myself that Thorpe is left-handed, staring at the bruises on his right hand to confirm. He's not guilty. He's not.

But then he slips something to Charlie, and cold fingers crawl up my spine. It's a Post-it note, lime green. *Exactly* like the one in my pocket that I totally forgot until now.

I force my shoulders down. Okay, back up the bus. Charlie is a decent guy. For all I know, that's a customer name. A girl's phone number. Hell, an order for a bacon cheeseburger at Clawson's. Still, there's something about the way they're watching Joel, something hateful.

Thorpe offers another one of his filthy grins to Charlie, and my arms drop heavy to my sides. What happened to the kicked puppy look? Guess it's all different when the boss isn't checking in.

Charlie tucks the paper Thorpe gave him into the back of his jeans like it's a dirty secret. Maybe it is. Alibi or not, maybe I'm missing something big.

* * *

I leave the bench like a hunted animal, my eyes darting behind me until I'm sure I'm out of sighting distance. I should have said something about what I found, but I was so flipped out about Thorpe. I could call Joel now, but what am I going to say? I'll have to admit to snooping, and since both of these notes could be nothing, I'll wind up looking paranoid.

Nice as he is, Joel is my *boss*. Me looking sane and reasonable in front of him is pretty nonnegotiable.

I head to the shade of a cluster of live oaks near the shops and restaurants, my knees loose and weak. The foot traffic is light today, so I lean back against the rough bark of one of the trees and feel myself go steady.

Okay. This isn't a crisis. Not yet. The coordinates and the paper could be coincidence. The bag-of-snakes feeling in my belly might be left over from the visit with the sheriff. All of this could be absolutely nothing. Or not.

Could be. Might be. Too many what-ifs and maybes. I rub my forehead where I can feel the stirrings of a wicked headache.

I pull up a map website on my phone and load the coordinates in. The map adjusts and reveals a spot in the middle of the Caribbean. I look at it and shake my head. What kind of coordinates are those? Third sandbar to the right and straight on till morning? I try again, double-checking each number. The same random location in the Caribbean shows up.

I need someone to think this through with me.

Mom's not even a possibility. After the sheriff visit, if I started going all Sherlock on her, she'd have a nervous breakdown. Dad's probably out on some random dock selling some random boat thing, and I'm trying to stay away from Deacon. That leaves Chelsea.

She'd be my first choice if she hadn't thrown me under the bus in a fit of grief-induced psychosis. A trio of seagulls flies overhead, and I close my eyes, listening to their cries. What's the big secret she doesn't want me knowing? God, there's so much I don't get about that. About the way she's been acting in general.

This isn't the time to hold grudges, so I call her. It rings six times before her voice mail picks up. I try again, and it's straight to voice mail, so she denied the call.

*Still pissed then.*

I take a breath and force myself to lift my chin. In thirty minutes, I'm supposed to hit Clawson's with Seth, and I'm not going to be torn to bits about this the whole time. Still, I'm not sure I'm going to be able to eat a burger either.

I fire off a quick text to Seth, who's all too willing to swap out Clawson's for the Cru. Good. Coffee I can definitely do. I head in that direction, forcing myself to keep a slow and steady pace to calm down.

The Cru is a dark, quiet hodgepodge of a restaurant with a deli counter on the left and a full-service bar around the corner to the right. It's also the only place in town to get a seriously good cup of coffee. Summer mornings are a madhouse, but we're lucky enough to have one of the long comfy couches in the back tonight.

I wipe down the rim of my coffee cup with my napkin while Seth dives into his ham and cheese sandwich.

"So," I say. "When did you switch to Team Chelsea?"

Seth half chokes, and I grin, whacking him on the back when the coughing goes on for a while. He finally holds up his hands to stop me.

"I'm good, I'm good! Boy, you don't dance around a subject, do you?"

"This week? Not so much. You sure you're okay?"

"Bruised, but fine."

"So, Chelsea, huh?" I say again.

He scratches the back of his neck and scoots forward on the couch. "Yeah. I don't really know when it happened. It wasn't you or anything. I wouldn't want you to think—"

"No, I get it," I say. "People change."

"Yeah, I guess you know about that." I shake my head, not sure what he means, but he goes on before I can ask. "I mean with your brother and all."

Everything in me bristles, but I force a light tone. "Landon is just trying to figure himself out. He's confused. There was a lot of pressure on him. It was doctor or bust, and not just from my parents. This whole town expected him to be our poster child or something."

"That's your hero worship talking," he says. Then he lifts his hands like he's surrendering. "Not judging. My dad's so big around here, you'd think he brunches with Jesus."

"It's gotta be nice though." I smile over the rim of my coffee cup. "At least you want to be a veterinarian like him."

"Not especially." Seth laughs, so I must be gaping. "You'll catch flies that way."

"Sorry." I straighten the pillow beside me. "I'm shocked. You're always at the shelter."

"Got to get my hours in. Walking dogs is better than changing geezer diapers."

"Wow." I take a drink of coffee to hide my frown. He has a career plan I'd love to have, and he could take it or leave it.

When I set the cup back on the table, Seth chuckles. "Emmie, you're looking at me like I'm confessing to a murder."

I wince. "I know, sorry. It's just—you had this all planned out. Third-generation equine veterinarian, right? Isn't your grandfather planning to retire when you get your license?"

He nods, puts his coffee down on the table. "Absolutely."

I put a paper coaster under his cup. "But you don't want it?"

"Well, I want the money." I must not hide my distaste, because he laughs again. "I like animals. Maybe not like you do, but well enough. The money's good, and I have a family advantage. It's business, Emmie. Gotta be sensible."

He's right. And I really should watch the way I'm looking at him. It's not like I'm doing something so different. I didn't grow up dreaming of law school. I adapted. I got sensible.

He crumples his sandwich wrapper, and I wince at the crumbs that spray over the coffee table when he tosses it in the basket. I resist the urge to clean them up, but I can't stop looking at them. Bits of bread. A shred of lettuce. It revolts me more than it should.

"So what are you up to for the rest of the night?" Seth asks. "Want me to call Caleb and his crew?"

His track friends? Nice enough guys, but without Chelsea

to chat with? I'd rather lick the underside of this table. I make myself smile. "Actually, lame as it is, I think I want to stop by Joel's office. He's out of town, so I'm checking in more often for calls and such."

"On a Sunday night?"

"Trust me, Joel's work never ends. People call day and night." Which is true. But really, I just want to make sure everything's in order. Because I want to do a good job for Joel. And because organizing brings me down a notch or two on the anxiety scale. And also because I maybe want to scan our files for any details on these coordinates burning a hole in my pocket.

"Joel's place is out in the east end, right?" He stands up. "I'll walk you over, maybe keep you company."

"Are you sure? I actually might do a little work. I don't want you to go out of your way."

"Maybe you'll give me some Chelsea tips while we walk," he says. "I'll help you collate copies or whatever when we get there."

Seth smiles, and I bare my teeth in a close approximation, discreetly scraping his crumbs into a napkin.

He heads to the counter to put a few bucks in the tip jar, and I mash my lips together, scrubbing at the table with my napkin. Why on earth would he want to hang out with me while I work? And how am I going to get out of this without being rude? I notice Seth watching and still my hand, crumpling my napkin in my fist.

Outside, the misery of the day has given way to a perfect night. There's a band playing at Dockside, and the air is cooler. Sweeter. We walk along the waterfront, where I tell him Chelsea is a no for flowers but a yes for letters and a definite yes for penuche from the Fudge Factory.

It's easy with Seth to pretend that Chelsea and I are fine, but I know we're not. We will be though, so I focus on that. We've hurt each other before, and we've always gotten over it.

"When you talk to her, maybe you can put in a good word," he says as we turn toward Joel's office. "Make sure she knows you aren't secretly pining over me."

"Trust me, she already knows," I answer.

"You wound me."

"Really? I think we're getting along a whole lot better now that we're not trying to date."

"We *were* dating, just not seriously," he says, leaning against the painted porch railing. "I was pretty good at it."

"Pretty modest too." I pull out my keys and look up at the small office. The flower boxes need cleaning. I should do that in the morning. Sweep the welcome mat too. Seth's still waiting on the porch, not catching the hint at all. We need more things to do in this town.

"Do you mind if I come in?" he asks. "You seem weirded out."

I hesitate. I have no idea how Joel would feel about Seth being here. I mean, it's Seth, but is that unprofessional? Probably not as unprofessional as standing here in the dark, hemming and hawing about it like it's a difficult question. Especially since deep down, I know the only reason I'd think about not letting him in is because I want to snoop.

I look at Seth, feeling like my mom is hovering over my left shoulder. Life would be so much easier without manners. My smile feels like it belongs to someone else.

"I'll just check the messages really quick," I say. "I can do the rest in the morning."

"Putting something off until later?" Seth clutches his chest. "You make me proud, Emmie. Hey, care if I use the bathroom really quick?"

I can't even flash teeth this time, but my voice stays perky. "Sure, come on in. I'll just…" *Think of ways to get rid of you?* "… check those messages."

We step inside, and I point at the bathroom just inside the door. Seth heads left, and I wait on the carpet in the main office until I hear the door latch. The light and fan combo whirs to life, and I move quickly, slipping past my desk, where for once, my phone's red message light isn't blinking. So I have maybe two minutes.

I could check the paper log on Joel's desk. He keeps a month printed out for easy reference. Maybe there will be some clue on that. Some really long-term charter I missed.

Only the lamp in Joel's office is on, but I can see his large footprints trailing through my vacuumed carpet, so he must have stopped by before Asheville. I step into his doorway and see a shadow hunched over the desk. My throat cinches tight.

"Joel?"

He looks up, and I stop dead. It's not Joel. It's Deacon, sitting in the big leather chair with a few Westfield files open on the desk. A thousand feelings hit me in that second, all of them beating furious wings inside my chest.

"What are you doing?" I whisper. "You shouldn't be here, going through Joel's files."

He stands up from the desk. He's freshly showered. In new clothes too. "They're *our* files," he says just as quietly, tapping at the Westfield sticker. "And I have a key."

"The sheriff is still looking for you," I say.

He sags, pushing his hand through his hair. "I know. Why are you here?"

I don't bother to answer. I work here. I'm supposed to be here. I don't feel like explaining myself. "What are you looking for, Deke?"

"I'm looking for coordinates."

I feel cold pouring down from my hairline until it pools in my belly. The toilet flushes, and Deacon moves around the side of the desk, brow furrowing.

"Is that Joel?" he asks. Then he looks me up and down. I can feel his eyes burning a trail from my silver necklace to my going-out-tonight skirt. "Wait, it's Sunday."

The sink turns on, and Deacon closes the distance between us.

His smirk flips my stomach. "You brought your *date* to work?"

"It's not a date." The bathroom door creaks open, and I switch off the lamp on Joel's desk. I don't know why. I'm not supposed to be helping him.

"Emmie?" Seth calls.

"I'm back here. Don't move!" I shout. Too loud. I clear my throat and try again. "I tripped over the lamp cord. I'll get it."

I hear the chime of an incoming message on Seth's phone. It's the best chance of not being seen. I press my palm to Deacon's chest, pushing him backward into the narrow space between the window and Joel's tall bookshelf.

We're close enough to whisper now, and his eyes are a flash of heat in the darkness. He doesn't like being tucked away like this.

"*Please.*" The word trembles out of me. "He could call Perry."

His face changes then. Maybe he sees the fear in my eyes.

"Emmie." My name is a prayer on his lips, and it goes straight to my knees. His heart—a steady *thump-thump-thump*—grows faster against my palm.

"Do you need help back there?" Seth calls. "Should I look for a switch?"

"No, I'm coming out!" I lick my dry lips, try to kick my voice down from panicked to annoyed. "It's just fiddly. You know these old houses. You can wait on the porch if you want."

I hear Seth shuffle to the door, but he doesn't leave. He's waiting for me.

There's nearly no light. I can hear Deacon breathing. Hell, I can practically feel it.

"I have to go," I whisper.

His fingers brush my hand as I pull it free. He turns away, and I can see his jaw clenched. I think he's trying to keep his word. To keep me out of it. But he's looking for coordinates, so the tables have turned. If I really want those answers, he might be my best shot.

I inch forward on the carpet, feeling the toe of my sandal brush one of his shoes. "We need to talk. I found some coordinates. Where can I find you?"

His lips part as he takes that in. Then he holds his breath, like he's not sure he should answer me. But he does. "That abandoned house where we found Hushpuppy," he says.

"Emmie?" Seth laughs. "You sure I don't need to send in a rescue crew?"

"Coming!"

I switch the lamp back on and stride out of Joel's office without looking back. I take a breath as I lock the door behind me, still feeling the warmth of Deacon's chest along my palm. My knees knock with every step on my way down to the sidewalk.

# CHAPTER TEN

. . . . . . . . . . . . . . . . . . . . . . . . .

I wake up to the smell of coffee and eggs and the sound of Mom and Dad talking in the kitchen. I've had the big downstairs bedroom since I was eight, but I'm not sure they've ever considered that my bathroom sink shares a wall with the dishwasher. I can hear every word they say when I'm getting ready in here. Sometimes that's way too much information for my pre-coffee brain.

Mom drones on while I pull my hair into a ponytail, mostly tuning her out. I'm brushing my teeth when she starts talking about me. Always harder to ignore that, but it's usually the same song and dance. She's proud of me. I'm a good girl, but I'm just so persnickety about things these days.

It's not *these days*. It's been this way since the Landon debacle, and I have a feeling I'm going to have to deal with it at some point, especially since just hearing her talk about it makes me want to scour my bathtub.

I frown at myself in the mirror when Dad agrees with her. It's not like I can argue. I know I'm flirting with something that looks a lot like OCD, but even that isn't enough to make me quit doing it. I put my brush away and close the medicine cabinet. Wipe down my sink and the faucet handles too. Wipe them once more before I force myself to stop.

"Sheriff Perry called me last night," Mom says.

I pause at the mirror. My reflection goes tight. And then pale.

"Has she been with Deacon again?" Dad asks.

"Not sure. He said he'd keep an eye on her for us though."

"Good," Dad says. "Those Westfields are trouble."

I don't like his tone. All the Westfields are trouble now? Why? Because Deacon drives too fast? Because Mr. Westfield cut Dad's maintenance contract? Maybe he's forgetting all the days I spent at their house, days when Dad was packing his things and splitting our family in two. A cramp in my jaw reminds me to stop gritting my teeth.

It's getting clearer every day that Perry isn't investigating anything. This case begins and ends with Deacon for him—but not me. I glance over at my laptop open on my bed.

I still don't know what to make of the coordinates. If my research is legit, then a few of the Westfield boats could make it down there, and there are some small islands in the area. But people don't charter clunky fishing boats for a pleasure cruise to a remote tropical paradise.

Is it a fishing thing? Some rare "not legal to catch here" opportunity that I wouldn't have a clue about? Definitely a Deacon question. Guilt still flits around my plans to see him, but I've been round and round with it all night. Deke might have answers, and if I don't get some of those soon, I'm going to start pulling out my bedroom carpet fibers, one by one.

I pause with my hand on the door, reviewing the mental to-do list I pored over all night.

Spend time with Mom so she doesn't worry.
Visit Chelsea.
Weed flower boxes and check messages.
Check in with Joel.
See Deacon.

Okay. It's showtime.

In the kitchen, Dad's reading the paper and Mom's chopping vegetables for something she's probably cooking later. I sit at the oak table, eating toast with too much butter, while we all chitchat about breakfast-appropriate things. The weather. The new boat engine Dad's all excited about. The estate sale Mom's shopping this weekend.

It's all as sunny as the kitchen itself. I pretend I didn't hear them talking about me, and they pretend they are still married. We're very good at this game.

I put my plate in the sink and head to the back door. "I'm going to head out to check on Chelsea. Run some errands."

"When will you be home?" Mom asks.

I shrug, aiming for nonchalant. "Probably late. I want to stop by Joel's office. Might see who's hanging out at the Cru."

Mom's lips go a little thin, and Dad looks up from the paper. It's as close to suspicious as they've ever looked with me. My shoulders go heavy, but I force a smile. "What's the matter? I said the Cru, but you guys look like you heard seedy meth lab."

Mom waves a dish towel at me, but her laugh is nervous. "No, sugar, it's all fine. Just…just check in on your phone."

I push her anxiety out of my mind as I head across the backyard. There's no help for it right now. If Deacon's name is cleared, they'll chill out, and they'll never even have to know I was involved.

The morning haze still hasn't burned off, so the air is thick and muggy. It might be one of those days where the cloud cover never clears. I slog through the humidity, focusing on all the ways this conversation might go with Chelsea. The inn is only a couple of blocks from my house, so I don't have much time to think. It'll end up the same anyway. Chelsea and I will talk. Holler a little maybe. Then we'll be friends again.

Maybe she'll even know something about the coordinates.

The Ann Street Inn is a two-story white beauty with a wide front porch. There are pretty tables for cocktails and rockers and lounge chairs with plenty of cushions. Most of us in the historic district have spent at least one night chatting on this porch with Donna and her guests. It's almost weird to see it empty.

I climb the steps and slip inside, spotting the narrow table with brochures and the door to the Queen Anne suite on the right. Faintly, upstairs, I hear the whir of a vacuum cleaner.

"Donna? Are you up there?" I call.

I knock on the wall by the banister, and the vacuum goes silent. Donna bumps something upstairs, swears softly. Then she rounds the landing at the top of the steps, breaking into a wide smile. "Hey, you! You here to see Chelsea?"

"Yes, ma'am."

"Shoot, no need for the ma'am here." Donna's the epitome

of life in Beaufort—always friendly, always smiling, and *always* ready for cocktail hour. "She's out back with a visitor. I think he's from Children's Services or something?"

I feel my brows pull together. "Children's Services? Oh no, did her aunt call?"

"Well, I didn't think to ask. But they'll have to figure out where she'll go long term, so maybe." She drops her voice to a whisper. "Her daddy's got a long road yet."

"Of course," I say, though I'd never thought about that. I just assumed Joel would get the guardianship, but maybe my mom was right about their aunt.

Donna looks back into the upstairs, toward the guest rooms most likely. "I'd love to sit and wait with you, Emmie, but I've got to get these bathrooms done. Grab a glass of tea from the fridge if you want to wait in the kitchen."

"Thanks."

I slip through the small living area, cluttered with thick-cushioned sofas, then past the huge dining room table on my way to the kitchen in the back. Tea's not a bad idea. I can pour us both a glass. It'll make this visit look more social and less "let's talk about your betrayal and your dad's possible attacker."

I find glasses on the counter and glance outside, spotting Chelsea at a chair just beyond the windows. The windows are open for air, but the blinds are tilted down enough to make it easy to see out without totally sacrificing privacy.

I like that it gives me the chance to see Chelsea, to brace myself for our talk. She's still with the guy Donna mentioned, so maybe

I should give them time. I don't recognize him, but he looks nice enough—dark skin, gray suit, and a friendly face.

"I don't know how long," Chelsea says, apparently answering something. I feel a little bad being able to hear them so well, so I grab a glass for the iced tea and start pouring.

"Do you think Emmie knows anything about this?"

My head jerks up at my name. What kind of a Children's Services question is that? What would *I* know about? Unless maybe she wants to stay with Mom and me? Hope unfurls in my chest.

"I don't know," Chelsea says, her voice cracking. "God, I hope not."

"But you aren't sure," the man says. "We have to be sure."

Chelsea sighs. "She works for Joel, not my dad, so I doubt it. I don't know though. It's not like I haven't kept secrets from her."

My stomach drops, and tea dribbles over the rim of my glass. I set down the pitcher. This isn't about where Chelsea is staying. This is about secrets. And somehow about me.

"Maybe I'll have a talk with her," the man says.

"Don't!" Chelsea's urgency startles me. "Please don't talk to Emmie. Not about this."

The kitchen goes narrow and dim. All I can see is the tea I spilled, rivers of brown liquid that pool into tiny lakes on the counter. I snag a handful of napkins with shaking hands.

"I can't make you promises, Miss Westfield."

"She wouldn't keep this quiet," she says. "Emmie can't handle secrets like this."

I'm wiping furiously, scrubbing at the mess on the counter.

"It's almost time," the man says.

"I know." Chelsea looks down at the table and sighs. "I should get back in there."

She stands up outside, and fear grips me. I don't want her to see me. I don't want her to know I heard them. I swipe the napkins into the trash and put my glass in the sink. I all but sprint out of the kitchen.

I'm at the front door when Donna starts coming down the stairs. "Emmie? You're as white as the wall."

"I'm so sorry, Donna. I think I might be sick. I'll come back." My gaze darts to the back of the house. I can't see the kitchen from here, but I don't hear anything yet. "Could you maybe not tell Chelsea? I…I wanted to surprise her."

"Your secret's safe with me," she says with a smile.

I stumble outside without another word, my stomach in knots and my world falling apart.

* * *

I dial Joel half a block from Ann Street Inn, but his line goes straight to voice mail. Okay, slow down. Think. Calling Children's Services will get me nowhere. Calling my parents will result in a paranoid mess. The police?

I pause at the corner, thinking that one over. I don't know if he was Children's Services or not, but Chelsea wasn't afraid. He obviously introduced himself to Donna. The only scary thing about any of this is the fact that Chelsea obviously has a secret. One she doesn't want me knowing about.

*Chelsea, what are you hiding?*

I remember in a rush. Deacon knows.

The office will have to wait. Everything will have to wait. I narrow my eyes and start out again, toward my house. I don't care whose secret this is—it's getting closer to me every second, and I'm tired of being in the dark.

I stop back by the house to pick up my bike—a second-hand beach cruiser with a giant metal basket. Mom and Dad are both gone, and I don't hear Ralph barking, so they must be out.

My tires crunch over the driveway and then onto the street. I swear I feel eyes on me the second I clear the shadow of my house. It's stupid. This isn't some big city. Sheriff Perry doesn't have the manpower to set up a tail for a seventeen-year-old girl. Heck, we can barely produce a sufficient police presence when things get crazy during the Pirate Invasion Festival every year. Still, I find myself looking over my shoulder at every stop sign.

I avoid the waterfront and take a couple of wrong turns, so it takes me almost an hour to span the four miles to the cottage up the creek. It's the quiet side of town, the part the tourists don't see and most of the rest of us don't think about much. The houses are farther apart and sometimes abandoned. Beaufort isn't a cheap place to live or an easy place to find work.

The old Carmine place had some sort of foundation problem. When the owner couldn't fix it, the house was condemned, and after he died, the whole thing turned into a blame game.

The place has been sitting vacant ever since. Chelsea, Deacon, and I found it shortly after Mr. Carmine died. Chelsea hated it—thought it was creepy to be wandering around an old dead man's house—but I thought he'd lived a good life here, and the peacefulness kind of stuck.

I could have come here every day.

I might have, if Deacon hadn't chosen it as his personal sanctuary too. I've ridden out here more than once to spot his motorcycle off in the high grass beside the gravel driveway. Chicken that I was, I kept right on pedaling, too afraid of what might happen if I spent time with Deke without Chelsea running interference.

Feels funny riding up this narrow, twisting road now, not bubbling up with that electric mix of hope and fear that I'll see him. This time, I'm just praying he'll be here like he said.

It's a good choice for a hideout. Close enough to give him access to town. Far enough away to keep people out of his business. Plus, with an attached dock, the property provides easy water access.

The house is ugly, tiny, and lost in a thicket of wildly overgrown shrubbery. Probably has a lot to do with why it's been in legal limbo so long. It's a one-bedroom hovel with a closet-sized kitchen and a bathroom so small, you could probably pee and shower at the same time. The plumbing still worked last time I checked, but the occasional critter gets in the bedroom window. And there's no electricity. Not exactly the Hilton.

I park my bike in the weed-covered driveway and head to the porch. That's what brought us here the first time. We heard something crying in this thin, awful way. From the road, it had sounded like a little kid. Chelsea was already skeeved out, but Deke insisted we look.

We found her trapped on the second step of the porch, one paw caught between two boards and raw from her trying to free it. The cat hissed and shrieked until even I was ready to call animal control and throw in the towel. Deacon just took off his shirt and wrapped her tight, holding her other paws down while he freed the trapped one. He carried her all the way back to Dr. Atwood's that night, rolled up like a little kitty burrito in his sweaty T-shirt.

I even suggested Burrito as a name, but Deacon was set on something more ironic. She's been Hushpuppy ever since.

There's no caterwauling today though. Just the steady breeze rasping through tall grass. I don't see any movement inside the windows. Nothing on the chipped kitchen counter or on the floor where a dining room used to be.

Still, I inch around the side of the cottage. I see a flash of silver-gray out by the dock first. My cheeks tingle. Deacon's little putter-around boat.

I find him in the hammock, stretched out and eyes closed while he sways just a little. I know from my own naps on that hammock that if I get much closer, I'll hear the creak of the rope against the metal ring. Is he sleeping? I take a second to watch his chest rise and fall in his white T-shirt, his brown arms propped behind his head.

The grass rustles when I start walking again, and he opens his eyes, surprise lighting his features. He lumbers out of the hammock, stretching his arms high enough for me to catch a glimpse of hip bone above his faded shorts.

"I wasn't sure you'd come," he says, smirking.

"We have a lot to talk about."

We walk to the dock where his boat is anchored, sitting side by side. The fabric of his cargo shorts brushes my leg and heat spreads over my skin, flash-fire fast. I look out over the inlet. The water's gone navy blue under the cloudy sky.

"Someone was talking today with Chelsea at the inn," I start.

"She's staying with Donna?" he asks, then he frowns. "Hell, I didn't even think about that. I figured she'd stay with Joel."

"He applied for emergency guardianship, but they'll probably reach out to family too. Donna thought this guy was Children's Services. But here's the thing—"

"It should be me there for her. I know."

I shake my head, wishing this were just a simple chewing out. Because this is worse than that. I watch a heron stalk back and forth in a patch of tall grass. I feel like I'm hunting too—for words. I doubt I'm going to find any that will make this easier to say. I scoot back on the dock, tucking my legs under me so I can turn to face him. "The guy with Chelsea asked about *me*, about whether or not I knew about something. They never said *what* exactly, but Chelsea begged him not to talk to me. It was creepy, Deke. He said it was almost time too."

"Almost time for what?"

"I have no idea."

His shoulders pull back, and a gust of wind tugs hair loose from my ponytail. I focus on the thin white scar on his chin and the tension in his jaw.

"Was she afraid of him?" he asks. "Was he threatening her or anything?"

I press my lips together. "She wasn't scared. Not one bit. She just begged him not to talk to me. She said I couldn't keep it quiet. Like it was a secret. Do you think she's hiding something about what happened to your dad?"

"You're seriously asking that?" His eyes are sparking, spots of pink burning high in his cheeks.

I swallow hard. "Deke, I know it sounds crazy—"

"It does sound crazy, Emmie," he says. "Chelsea's so wholesome she should be on one of those nutritional posters. She's a Girl Scout. A youth group leader!"

"I know that! You don't think I know that?" Our shouting startles the heron, which lifts off with a steady beat of long, wide wings. I blink away my sudden tears. "She's my best friend, but she *is* hiding something. Hiding it from me specifically. You said so yourself."

Deacon stands up, pacing back and forth on the dock. It's like he's putting pieces together. Of course he is. He knows the big secret; I don't.

I square my shoulders, though tears are blurring my vision. "It's been the three of us forever, Deke. Forever. And I'm *dying* watching you both go through this, but I can't help, because there's obviously some huge chunk of your lives that neither of you trust me with."

"I trust you." He crouches in front of me. Touches my shoulder. My chin. Turns me to face him. "*I* trust you, Emmie."

He grazes my cheek, one calloused finger running temple to jaw. He's waiting for me to say something, but I can't. His

145

touch is sucking all the oxygen out of the air and changing everything between us.

"Then tell me the truth," I say finally.

He takes a breath, and I can see a war waging behind his eyes. Then his mouth goes soft and his brow goes smooth. If surrender had a face, it would look like this.

"I'll tell you everything," he says. "But first I have to show you something."

# CHAPTER ELEVEN

· · · · · · · · · · · · · · · · · · · · · · · · · · · ·

Deacon heads into the house, and I walk to the space where the dock meets the yard. A little crab struggles at the edge, one claw pinned between the boards.

"Little buddy," I whisper, trying to ease his claw out without getting pinched by the other. The wind is ridiculous. Half of my ponytail is flying loose around my face. I gently free the crab and then yank my hair tie out while I watch him scuttle into the safe shadows under the weathered planks of the dock.

Deacon returns with a battered, brown Westfield Charters envelope. It's covered with greasy smudges I really don't want to think about. He offers it and laughs when I recoil.

"You sure I'm the right guy for you to be hanging around?" he asks.

"I ask myself that every day, Deke."

That makes him laugh harder. "You do know what I do for a living, right? Do you ever think about the kinds of *residues* that might be lingering on my hands?"

"I choose not to dwell," I say, and he waggles his fingers toward me like it's some kind of threat. Hardly. If he keeps it up, I'll start bobbing like one of those cobras in a basket. His special Emmie superpowers annoy me to no end.

I finally swat his hand away, because I like that last shred of my dignity. "All right, what do you have in there?"

His smile vanishes as he opens the envelope, pulling out a stack of receipts.

"Where did you get these?" I ask.

"From the lockbox on the main boat up in Morehead City."

They don't have an office in Morehead, just a closet-sized, fold-up counter where they can lock the register at night.

I look up at him over the receipts. "Wait, you stole these?"

He rolls his eyes. "Yes, Emmie. I stole a pile of receipts. Hide your women and children."

"Don't be a smart-ass," I say, looking them over. "Joel and I need these to do the accounting for—wait, are these coordinates?"

My fingers trace the handwritten numbers on the bottom of a receipt. Deacon's stomach growls, and I look up. He points back down at the receipt. "They all have coordinates. I need you to see the last one."

I flip through. The coordinates are jotted down everywhere. Some on the bottom. Some on the side. They're all different, but I know why the last one is important at one glance.

*15 62, 25 30 (Emmie)*

My pulse jumps. "That's my name. Why is my name on that? Where is that?"

"About sixty miles southeast of Washington, DC."

"Sixty miles from DC? Why the hell is my name next to coordinates near Washington, DC?"

"That's why I wanted to talk to you. Did you arrange any charters for that area?"

"No. They're all in state." A dull ache throbs at the back of my neck. I head over to the hammock, sitting down sideways. "I found coordinates with my initials in the dockside office. It's at home, but I checked and it's for a pretty random spot in the Caribbean."

Deacon joins me, and the hammock swings hard, the scratchy rope rubbing at my thighs. "The Caribbean? I don't get it," he says. "The coordinates aren't the kind of places you'd imagine charters heading. No resorts or beach towns. Just random spots along the Carolina coast, some up into Virginia. I was trying to figure it out from our client files."

"Maybe I should check the dockside office again," I say.

Deke shakes his head hard. "Emmie, you should steer clear of that place. Believe me, some of the guys working on our boats are worse than the shit we scrape off the hull."

"I know. Thorpe cornered me in there."

Deacon's whole body goes stiff beside me. "He *what*?"

I kick at the ground to swing us, careful to avoid a glass jar full of shells. "It's fine," I say, trying to lighten the mood. "I'm fine."

"Did he touch you?" His voice goes to gravel, and his eyes grow dark. "Because so help me, if he even *looked* at—"

"No, it wasn't… I mean, yeah, he was gross. Joel kind of saved me. It wasn't that bad."

"Him even breathing in the same space as you is that bad."

Warmth floods over me at his sudden intensity. He can't look at me like this, not when we're mashed together on a hammock with the wind blowing my hair into his eyes.

"I'm okay," I say. "Really."

He opens his mouth, and his stomach growls again, loudly. I laugh, and he flips me off playfully.

"When's the last time you fed that thing?" I ask.

He's as close to blushing as he ever gets, one corner of his mouth curled up. "It's been a while," he admits. "I finished off the gas station crap yesterday morning."

"Yesterday!" I gape at him while he shrugs.

"It's not that big of a deal."

"Yeah, starving to death isn't a big deal at all."

He chuckles. "It's not exactly the Great Outback. I've got a pole in the boat. I can catch something if it gets dire."

"And then what? You're going to just gnaw into it raw? Maybe bust open a coconut for water? This isn't the zombie apocalypse, Deke."

I stand up, about as gracefully as a greased pig on an ice rink, and brush off the back of my shorts.

"Wait, what are you doing?" he asks. "Are you leaving?"

"Yes. New plan. I'm getting you some supplies. You can't survive on energy drinks and whatever you fish out of there." I wave at the inlet for emphasis.

"Emmie, this isn't a camping trip. I got myself into this. I can skip a couple of meals."

"And drink salt water?"

"The water's still on in the house. Don't know who missed that, but I'll take it."

"Those faucets might be spewing chemical terrors unknown. You'll probably end up with some rare psychological disorder."

His grin turns his face into something magazine-worthy. "I think my raging blood phobia covers the psychological part, don't you?"

Deke's glib expression slips, just enough to show me the raw bits underneath. My throat goes tight looking at those bits. "You'll get better. You can handle the fishing stuff now, right? That used to freak you out."

"Fish aren't human," he says. Then he scuffs the grass with his battered boat shoe. "It was because of when I found her. I never told you about that either, did I?"

I shake my head, because aneurysm is pretty much all I knew. The details have always been vague, brushed over with murmurs about how tragic and terrible it all was. *So very unexpected.* Mom liked that phrase best.

"You don't have to explain," I say.

"No more secrets, right?" He takes a breath. "Mom was drying her hair, and we were running late for my baseball game."

I smile, remembering his uniforms, wide-brimmed caps and dirty white pants. They used to have trophies in the living room. I wonder what happened to those.

"Felt like she was in there forever," Deacon says. "I was getting so mad because we were late. I yelled, but the hair dryer kept running and running, and all of a sudden, I could tell it didn't sound right. It was too low. Like she was sitting on the floor."

*Or lying on it.* My eyes feel hot with the promise of tears, but I blink them back. Deacon stands up, moves his gaze to the inlet, where the heron is back, studying the water.

"I started hollering," he says. "Banging on the wall. I tried opening the door, but she was… I couldn't. But I could see the blood right away."

The phantom drone of a hairdryer presses against my ears. I can imagine it so clearly. *Too* clearly.

"It was everywhere, Emmie. On the sink. Running down the cabinet. She cracked her head on the faucet. That's what they think—" His breath hitches. The sound hits me like a fist. "I couldn't get inside. I couldn't—the door wouldn't—she was in front of it."

"Deke…" I tug at his shirt and see a flash of his watery eyes before he pulls me in.

This is nothing like our other rare hugs. It's bruising and broken, and I can't hold him tightly enough. Both of us are breathing all wrong. Jagged and harsh, like the air won't go in or come back out.

He releases me before I'm ready. "Sorry," he says, swiping at his eyes. "I'm sorry."

"Don't be. Please."

"I shouldn't have…" He shakes his head. "Shit, that's not what you're here for. I need to tell you about my dad."

"I'm here for *you*," I say. Then I smooth my hair behind my ears and watch his face shutter off once more. His eyelashes are still wet. Seeing it hurts. I don't think I can watch him go through another painful secret right now. He needs a second. Hell, I need a second.

"Deacon—"

"I'm going to tell you. I'm just regrouping. It's kind of about Dad's baggage from all of that, I guess."

More about his mom dying? I touch his arm. "Let's take a breather."

I glance back at the house, where there is no food and the water scares me. I could be to town and back in an hour.

"How about that supplies run?" I ask. "I'll go into town and grab some lunch. When I come back, you can tell me the rest, and then we'll make a plan."

My shoulders sag with relief when his smirk returns. "Should you get color-coded folders? Will we need a label maker?"

"Keep it up, and I'll make you draw up a flowchart."

I turn to leave, and he grabs my hand, pulling me back. "Emmie, be careful. Your name is on that receipt, and we don't know why."

\* \* \*

By the time I get to town, it's clear what all that wind was about. A storm is rolling in. They come in quick on the coast sometimes, turning the sky over the water thick and gray. Flags on the boardwalk snap, and the leaves on the live oaks flip backward. I need to get to the store quickly or I'm going to get drenched.

The temperature has dropped, and goose bumps rise on my arms. If Chelsea were here, she'd tell me Pacheco has arrived. It's a Venezuelan saying her mom used to use anytime it got chilly.

I slip into the grocery store, a small, aging shop set in a narrow lot on Front Street. Bells tinkle overhead, and the lights flicker and go dim as the door closes behind me. I feel distant thunder, a low rumble that shudders through the ground.

Someone swears in back where the registers sit. "Damn lights! I'm going to fire up the generator, so go on and shop, everybody."

I have no idea who *everybody* includes, because the narrow aisles are flanked by tall shelves, but the place is silent as a tomb, other than the cashier muttering in the back office. I pull a plastic basket from the stack by the door and head down the farthest aisle.

I stop by the juice boxes to count the cash in my wallet. Twenty bucks. Should be enough. The door jingles, and heavy steps shuffle in.

"I'm still open." The clerk's voice is thready and distant. "Be up there in a sec."

The shopper doesn't respond, but I have no trouble tracking his heavy shuffle through the store, even when the generator grumbles to life out back. The person who came in is staying close to me. Always one aisle away.

*You're imagining things.*

Am I? Because there's a crack between the shelves, and I'm sure the dark shape blocking that crack is a large man. Hard to be sure in the gray filter of emergency lighting though.

I turn away and grab a bunch of bananas from the tiny produce section, ignoring the chill climbing up my arms.

Thunder rolls outside as I turn the corner. I need easy stuff. Granola bars or something. Then I hear it again. *Shuffle step. Shuffle step.*

I scan the dimly lit shelves, grabbing a box of granola bars and some chips. I even find a sandwich on the salmonella spinner that looks to be on the right side of the "sell by" date. We need drinks though.

I round the aisle, and the footsteps that stopped start up again. I stop. They stop. Okay, coincidence is looking less likely. This has a stalker vibe.

*Did someone see me come in here?*

My skin goes cold as I try to think about the short ride down Front Street. My mind blanks on all the details I desperately want. Unfamiliar cars. People watching me on the street. What did I miss?

My gaze moves to the shelf that separates me from the next aisle. I take four experimental steps to the right. Two more and mystery man shuffles my direction.

Mystery man could be Sheriff Perry. If he saw me with Deacon. If he saw me at the house, he could be here to arrest me.

*Oh crap. Crap, crap, crap.*

My palms go slick and prickly on the basket handle. I'm breathing fast and shallow, like something's pushing on my throat.

Do I run? Call someone? I want out of here. I move fast for the register. I'm safe there, right? He couldn't just arrest me at the front counter beside the chewing gum and Slim Jims. Could he?

It's the kind of logic that I used at seven to convince myself my threadbare sheet would protect me from the monsters under the bed. Just as long as my feet were covered, I'd be okay.

I push my basket to the center of the counter and drum my

fingers, impatient for the clerk. The whole store is behind me. *He* is behind me, somewhere in those aisles. I glance around and find nothing. My head snaps forward. C'mon already.

*Shuffle step. Shuffle step.*

The hair on the back of my neck stands on end.

He's in the middle aisle. He's coming closer. Closer.

I put my items on the counter with shaking hands. The clerk, twenty-something with a scruff of sparse facial hair, returns and starts ringing up my purchases. I look straight ahead, hoping I won't be recognizable from behind. Long, blond ponytails aren't hard to come by around here.

"Sorry about that. Damn power."

I smile. "Yeah."

The shuffling is just behind me now. I watch my purchases move across the counter as the clerk rings me up. Bananas. Granola bars. Gatorade. Water. No more shuffling, but I can feel him back there. I take a breath, smelling leather and cinnamon. My heart lodges in the space between my tonsils, banging out a desperate SOS message with every beat.

"Be right with you, man," the clerk says, nodding over my shoulder.

I deflate a little. Not the sheriff. The clerk wouldn't call someone in uniform "man." Plus, why would the sheriff sneak around? He doesn't have anything to hide.

It's not Thorpe either, not unless he's bathed and picked up dental hygiene in the last few days.

I look up, catching a glimpse of myself in the surveillance camera monitor behind the register. I hadn't noticed it before, but now

I'm zeroing in. You can see me clear as day—so much for keeping my back turned—but the man behind me is mostly out of focus. I can be sure he's average height and build and he's wearing a suit jacket and a white button-down shirt. Business guy.

He leans a little left, and I see his dark skin and hair in the monitor. My limbs go heavy with dread. It's the guy from the Ann Street Inn. The one who was talking to Chelsea about me.

*Just turn around. He can already see you. He already knows who you are, and you want to know who he is.*

"That'll be sixteen forty-five."

I dig out my wallet, and a cell phone chirps behind me. *His* cell phone. It chirps again when I hand the bill over.

"Yeah?" The voice behind me is gruff. Familiar. Definitely the same guy.

I hear nothing from his phone, but my ears strain like radar dishes until he speaks again.

"I'm in the middle of something," he says.

The clerk's wrestling through the drawer. Swearing.

"It might be," the man says. In the monitor, he steps back. Turns and walks away. "Yeah, I'm on my way."

"Hang on a tic, miss," the clerk says. "I gotta get a roll of quarters from the back."

I nod absently, but mostly I'm watching the monitor, where the man in the gray suit is heading for the door, cell phone still pressed to his ear. When I lose sight of him on the monitor, I look over my shoulder, seeing nothing but dark hair and the suit jacket disappearing out the door. The bells jangle behind him, and then he's gone.

I don't know what the clerk is doing in the office, but it takes way longer than *a tic*. I don't care. I'm too busy holding on to the counter while I try to remember what breathing is and how I'm supposed to do it.

The cashier swears, and it sounds like something falls off a desk. Then he answers the phone. At this rate, it'll be dark before I get back to Deacon. Or pouring down rain. As if on cue, I hear the roar of a hard rain on the roof.

Terrific. I'm going to end up with a case of pneumonia to match my felony for interfering in a police investigation.

The clerk finally returns with my change, pocketing his cell phone before he hands it over, his gaze moving to the window. "Dude, it's pouring out there."

My smile feels like a rubber band pulled too tight. "You think?"

I grab a couple of extra plastic bags, tying my phone inside to keep it dry. I stall after that, waiting a few minutes with the futile hope that the rain will let up. So naturally, it hails.

It doesn't last long—hail never does—but it's still pouring when I push open the front door. The man in the gray suit could be waiting for me, but I've scanned every inch of the block I can see from the window, and I'm pretty sure he's gone.

I'm shoving the bags into my basket when I spot a plain white card with black ink melted into gray streaks.

I pick it up and blot it on my sleeve. Something was written here. Most of it's gone, but I can read a few words.

*Emm*

*Stay away fr*

*Call 6 8 4*

There are smudges next to the *fr* that I'm guessing spell *from*. And I'd bet the numbers at the bottom are a phone number, but three digits isn't enough to help me make a call. None of this is enough to help me with anything.

But it's doing a darn good job of scaring me half to death.

This card wasn't in my basket when I went into the store, so it's from him. I know it is.

He was looking for me. Waiting for me to come back to town. But for all the terror I went though, all he did was leave a note. I turn the card left and right, but nothing else is legible.

I don't know if he's trying to help or laying out a threat.

I search the street, but it's hopeless. Traffic is heavy from tourists rushing to their cars, crawling down Front Street to escape the storm. There's nothing but headlights and windshield wipers. The man could be sitting in one of those cars.

He could be watching me right now.

# CHAPTER TWELVE

. . . . . . . . . . . . . . . . . . . . . . . . . . .

Deacon is on the porch when I get back. He's on his feet the second he sees my bike, and I can tell he's surprised to see me.

He jogs into the yard, though it's still pouring buckets. "You rode in this? Emmie, you're soaked!"

Well, so is he now, but I'm shivering too hard to say so. I manage to hand him the note, which is pointless. Hardly any of it's readable now, and I can tell by his confused face he has no idea what he's looking at it.

"The guy who w-was talking to Chelsea l-left it while I was in the store. I-I think he was waiting for me."

I'm shivering violently now. I don't know if it's from the rain or my nerves. Deacon's white shirt clings in ways I'm too cold to fully appreciate, but I'm thankful when he takes the bags. "Get inside. We need to find you dry clothes."

I'm stiff and slow getting up the porch steps, and managing the knob with my half-frozen fingers is nearly impossible. I stop just inside the door, dripping the Mississippi all over the sloping wooden floor. Deacon's right behind me, shutting the door and dropping bags on the kitchen counter. I wince at the trail of water and mud he's leaving behind him, but he obviously doesn't care.

He heads to the single tiny bedroom, where I can see a sleeping bag and the backpack he grabbed from the boat shack. He finds a black shirt and a pair of boxer shorts I picked out and brings them out to me.

"I can't read the numbers. Did he seem dangerous?"

"No." I shudder. "B-but I don't trust him. Why wouldn't he have talked to me right there? Why wait until he could get me alone?"

"Children's Services won't conduct interviews like that in front of people. Too many privacy laws." Deacon frowns, looking thoughtful. "Do you think he followed you here?"

"N-no. I took the long way. I was careful. I stopped once to try to call Joel. He didn't pick up."

"You stopped? In this?" His shoulders droop. "*Emmie.*"

Another wave of violent shivers hits, and he moves in, handing me the clothes so he can rub my arms with both hands.

"You've got to get warmed up," he says. "Sorry I don't have shorts, but the boxers are clean. There's an old beach towel in the bathroom, and I think there's propane in the tank. I can get the water heater going if you want."

Warm water sounds divine. My thoughts cut off when he tugs his own sopping shirt over his head, hanging it over a rusty folding chair in the corner. I don't know what they do to this boy on those boats, because he is nothing but carved abs and sinewy arms. It's ridiculous.

If I take him up on that shower, he'll be out here. Looking like this. While I'm naked in the bathroom. Yeah, there is just no way. *No way.*

I wrap my arms over my middle, and his face softens. I think he gets it because he looks away, and maybe it's the light, but I swear his cheeks are a little pink. He clears his throat, and I stare at the puddle around my feet.

"I'll probably just change," I say, holding up the clothes gratefully.

He nods. Definitely blushing. "Me too. I'll be in the bedroom. Pretending this wasn't awkward at all."

That makes me laugh, and laughing makes everything more bearable.

He slips into the room, flashing a smile that thaws me from the inside out. Then the door closes and I'm alone. I squelch out of my shoes and peel off my dripping socks. The door stays closed, but I watch it all the same as I slip into the bathroom to shuck my soaked shirts and shorts. My bra and undies are drenched too, but taking them off is out of the question, so I pull on the dry shirt he gave me, which thankfully covers most of the boxers.

The beach towel is hanging over the bare curtain rod above the tub. Seriously? I was supposed to bathe in here, with a two-inch gap beneath the door and no shower curtain? He's lost his mind.

I hang up my clothes and use the towel to wipe off the drips my hair left on the sink. Then I start on the mirror. I force myself to stop, because this is not the time to clean. Back in the living room, I move for the grocery bags, but where do I put things? I scowl at the single remaining cabinet, which is closed. I'm not about to reach into that abyss to see what might crawl out, so I leave the bags where they sit.

The bedroom door is still shut tight.

I smirk. "Are you planning on taking a nap in there?"

The door cracks. "You finished changing?"

"Yes." I untie plastic bags again, glad my phone made the second half of the journey without crapping out. I text Joel another request for him to call me about Chelsea. I don't want to annoy him, but this definitely feels like an emergency.

"I'm trying to reach Joel," I say. "I think he needs to look into this guy. Do you think I should text Chelsea?"

"Not yet. Let's talk first." Deke sighs, pushing his wet hair back from his forehead. He slips into the tiny kitchen with me and he's so *focused*. I can feel all the places he looks at me, and every last one of them burns.

"Okay." My voice cracks. "I'm ready to talk. To listen. Whatever."

Deacon nods, putting a hand on the counter beside my hip. The sink drips, and my heart stutters.

"I need to do one stupid, selfish thing before I say this to you," he says.

I pull back, wary. "What thing?"

"Only if you want me to."

My palms are tingling. I press them into the cabinet doors behind me, and Deacon moves his hand closer. His thumb grazes my hip. I suck in a tight breath.

"Oh," I say, the word catching in my throat.

His answering smirk unravels me. He slides his palm to the middle of my back, and I'm in free fall, hurtling and spinning like I'm lost in space. But he's pulling me in. Just like always.

His forehead dips to touch mine, and I feel my pulse in my throat like a hammer.

"Why now?" I ask.

"Because I want to and you want me to. Because you might change your mind after."

*After?*

I push at his chest. He relents in an instant, pulling back. Surprise and worry cloud his expression. There's an unnecessary apology forming on his lips, so I hold up a hand.

"Please don't. You're right about what I want"—I force myself to meet his eyes—"but what I *need* is to hear the truth. Now."

He takes a step back, and I feel his absence like an old wound. He leans against the counter across from me, pulls his shoulders back a little before he starts.

"My dad has a drug problem," he says.

It takes everything I have to not laugh. The idea of Mr. Westfield—in his short-sleeved button-down shirts and battered boat shoes—even thinking he would know where to get drugs is too ridiculous.

But Deacon isn't laughing.

Not even close.

\* \* \*

The rain has finally eased. A sliver of blue sky peeks through the clouds outside the back window. Deacon's pacing the stamp-sized kitchen now, and I know he's waiting on me to say something. Anything maybe.

I lick my parched lips. "I had no idea. None."

"Of course you didn't. Chelsea's done backflips to hide all this from you."

I blink, as if somehow that'll clear the fog settling over me. It doesn't. "Okay, tell me more. What does he use? When did it start?"

"Pain pills. Prescription stuff like Percocet, Vicodin—even morphine a few times when he got his hands on it. It started with a back injury after Mom died."

"Does he use all the time? Is this an everyday thing?"

"No. He's been clean on and off. Sometimes for months. We found out he had problems even before Mom, back in his teens. Valium, sleeping pills—he stole whatever he could find." Deacon's still pacing, burning nervous energy. "Anyway, Mom was a good Catholic girl from Caracas. She made it clear she wouldn't be dating someone with that sort of habit. I know everybody says you can't get clean for somebody else, but he did. Stayed sober for fifteen years. And then Mom died."

I rub my hand over my face. I still feel numb. "Who knows about this?"

"Chelsea, me, and Joel." He laughs, but it's joyless. "It's pretty easy to hide. People think drug addicts are hollow-eyed vagrants. Nobody thinks of the middle-aged guy next door."

I raise a hand to stop him. "Joel knows?"

"Yeah. He's been good to us. Paid for a couple of Dad's stints in rehab. He says he had a rough go when his wife and daughter died—I guess it bonds them. He had to cover Dad on some tax problems after a bad episode, and he's helped ever since. He never wears out like I do. I'm sick of protecting him—but not Joel and definitely not Chelsea. Chelsea would lie forever for him."

I swallow hard, but his words go down like a jagged pill.

"Do the police know? Do they think the attack is related to drugs?"

"Deputy Nelson is the only one who knows he uses. He saw him overdose last year. I think he could have pushed the issue, but he was decent. Dad was going into rehab again, and Nelson turned the other way. I think he knew what the sheriff would do if he found out."

"The sheriff? What would he do?"

A group of gulls flies over the house, screeching. We turn to watch them flap over the water, sending the herons into irritable dances in the grass. When I look back, Deacon continues.

"Perry hasn't exactly kept his bad opinion of us quiet. He thinks Dad has a waterfront monopoly. After the marina wreck I covered for him, things just got worse."

I straighten. "Wait…covered? Did your dad wreck the boat?"

"I forced Dad into that. I was seventeen, so no permanent file. If he had taken that on his record?" Deke shakes his head, looking grave. "Perry would pull his license, his membership in the council of commerce. He'd do everything he could to ruin us."

I press my lips together, wondering what the sheriff will think if Joel's investor comes through. Three locations on the Carolina coast? I doubt that'll sit too well.

"Do you think he'd go so far as framing you?" I ask.

"I don't know. I don't like the guy, but I don't see him as a dirty cop either. If you look at it from his angle, the pieces fit nicely.

I've got a record. I was there that night. I look guilty. And there aren't any other suspects without alibis."

He pauses, his jaw going tight. I watch his fists clench and relax. Clench and relax.

"Dad had been clean for six months," he says. "Chelsea was sure it would stick this time. But then there he was in the office at home, so out of his mind he barely recognized me."

The image sits heavy on my chest. "That's when you hit him," I guess.

He swallows hard, looks at his feet. "I was furious. I've covered so much shit for him. Almost didn't graduate because of him. I just lost it. Then I felt like crap and went back."

I move away from the counter, pushing my hair behind my shoulders. "Deacon, this is awful. You need help."

"I know I do—but who? Joel thinks I did it. Perry thinks I did it. Hell, *Dad* thinks I did it. Chelsea's probably too flipped out about me hitting him to know what she thinks." He sighs. "I thought rumors would come out, that someone would have heard something by now."

"Do you still think it's somebody that works for you guys?"

"It's a good bet. My gut tells me it involves the boats. It's the only thing Dad has that's worth anything. We've got five regular guys between here and Morehead City, but I'm pretty sure the police would have looked into all of them. My money's on our seasonal guys."

"The ones who only work on call?"

Deacon nods. "There are probably a dozen of them, and we don't know them quite as well because they come and go. At least a few of them might have considered the opportunity the boats provide."

"What kind of opportunity?"

"Smuggling," he says. "Our boats move without much attention. We're not exactly a threat. Which is the kind of thing some of these guys look for."

"The coordinates," I say. "You think that's where they're taking stuff?"

Deacon shrugs. "Makes as much sense as anything else I can come up with. But random coordinates aren't enough to prove anything. I need something to give Perry. Not evidence—I'm not that stupid. I just need to be able to offer a reasonable lead. Something that convinces him I'm not just trying to save my own ass, you know?"

We slip into the living room, sitting side by side against the wall.

"Do you think the guy with Chelsea ties in to this?" I ask.

"I doubt it. Children's Services checks in after any bad relapse. Last time, you were probably too young, but they interviewed our teachers and doctors, set us up with counselors. I'm sure they're around again, and since Chelsea seemed comfortable, he's probably legit."

"But why would he want to talk to me? And what would he want me to stay away from?"

Deacon frowns. "I don't know. Maybe someone who was dealing to Dad? Maybe it's someone you might run into at the office? Either way, he'd want to talk to you because you're part of her support network."

It does fit. Except I'm *not* part of her support network, am I? Not really.

My cheeks burn. I stay quiet, because I don't trust my voice right now. I leaned on Chelsea so hard when my brother left. I needed her. And I always thought she needed me too.

Deacon scoots closer to me, still smelling like salt water. Still looking like everything I've ever wanted in my life.

I shiver, not because I'm cold but because I feel small and young and incredibly stupid. All these secrets were swimming underneath me, but I never looked down. How did I love them both so much and know them so little?

My laugh is bitter. "God, I'm such an optimist. How could I not see this? I'm so sorry."

"What? Emmie, no."

I turn to him, the carpet rough under my legs. "You and Chelsea—you were suffering. The signs were there. Those nights Chelsea didn't want me staying over. The times you'd seem so angry about your dad sleeping in. There were clues, Deke. How could I not see this?"

He nudges me with his knee. "You *always* saw. Better than that, you knew what to do. From the lilies on Mom's sailboat to the blood thing. You've been there every time I needed you, and you've been there for Chelsea too. You let her feel normal. You let her forget."

"Maybe," I say, trying to accept it. I still can't help feeling like I failed her.

"Hell, you're neck deep in our shit show now." Deacon sighs. "I should be sorry about that, but I'm not."

"What do you mean?"

He touches the side of his head to the wall. Even in shadow, his eyes are electric. "I mean that even though I'm sorry it's hard on you, I'm not sorry enough to send you away again. I need you, Emmie. Your steadiness. Your help."

I let out a sigh that's as shaky as my legs. His fingers trace my sleeve down to the bare skin of my elbow. One touch and I'm hungry for more. I crave him the way green things crave the sun.

If I move two inches, I will kiss him. He will kiss me. I can feel the certainty of it sitting between us. The want for that kiss is so sharp, it cuts deeper with every breath.

But what comes after that? What happens when he doesn't need me anymore? Or is that all I'll ever be—the steady one, the supportive girl?

My phone rings on the counter, a god-awful clucking chicken that pecks bullet holes in this mood with its digital beak. I all but leap to my feet, heading to the kitchen to fumble the volume back to vibrate as I glance at the screen.

"Oh, thank God." I heave a sigh of relief as I answer it. "Joel? Are you there?"

# CHAPTER THIRTEEN

. . . . . . . . . . . . . . . . . . . . . . . . . . . . . . . . .

You have no idea how happy I am to hear from you," I say, pressing the phone to my ear. I throw the door open and step outside for better reception. The grass is wet and cool around my feet, but the sky is showing wide patches of blue between the clouds.

"I'm so sorry, I've had no reception at all. Are you all right?"

"Yes. No. I don't know." I walk a loop around the yard, tugging Deacon's boxers lower on my thighs while I fill Joel in. I go over the coordinates we found with my name, the way I saw Thorpe and Charlie watching him, and the Children's Services guy with Chelsea.

His quiet stretches long enough that I'm afraid I lost the connection. "Joel, are you still there?"

"Yes, yes," he says, voice a little rough. "I'm not sure what those coordinates are about, but I'm concerned about Chelsea. I haven't received any calls from her, and that *woman* from Charleston—" He collects himself with a breath. "Daffy's sister can be protective. She worries with their mother gone and all, but Chickadee won't want to be away from her dad. I need to look into that right away. Did you catch the gentleman's name?"

"No. He did leave a note on my bike outside the grocery—"

"Did he leave any contact information? A number?"

He brightens at the news, so it stings to have to let him down. "No. It rained buckets and the ink smeared. It was just a hand-written note."

I look back at the house, making sure Deacon's not in earshot. I can still see him through the window. "Joel, Deke seems sure he's from Children's Services, and I don't want to scare him, but I'm still not convinced. The note said to stay away from something. I couldn't read what."

Another pause. "Well, I don't rightly know what that was about, but I plan to find out. Did he follow you? Threaten you?"

"No, not at all. It just…the whole thing feels weird, you know?"

"Well, not to worry. I'm sure we'll figure it out. The family has been through so much."

I look down. "Deacon told me about his dad. I know about the drugs."

He goes very quiet again, so I tell him the rest, about Deacon's theory with the seasonal guys, about the possibility that the boats are being used for smuggling, even about how Deacon is afraid to come in because he knows there aren't any other suspects yet. The sentences all trip over each other, but Joel doesn't interrupt. He listens until I'm finished.

The quiet stretches. Deacon's still inside—eating, I hope—so I plop down on the side of the dock again, letting my feet dangle over the water.

"You're awful quiet," I say.

"It's a lot to digest."

"You think we're crazy?"

"No. No, I don't. I just can't imagine how we'd have missed something like this. I need to get back to town to look through staff records, that much is clear. But I can't leave Mr. Trumbull just yet. With all this going on, we may need his expansion more than ever. I confess I'm worried about the future of Westfield Charters in Beaufort. Emmie, I'm sure you realize this is all very private family information. Discretion is key."

"I would never breathe a word of this, Joel." I lift my chin, though there's only a lonely pelican on a nearby post to see me. "They're like family to me."

"I'm sure they are. Now, as for these coordinates and these theories, I think you need to go directly to the police," Joel says. "Take the receipts and anything else you found and go today. Right now. If someone hurt Daffy to protect their crime, they might hurt you too, so you promise me that you won't delay."

I wince, pulling my legs up until I can rest my chin on my knees. I hear Deacon's footsteps behind me, and it strengthens my resolve. "Joel, if the sheriff finds out I'm with Deacon, he'll arrest him. You know he will."

He pauses for a moment, deliberating probably. Then he's back, crisp and firm. "Go to one of the deputies. Find a deputy."

"And if Sheriff Perry sees me?"

"Let's just hope it doesn't come to that."

We exchange our farewells, and Joel reminds me to go quickly. As soon as we disconnect, Deacon sits down next to me.

"He wants you to go to the police?" he asks.

"Yes. But I'm going alone. I won't tell Perry where you are."

"I know."

"I'm staying with my dad tonight, but I'll be back tomorrow. Can I call with news?"

He cringes. "I…uh…ditched my cell phone. Didn't want them to track my location."

"Then I guess I'll just have to come back in person."

His smile dances the line between wicked and sweet. "Definitely my preference."

He walks me inside, where I slip into the bathroom to change back into my clothes. My shirts are still damp, and getting my denim shorts on is an exercise in misery. I pause to look at my reflection. I'm red-faced and my hair is a mess. I rake through it with my fingers but give up fast. It's pretty hopeless.

Outside, Deacon's leaning against the front door, arms crossed over his chest.

"Did you change your mind about me?"

My brow furrows as I cross the room. "What?"

"The secrets. The truth about my dad. Did it change your mind about what you want?"

Heat rolls up my body in a heavy wave. I'm sure I'm crimson from neckline to hairline, and I don't know what to say, so I stay silent.

Deacon stalks toward me. "Because I've been thinking about kissing you all summer. Almost did it that morning in Joel's office. When I said some stupid thing about flirting with you and you blushed just like you are right now."

And that's helping the blushing problem oh so much.

I feel his hand on my face, and then he's tilting my chin up. "I want to kiss you, Emmie. Because you give me shit and you plan too much and you try to fix everything. Most of all because you're here, believing in me when the whole damn world has walked away."

I can hear the sink drip in the kitchen. My own heart thumping like a bass drum. He walks me backward until my shoulders bump a wall. Then he leans in again and takes my wrist in his hand. The fire in his eyes burns right through me. He looks at my mouth and sweeps his thumb over my pulse point. I swallow the fist-sized lump growing in my throat and feel his nose brush my cheek.

"Say something, Emmie."

I feel his words more than I hear them. My response is a shudder of air, and he waits while my heart drums him a prayer. Hours pass—days maybe—and then his mouth touches mine. It's the lightest feathering of lip against lip, and it's enough to make streaks of light burst behind my eyes. His thumb circles the inside of my wrist, and everything in me aches.

He pulls back, forehead pressed to mine. His fingers tremble on my cheek, and I am lost. Suspended in this drugged moment of *almost*.

"Yes or no?" he asks.

I kiss him. There is no easing now, no gentle exploration. This is a desperate, almost painful pressing of lips, my hand fisted in his hair and his fingers clawing my hip so hard I can feel the scrape of his short nails against the denim.

I taste sunshine, salt, and Deacon. It is more than enough and it will never be enough. We push and pull, his hands sliding down my neck while mine clutch his shoulders hard enough to leave marks.

Deke pulls back with a soft hiss. He has swollen lips and hungry eyes. I want more. So much more it scares me.

I swallow hard and stumble sideways to the door before he can speak. I fling it wide and sprint to my bike. He calls my name more than once, but I don't look back.

The long way would be safer, but I'm too rattled to care. My mind is supplying an endless stream of sensory input—from the feel of his scratchy chin to the taste of his mouth—but I push every last one of them back. I need time to think. To process.

And right now, more than anything, I need time at the police station so that we can finally get some help.

I turn left on Live Oak, and water sluices out of my seat, dribbling down my leg. I scowl and speed up, feeling the wind sting my slightly chafed chin. I catch a glimpse of my reflection in a passing car and nearly veer off the road.

Okay. I need to get myself together. I look like a lunatic. A lunatic who's recently been seriously and thoroughly kissed. Not exactly the impression I'm hoping to make when I head into the *police station*.

A mile later, I round the corner onto my street, mentally sifting through outfit choices. The white button-up might be too overt. My baby-blue dress? Too immature. I lift a hand to wave at Mrs. Baymont, who's working in the garden.

Oh crap, what if Mom's home? Because I'm almost definitely sporting make-out hair and I'm not sure that will fly.

My house comes into view, tall and white and—

Cold slams into me like a wall. My foot slips off my pedal and my belly flips.

The Children's Services officer is on my porch. He's *on my porch*. Waiting for me.

# CHAPTER FOURTEEN

· · · · · · · · · · · · · · · · · · · · · · · · · · · · ·

My bike wobbles and I stop abruptly, feet slapping the pavement. I wince as the pedal scrapes my ankle, but I don't look down. I can't tear my eyes off the house. The porch. The well-dressed man who's checking his watch.

Maybe I should talk to him. I could assure him that Chelsea won't do this alone—that I'll be here for her. I could find out what the heck he wants me to stay away from. Cicada song rings in my ears as he sits down on our porch swing. His pants ride up on his ankles, and my eyes drag to a dark bulge above his right shoe.

What is that? A cast? A brace? He tugs his pant leg free of the black lump, and something glints. Metal, I think.

Is that a gun?

Dread turns my limbs heavy. Children's Services officers wouldn't carry guns.

My feet scuffle, fumble for the pedals of my bike. I don't know what that is or why he's waiting on my porch, but my mom isn't home, and I don't hear Ralph barking. I'd be alone with him. Alone with a stranger and the thing on his ankle that might be a gun.

He turns toward me, and our eyes meet. His hand grazes his pant leg, and my pulse rush-thumps in my throat. He smiles, and it seems completely genuine. Friendly even. But Mr. Westfield seemed like an upright, drug-free guy. And Landon seemed like a brother who'd never leave.

I don't trust things for what they seem. Not anymore.

*Run.* The word pounds into my mind with every beat of my heart. He's waving at me now. Shouting hello. I'm not playing this game. If he wants to talk, he can follow me to the police station, because that's where I'm going.

My joints are loose, every limb moving off pace as I get my bike going.

He calls after me. "Emmie, wait up!"

His voice is pitched to friendly, but I keep pedaling. I don't know where Chelsea is. I don't know this man, and I'm definitely not convinced he's Children's Services now.

I think of calling 911, but my phone is zipped in the plastic bag in my pocket. I don't think I can get it out while I'm riding. Not without slowing down. It's four blocks. I can make it.

An engine rumbles to life behind me, and my stomach bottoms out. I chance a quick glance over my shoulder, catching a glimpse of a silver sedan backing out of my driveway. He's turning my way. My bike swerves, and I whip back around with a gasp.

He's coming for me.

I hang a left into an alley, picking up speed as I pass trash bins and brick walls. Another alley and another turn, weaving my way out of the residential area and toward the restaurants and stores. I peek through the spaces between the buildings where I can see the main road. I hear him behind me, so I know this is no coincidence. He is chasing me.

I pedal harder. One block. I'm one block from the police station.

He's close enough that I can hear the crunch of his tires on the pavement. My thighs are burning. I can't keep this up, and he's coming. Coming fast.

Is he going to hit me?

I swerve off the road into one of the narrow spaces between the buildings. I can't pedal through here. I can barely fit myself. I dump the bike and stand on quaking legs. The car stops, and I hear the whir of his window rolling down. Running is impossible. My legs give, and I stumble left, the brick wall scraping a painful line up my left arm.

I have to go. *Go!*

"Emmie, my name is Vaughn. I don't mean you any harm. Just stop running and I'll explain. I just want to ask you a few questions."

No chance of that. He can *explain* to the police. I feel my body giving out as his car rolls forward again. I sprint with the last bits of my energy, but I can hear his engine nearby. He's going to try to go around the block, cut me off at the main road.

I emerge from between the buildings and turn right, a stitch knifing through my right side. I press my fingers at my ribs, panting as I find the red brick courthouse with white columns and a cupola perched at the top. The sheriff's station is right beside it, a brick box as plain as the courthouse is pretty. I'm almost there. So close.

My legs are lead heavy, and I can't run. I clomp gracelessly down the street toward the sheriff's department sign. I look back, but Vaughn—if that's really his name—is at a stop sign half a block away. I see his dark head above the steering wheel, his mouth downturned.

I try to speed up, but there's nothing left. Nothing. One more look back. He's still at the stop sign. Looking at me. Looking at the sheriff's station. I keep moving until I'm at the station doors, flinging them open. Air-conditioning closes around me. I stumble across yellowed tile and reach a tall counter with the sheriff's seal beneath it. I sag against it, gasping one ugly breath after the last.

"Hello? I need help! I'm being followed."

A busty woman with dark eyes and fuchsia lips comes up to me. "Settle down, I'm right here. What can I do for you?"

"I need to speak with an officer." My heart is still pounding, sweat rolling down the sides of my face, the back of my neck.

"I *am* an officer. What can I help you with?"

"I'm being followed." I glance back out the glass doors. I can just barely see where the car was waiting, but he's gone now.

"By who?"

"I don't know. He said his name is Vaughn. He—I saw him with my best friend—I think he might have a gun."

"You need to just calm down, miss. I'll get you some forms, and you can have a seat."

I brace my slick hand on the high counter. "I'm too freaked out to fill out a form. I need help. I need to talk to some—" My words cut off on a gasp. I can't catch my breath. It's not getting better.

The woman's speaking, but my pulse is still fast and thready. A wave of nausea rolls through me. I close my eyes, trying to get myself together.

When I open them, I can see Fuchsia Lips isn't pleased. "You're going to need to calm yourself down before I can help you with anything, young lady."

"Hey, Brenda, what's going on?"

I smell bad coffee and cheap aftershave. I open my eyes to see Deputy Nelson, his moustache working as he chews what I'm guessing is a bite of the bagel in his free hand. He looks wholesome, solid, and just a little bit country.

My next breath slows.

"Miss, what's going on?" he asks. "I'm Deputy Nelson."

Brenda cocks her head. "She flew in here with her hair on fire about someone following her. Some Vaughn. Says he's armed or some such."

"I think," I say. "I'm not positive, but it looked like a gun, so I ran."

"That's what a sensible person does." Nelson swallows his bagel, his brows pulling together. "How was he following you? On foot? And what time did this happen?"

I shake my head, feeling steadier. "Just now. He was in a car. He followed me here."

"He followed you *here*?" He quirks his head at that and takes the paperwork Brenda had gathered for me. "I'll go ahead and take care of her." Then, to me, "What's your name, miss?"

"Emerson. Emmie."

Nelson nods. "All right, Emmie. Let's go outside and see if we can spot that car that followed you."

Reality floods in with the daylight outside. I'm...disgusting. My clothes are damp, and my hair is dripping with sweat. I try to smooth it with my hands while Deputy Nelson gestures at the parking lot with his coffee cup. "Do you see the car out there?"

It's hard to look past the bagel pinned against the papers under his arm. I really hope he doesn't want me to fill those out later. There will be crumbs everywhere. But even after a thorough look at the lot, I can't find the silver sedan Vaughn drove.

"No. No, he's not here. He stopped at that intersection. I think he saw that I was coming in here and he decided to leave."

"What can you tell me about the car and the driver?" he asks and then he looks over at a bench. "Why don't we sit down? I can finish up my bagel and you can tell me what happened."

I hesitate, looking at the building. Sheriff Perry could be in there.

"We could go inside if you want," he says. "This is a little unorthodox."

"No, it's great! I'm sorry. I'm still just shaken up. The fresh air will do me good."

"That's the spirit." He pops his bagel in his mouth and digs around in his shirt pocket, pulling out a pen. I cringe at the smear of cream cheese left on his moustache.

"Let's start with the car."

I take a deep breath and reach in my pocket for the bag that has my phone and the receipts. "Actually, if it's okay with you, I think we should start before that."

I tell him everything. Almost everything at least. He knows about Deacon's dad, of course, and doesn't look too thrilled when I talk about Thorpe and Charlie at the docks and the coordinates I found. He's even less thrilled when I mention running into Deacon at Joel's office and show him the coordinates *he* found.

I skip over the abandoned house because I'm not about to leak that to anyone who might tell Perry. Instead, I tell him about Vaughn—seeing him at the inn, the things he said to Chelsea about me, then him leaving me the note that got ruined and showing up on my porch today.

"Deacon believed he was Children's Services because Mr. Westfield is…troubled." My shoulders droop. "It made sense until he started chasing me around Beaufort."

"Did he threaten you at any point? Pull his weapon? Try to corner you?"

I shake my head slowly. "No. He just followed me all the way here—told me to stop so he could talk to me."

Nelson jots down a note at that.

I sigh. "Look, I know that Vaughn seems unrelated, but I can't help but feel like this is all tied up with Mr. Westfield getting hurt. I don't know if he's threatening Chelsea or working with Thorpe on some sort of smuggling thing. I just know it's scary."

Nelson puts down his pen and looks at me gravely. "Now, I suppose I don't have to tell you how foolish it is to be investigating an assault, Emmie."

I wring my hands. "I know."

"That investigation is police business."

"I know that. I do. But I'm so afraid."

"Afraid of what?"

"Afraid that the people who really hurt Mr. Westfield aren't going to get caught. I think something bad is happening with those boats. One of those guys is using them for something. Maybe smuggling drugs. I tried to tell Perry, but he believes I'm just covering for Deacon."

A look I can't decipher passes over Nelson's features. He finally wipes his mouth with a napkin and swallows. A beat passes before he speaks again. "Make no mistake, Emmie, I'm going to have to tell the sheriff about this conversation."

"He won't listen." My body starts to tremble, and tears spring up like they've been ready to burst all day. Maybe they have. I scrub my fists over my eyes. "I know Thorpe has an alibi, and maybe he didn't hurt Mr. Westfield, but I can't shake the feeling that he's involved. There's just something about him." My mind drags back to that encounter in the shack, making me shudder.

"Like you said though, he has an alibi. All of the men who work for the Westfields have been checked over."

"What about the seasonal guys? Did you check them?"

Nelson sighs. "You know, Emmie, when things are hard, sometimes we see what we want to see, even if it's not real. We need to get Deacon in here. We'll just talk."

"I won't be able to find him now. He doesn't have his phone anymore." The lie is easy. I don't even flinch. Maybe it's because it's buried in so much truth. "I know Deke *looks* guilty, but no one will even listen to the possibility that he isn't."

"I'm listening right now," Nelson says. And he is, warm brown eyes fixed on mine. "I'm not saying Deacon is guilty. I'm telling you we need to talk to him. That's all."

I nod half-heartedly, and Nelson taps my arm when I sniffle. "Emmie, don't lose hope. This investigation is not over yet, do you understand?"

I nod, feeling lighter. Hope is dangerous, but I cling to it all the same.

"I've already had one conversation with Mr. Thorpe," Deputy Nelson says. He pauses, jaw *click-clicking* as he swallows. "You can be sure I'm checking every possibility there. As for this man who followed you, I'd like to check in to Children's Services, but I'd also like to check to see if anyone might have hired an investigator."

I wrinkle my nose. "An investigator?"

"A private investigator. As you said, Mr. Westfield is troubled. If Chelsea has concerned family, it's a possibility."

I scrub at a spot of dirt on my shorts with my fingernail. "So what do I do?"

"You come inside with me."

I hold back a shiver. "Are we talking to the sheriff now?"

"Tomorrow," Nelson says. "And he'll be in a good mood, because he's picking up a new fishing boat in New Bern today. If I find something, Sheriff Perry will hear me out. Trust me on that, Emmie."

"I'll try."

"Good. Now we need to call your parents. There's paperwork."

"My parents?" I rub the back of my neck. "I really don't want to call my parents."

"You're a minor. I'd be neglecting my duty as an officer if I didn't call them."

I stand up then, chewing my lip. "Then just my dad. Not my mom. Please."

His laugh is easy. "Your dad will work just fine."

I follow him in, grateful that he agreed. Of course, it's only temporary. At some point, Mom *will* find out about this. And there will be no coming back from the place that takes her.

* * *

Dad is a strong, silent presence at my elbow throughout the interview at the police station. I appreciate the quiet until it drags on, stretching through the awkward car ride to pick up my abandoned bicycle and then through the stop at the grocery store.

By the time we're back at his condo, I'm wound up so tight my spine aches. We bring the groceries inside, where Ralph greets me with a happy bark. It's a tiny one-bedroom flat with an L-shaped kitchen and a balcony overlooking Front Street. The view of the water is nice, but the place is so cramped you practically have to walk sideways to get down the hall.

When it's quiet like this, it feels like sitting in a shoebox.

"Dad, are we going to talk about this at all?"

"Let's get started on that chowder first," he says, and I know right then and there, this is bad. Dad's usually one to downplay the little stuff, but this isn't little. And the line of his shoulders tells me he's holding his temper with both hands.

He starts chopping bacon on the counter, and I put a soup pot on the stove, adding onions and butter. Ralph is curled into a Volkswagen-sized heap in the doorway, and Dad's moving on to carrots now. It'd be a little domestic dream if there wasn't a six-ton elephant squeezed into the infinitesimal space between us.

I take a breath to steel my nerves and immediately cough, the onion on the stove stinging my eyes. "Dad?"

"Hm?"

"I really think we should talk about what happened at the station."

I hear his knife chop a little harder at the carrots. "What about, Emmie? The fact that you've been talking to Deacon against our wishes? Or maybe we can talk about you sneaking around the docks like Nancy Drew. Or we could go over the man who chased you today and the fact that you actually expect me to *keep* all this from your mother."

I tap the spoon on the bottom of the pot. "I don't! I just—I wanted to get the facts straight first. I wanted to see what Deputy Nelson found out before I terrified her. It could be that he's just a PI, like Nelson said. It could be nothing."

"It *would* be nothing if you'd stayed away from that boy."

"We don't know that. He has nothing to do with Vaughn." I grind my teeth together, stirring the onions and butter and listening to the sizzle. "I wanted to help my friend, Dad. I was afraid for him. I still am."

"You should be afraid for your mother." He moves into my peripheral vision, throwing away the empty carrot bag. "Can you imagine what this is going to do to her, Emmie? She's going to be convinced she's failed as a mother because both of her children are turning out bad."

"I'm not turning out bad!"

"Of course you're not, but she won't see that. She'll see another humiliating mess, only this one's revolving around *you*. God forgive me, but I'm grateful as hell that her mother isn't here to rub this in."

My face is hot, and the onions are browning. I scrape at the pan, furiously jabbing at the bits that stick. "Well, maybe Mom should stop caring about what her mother would have thought. Maybe she should just let us be what we want to be."

"Don't start. Your mom and I don't dictate your future, and we've both heard plenty of that crap from your brother."

"No, you don't dictate it, but you've *always* expected it. Especially with Landon," I huff and turn down the heat. "I know he's made some mistakes, but I get it. I get why he left us."

Dad snorts. "You don't *get* as much as you think you do about Landon leaving, because we've protected you from it."

"Then stop protecting me. Tell me what he did."

"You have to show me that you don't need to be protected!" He takes a breath, lowers his voice. "You're a smart girl, but there's still a lot you don't know. Especially about the Westfields."

I cock my head. "I know the sheriff is hell-bent on blaming Deacon for what happened that night."

Dad's mouth goes hard. "The sheriff is a good man, Emmie. He takes care of this town. Supports the local businessmen and keeps us safe. He looks out for you. He's been watching over you, worried that this boy would get to you. He was right."

I shake my head, biting back a hundred nasty responses.

Dad goes on. "As for Deacon, if he's anything like his father, he's bad news." He takes over the pot, nudging me gently aside. "Just steer clear, Emmie. Let the police do their job."

"And just walk away from him? Leave him totally friendless? Is that what you expect?"

"I expect you to use your head instead of your heart for once." He reaches behind him for the cutting board, scrapes the carrots into the pot. They hiss, and my eyes burn.

"We'll tell your mom in the morning," he says. "You can stay here tonight. Until they find out who this guy is, I want you close."

I nod and pick up a washcloth. I wipe at the stove knobs and then at the counter by the sink. My vision is blurry with tears, but I keep scrubbing until my dad's hand covers mine on the rag. I stop, letting out a shaky breath.

"Hey," he says, sounding much softer. I turn to look at him, and he touches my hair. "I'm sorry I'm coming down hard on you. I know this isn't easy."

"But you think he did it. Like everyone else."

He tilts his head, like he's not sure how to answer. "I think if Deacon is innocent, the truth will come out."

I turn to look at him. "Will it?"

He doesn't answer, so I mash my lips together and glance out the window. Outside, boats are gliding into the harbor for the night. Two miles down that same stretch of water, Deacon is alone in a dark house. Waiting for me.

"I'm going to bed."

"Let's eat first," Dad says, coaxing me back to the stove. I want to push him away. Run right out the door to Deacon.

But Dad is trying so hard right now. He puts his arm around me and sighs. "I know I'm the bad guy tonight."

I sniff. "You're not."

The bad guys are probably on the docks right now. Getting away with everything.

By the time I go to bed—Dad forces me to take his room and he sleeps on the couch—I feel seasick. Wrung out. It's too late to call anyone now, so I stare at Dad's bedroom ceiling, imagining Deacon in the tiny, dark house. He's probably in that sloping bedroom, no bed, no phone, no way of knowing if I'll ever come back.

A soft hum of activity and noise rises up from the harbor. It's the Beaufort lullaby that usually sends me to dreamland. Not tonight. Real sleep begins when dawn is turning Dad's bedroom window pink. And it ends with a banging on the front door.

# CHAPTER FIFTEEN

· · · · · · · · · · · · · · · · · · · · · · · · · · · · ·

Dad clears his throat and shuffles toward the door. Three more hard, fast knocks and I bolt upright, hand at my chest to hold my pounding heart in.

Someone outside is speaking. High-pitched voice. Familiar. *Mom.*

I flop back to Dad's pillow with a sigh, hand still over my heart. I hear him thumping and her clicking across the floor in one of her thirty-six thousand pairs of heels, I'm sure.

"Now calm down, Mary. She's still asleep."

"Then wake her up!"

I feel pinned to the bed, but I force myself up. I'm in a ratty T-shirt, but at least I managed a shower. I pull my hair into a too-tight ponytail and make my dad's bed. Smooth the sheets twice.

When I emerge from the bedroom, I find my parents by the couch. Dad's hair is mashed, and his eyes are puffy from sleep. Mom is the picture of business casual in a beige tank dress with a white sweater over top. It's friendly and approachable—like all of her shop clothes—but she's wearing an expression that could turn away a Labrador retriever. Even Ralph is keeping his distance, his big dark nose resting against the couch arm.

"I'm here," I say when no one speaks. "What's going on?"

"What's going on? Well, isn't that a marvelous question? The sheriff called this morning." Mom's eyes narrow, and my fingers curl over the back of the couch.

"Look, Dad was there when I talked to Deputy Nelson. Don't freak out. We were going to talk to you this morning."

"Were you?" Mom's voice is poisoned honey. "Well, it was *so* much better to be blindsided with all of this by a call from the sheriff."

I flinch.

"Get your things," Mom says. "The sheriff wants you to come in for a few questions."

My stomach drops, and Dad cocks his head, lifting a hand. "For questioning? Now hold on. Are you sure? Because Emmie was very forthright at the station."

The look she gives him could light a fire. "Yes, Tim, I'm sure." Her eyes cut to me, and I wince at her expression. "Get cleaned up and get your things."

"Mo—"

Her raised hand cuts me off. "Don't. I don't want hear a word you have to say right now, Emerson. Get cleaned up so we can get down there."

Dad drives us to the station, though it's a ten-minute walk at best. I don't complain though. The pressure of the silence in this car is already too awful. One word and the windows would probably blow.

We pull into the parking lot, and my gaze drifts to the alley where I abandoned the bike. Then to the bench where Nelson and I sat, talking about coordinates and the man who chased me.

Anger pricks at me like needles, turning my mouth sour. I was stupid enough to believe things would turn right after that. That Perry would see reason.

Dad turns off the engine, and Mom tells me in a clipped voice that I will march in there and answer those questions with absolute honesty, am I clear on that?

I am.

My legs turn to dead weight when Dad opens my door. I push myself up on them anyway and watch my feet move, one in front of the other, until I'm standing at the police station doors like yesterday.

This time, Brenda gives me a very different look. Her lips go thin as she picks up the phone. She says something quietly, tells us in a no-nonsense tone to have a seat.

Three rows of chairs stretch across the room, all connected and all bolted to the floor. There's a tear in the fabric of one of the seats on the left and dark smudges ground into every armrest. My breath goes shallow.

I don't want to sit in those chairs. My stomach is almost rolling just looking at them.

I hear a jingling behind me, and the blond officer I remember from the docks approaches. I change my mind about not wanting to sit, but he beckons us forward. My parents and I follow him deeper into the station, past police officers sitting in cubicles and huddled around the coffeemaker. I see a glass-walled office in the back of the building.

Perry and Nelson are in there. Nelson's getting the third degree from what I can see. He's in trouble because of me.

He looks past Perry's big shoulder, spots me through the glass, and gives me a sad look. I curl in on myself as I walk, arms wrapping around my middle.

"Y'all can just wait in here," the officer says, ushering us into a plain, windowless office. Perry's office? Maybe.

The door closes, and I feel like my throat is swelling shut. I look around, trying to calm my nerves. There's a dusty bookshelf in the corner and a houseplant next to the computer on the desk. Several of the leaves have fallen. I reach for them and feel a tug at the back of my shirt.

"Sit *down*," Mom hisses.

My shoulders jerk at her tone. It's too late to pretend I'm the good girl now—good girls don't get called to the police station—but I nod and stay quiet anyway.

There are four wooden chairs across from the sheriff's desk. I pick the one farthest from my mom and perch at the very edge. The room smells like mildew and metal. Every breath of it wrings my stomach like a sponge. Questions race through my mind like bullets.

*Did they arrest Thorpe?*

*Did I do something to break the law?*

*Did they find Deacon?*

That last one sends my heart into my feet. Dad pats my shoulder, and I jump, only half stifling my yelp. The door swings open before I can apologize, and Perry strolls in, one hand on that belt of tricks and the other holding a jump drive.

Mom takes a shuddery breath, and I see Dad touch her shoulder.

I have to look away. Dad was right. How could I do this to them? After everything they went through. All those horrible picnics and parties where someone would ask about Landon and they had no choice but to keep their smiles on and their explanations vague.

And now this.

The sheriff sits down at the leather throne behind his desk. He pulls out a file, flips through pictures, doesn't even acknowledge us. I've read enough about criminal justice to know an intimidation tactic when I see one, so I try to ignore him, looking elsewhere. Dad's left shoe is untied. Mom got a haircut. Every single surface in this office needs a come-to-Jesus meeting with some bleach and a scrub brush.

"Well," Sheriff Perry says finally, clapping his meaty hands together in front of him. "This is quite the situation you've gotten yourself into, Miss May. I hear you had quite a bit to say to my deputy yesterday afternoon."

No more Emmie now. So I'm in trouble. My insides shrivel like newspapers in a fire.

The sheriff softens when he looks at my parents. "Mary, Tim, I'm sure sorry to call you down here today."

"Don't be silly. We'll do whatever you need," Mom says. She's aiming for debutante charm, but it's all desperate parent coming out.

"Well, I'd like to show you a video," he says. "Some surveillance footage."

Surveillance of what? The house? There's no chance. The climbing wall? When we were down at the waterfront? My throat tickles and scratches.

"Do you know what video I might have here, Miss May?"

I shake my head because I have not one clue, but the sheriff goes on. "I felt this particular section was very enlightening."

He turns the monitor and puts a jump drive into the computer, and I sit, doing my best impersonation of a steel beam. I know I didn't do anything video-worthy. Logically, I know that. But I'm staring down the face of *very enlightening* and I'm wondering if I forgot something. My hands are shaking in my lap, so I shove them under my legs. They're slick against the wood.

"Here we go," the sheriff says when the video finally blooms to life.

I don't quite get it for a minute. It's footage from a traffic camera, I think. It's Front Street. Across from the grocery store. And it's raining.

My stomach tumbles end over end. It's the night in the store. With Vaughn.

But if they caught Vaughn—if he's in trouble—then why am I here?

I watch the video roll, watch myself come out and hunch under the onslaught of the rain. I pick up Vaughn's card from my bike basket—

"That's the card Vaughn left for me."

"We're looking into that gentleman, but that's not why this footage is interesting."

The video rolls, and I put my two bags in the basket. Perry pauses the video.

"See that right there?" he asks.

He taps again, loud enough to make my shoulders hitch. He's tapping at the bags. At the groceries I bought.

"Now, I know you can't see through the bag, so I contacted the store for sales records. One bunch of bananas, a box of granola bars, a large bag of barbecue potato chips, two large bottles of Gatorade, water—"

Dad's brow furrows. "I don't understand. Did she steal those items?"

The sheriff shakes his head. "No, she paid. But do either of the two of you recall seeing Emmie with any of these items in your house? Seems like a lot for a little thing like her to eat on the bike ride home. In the pouring rain no less."

I swallow against the boulder forming in my throat. My mom puts it together first. The crease between her brows relaxes, and her shoulders droop. Something in me aches.

"Deacon. You were taking it to Deacon." Mom's voice is a croak, and when she looks at me, I can already see tears welling in her eyes.

I twist in my chair, my hands slipping against the wood. I pull them to my lap, but there's nothing to say. Not one word I can think of that will undo what's happening to her right now.

The sheriff heaves himself out of his chair and steps to the plastic jug of water in the back corner of the room. I hadn't even seen it before. He offers a paper cup to my mom and pats her shoulder. My gaze jerks to the gleaming silver watch strapped to his meaty wrist. It's the only clean thing in this room, and it's a far cry from the ratty Timex he had last time I looked.

He clears his throat, dragging my attention back. "See, Emmie told Deputy Nelson she'd seen Deacon more than once, but she doesn't know where to find him now. Funny that she wouldn't, since I suspect she delivered groceries to the boy that afternoon. You *did* deliver these groceries to Deacon Westfield, didn't you, Emmie?"

Heat is rolling through me over and over. I'm sweating, picking at the hem of my shirt. It's too late to lie. I know my face is a dead giveaway. "Yes, I did. Vaughn was in the store when I shopped. He left before me. I found a note in my basket that told me to stay—"

"We're looking into Vaughn, but so far, there's not one thing that indicates he's committing a crime or interfering with a police investigation. But this shopping trip of yours? Now that's another story. I asked you to call me the moment you saw that boy."

Mom holds her breath. Dad closes his eyes. I feel like my insides have been replaced with cold, heavy stone. Perry isn't going to look at anyone else. His mind is made up.

The sheriff leans across the desk, his leather chair squeaking and that awful mold-and-metal smell filling the air. "Do you know where to find Deacon Westfield, Emerson?"

I flinch, noticing the glint of his new watch again.

"That's you in the video, isn't it?" he adds.

Anger slips inside me, cracking bits of me open. I hate the sheriff for playing dumb. I hate myself for the look my mom is wearing. Not the slow-dawning sadness that shadowed her eyes with every unreturned call or email to Landon. This is horror. The sharp, breathless shock of discovering the unthinkable. Her daughter is a liar.

Perry is doggedly silent. Determined to get his answer, I guess. I grip the edges of the chair hard. "You know it's me in the video."

"See, the truth is easy, Emmie. It wants to come out." His smile makes me think of hungry dogs. It's everything I can do to hold in my shudder. He looks down at the desk. Taps it with a thick finger. "Where did you take these groceries?"

"I met him at an intersection outside of the historic district." The lie feels silky on my lips. "I wanted to help. I was worried for him."

Mom covers her mouth, and Dad's fingers curl gently on her arm.

"Now, Emmie, you're a good girl with a soft heart. Boys like Deacon use that to their advantage."

I can see the hope dawn in my mother's eyes. I don't want to see that. I want to be strong and her pain will break me. The sheriff tilts his head, the office lights turning his hair to muddy straw.

"Did Deacon use your feelings to his advantage? Did he coerce you into bringing him those groceries?"

*Coerce.* I pause, rolling the word over in my mind. It feels important. I don't think he used it by accident.

I need to get him to look at those coordinates. This might be my last chance.

I lean in. "Deacon found coordinates in the office. And I did too. I told Deputy Nelson that we think someone might be smuggling—"

"Emerson May, I've already told you not to change this subject." Perry holds me in a stony gaze. "You need to stop thinking about what this boy told you to say and start thinking of the truth. I want to help you. I do. But you have to help me first. Where is Deacon right now?"

I clamp my mouth shut because I don't like this game anymore. Every card I'm dealt has Deacon's guilt spelled out in black and white. No matter what I say, Perry will use it against him.

"Where is he?" The sheriff is louder now, every word jabbing into my head.

Heat flares up my chest, and my mouth fills with sand and cotton, but I raise my head to meet his eyes, and I know. I won't tell him. So help me God, he will not drag that out of me. Not even if he puts me in handcuffs right here and now.

"Emmie." Mom sounds breathless and teary. "Answer Sheriff Perry, please."

My silence says everything and nothing. The sheriff's lips thin until his mouth is a jagged crack splitting the skin above his chin. My parents stare at me, and I stare at the pores on Perry's wide nose.

"Mr. and Mrs. May, perhaps I'm not speaking plainly enough for your daughter. This is a very serious situation. There is a warrant out for Deacon Westfield's arrest."

He lets that settle in the air. I don't breathe, don't flinch. On the inside, I'm coming to pieces, but I don't let myself react.

Perry takes a breath. "Anyone interfering with the investigation is subject to prosecution to the fullest extent of the law."

Cold sweat rolls between my shoulder blades, but I keep my chin high. I will *not* let him do this. This isn't justice. Not even close.

There's a knock at the conference room door, and then it bursts open. I see a frazzled-looking Deputy Nelson, who offers me an apologetic look. I try to give him a smile, but it just trembles right off of my lips.

And then I see the tall man standing behind him.

White hair. Blue eyes. Still straightening his tie as he strides inside.

My mom's sigh is the clearest *thank-you* I've ever heard. My shoulders drop six inches, my chest unbinding. Joel's never had better timing in his life.

\* \* \*

"I heard you were out of town, Joel." Perry flashes a smile I don't buy.

Joel isn't returning it when he nods. "Sheriff. If you don't mind, I think my clients could use some legal representation here."

I can't quite follow all the legal jargon that flies between them for the next five minutes or so. There's something from Joel about me being a minor, and then something else from Perry about a conflict of interest. That part I imagine has something to do with Joel representing Mr. Westfield before.

Joel offers to call down another attorney, and even though no one's raised a voice, it's clear a gauntlet's been thrown. If the sheriff's face is any indicator, he *really* doesn't want that to happen.

Maybe Joel is starting to think the sheriff is taking things too far with Deacon. Maybe he learned something about the seasonal guys. If I can get him alone, talk to him, maybe I'll understand what the hell is going on.

Joel stabs a finger onto the desk and lowers his voice. "Now, unless you're charging my client, I think we're done here."

The sheriff snorts. "Oh, sure, sure. I'd love to give y'all time to get your stories straight before we get our answers."

The look Joel fires Perry could wither someone's lawn, but the sheriff raises his hands and gives his best nice-guy impression.

"I'm just trying to get to the bottom of what happened to James Westfield. I'm trying to bring justice to all of this."

"James Westfield is my best friend. No one wants to know the truth more than me. And I'll do whatever it takes to find it." Joel tilts his head at the sheriff, offering an expression that is nowhere close to a smile. "We'll set up a time to meet again, Sheriff."

Joel ushers us outside. It's sunny and bright, only the barest wisps of cloud interrupting the cobalt sky. My hands are still tingling and numb. I shake them hard and breathe in the sweetness of fresh air.

"Mary, Eddie," Joel says, squeezing Mom's arm and mine in turn. He leads us to the edge of the parking lot, under a thick-trunked tree. Then he turns to include Dad in the conversation too. "I'd like to set up a meeting to talk about this, but I want you to both know, Emmie is going to be just fine. He's using scare tactics and nothing more."

"She took things to that boy, Joel," Mom says. It's like I'm not here. And Deacon's no longer my best friend's brother; he's *that boy*. I open my mouth, but Joel gives me a sideways look, a silent plea to wait.

"Now, Mary, she's a good girl who wants to help. The important thing to remember is that no judge in the world is going to stand behind flimsy charges being thrown at a girl like Eddie. This will blow over. Now, we'll meet up tomorrow. I've got to get a big client situated, and I've got to look into what's going on with Chelsea, but I'm free in the afternoon."

Dad nods. "If you think that's soon enough."

"It absolutely is. I'll call the sheriff to set up a meeting." He smiles at my mom, touching her arm again, sparing a quick smile to a group of teens walking past. "This is all going to be fine."

Joel looks like he's going to walk away, but I grab his arm. "Joel, wait. How did you even know I was here?"

"Your mama texted me." He smiles. "Lucky I was already on my way back. I've been at the courthouse trying to find some contact information on Chelsea. Sounds like that aunt of hers had her brought down to Charleston like I feared. And they've moved."

Mom clucks, eyes clouding over. "I just knew that overbearing woman would do something like this. Taking her away from her daddy right now."

Joel nods, revealing the dark circles under his eyes. "Trouble is, I can't even reach Chelsea to see if she's all right. They aren't releasing their phone number or address. People are being very secretive about the whole thing, so maybe they've hired an attorney or a private investigator. I think they're trying to stir up dirt, maybe keep Chelsea down there for good."

"Private investigator? Do you think it's the Children's Services guy? He said his name was Vaughn."

"I didn't get a name, but that'd make a lot of sense. PIs have no boundaries at all. He'd chase down anyone he thought could dig up nasty things on the family. We'd be smart to steer clear of him. I'm hoping to get him run out of town, but it's been hard to pin down specifics."

Mom touches her chin. "I sure hate to hear that. He wouldn't hurt Emmie, would he?"

"Definitely not, but he would dog her around. Swagger and generally intimidate her."

"Sounds about right," I say, my mind replaying the sound of his tires behind me. "Is there anything I can do?"

"You just rest up," Joel says. "I'm going to get Mr. Trumbull settled for his trip and then we'll meet up tomorrow."

"He's here? In town?" I flash back through the investment talk we had. Is there any real chance that will still work out? It seems impossible, the idea of something good coming out of this terrible time.

"He's on his way down, and I want his trip to go off without a hitch." He gives me the barest wink, and my spirits lift. "I'll text you as soon as I'm available. It's all right as rain, Emmie. Right as rain."

I smile for the first time since waking up, but my good mood doesn't last. Joel hops into his car, and I feel the low, familiar ache return. My parents are waiting behind me, stunned. Weary. Broken. I've seen them this way once before, and I vowed to do everything in my power to protect them from it ever happening again.

Dad goes to get the car and refuses to let me walk with him. The heat beats down like a punishment, or maybe that's just the air rolling off my mother. She won't even look at me. Just tucks at her hair and stares vacantly at the parking lot.

"I'm sorry," I say.

"I warned you to stay away from that boy." Her voice is cold and clipped.

My eyes burn, and my voice drops. "He's my friend, Mom. I thought helping friends was the right thing to do."

"Anything involving Deacon Westfield is wrong, Emmie. Don't you see that?"

She looks at me then, eyes red-rimmed. And yeah, I see it. She's my mom. She wants me to have the things she lost. A law degree. A suit-wearing, big-money husband. A big brick house. A life that would have made Grandma proud.

Trouble is, she never asks if I want that life. And I never admit that I don't.

"I don't want to make you unhappy," I say.

"Then walk away from this right now. This is…" She takes a shaky breath, clenches her fists. "This is you with your brother all over again."

Her anguish tears a hole through my middle. "Mom. You don't have—"

"No, I do. I need to say this, and you need to hear it. You try to save everything, Emmie. Dogs, turtles, *people*. You want to fix our family and this town and that boy so badly, and it blinds you from it."

"Blinds me from what?"

"From seeing that some people choose to stay broken." Her voice cracks then, tears slipping past her carefully lined eyes. "People like Deacon, like your brother. They don't want to be saved, sugar. They don't want to be saved at all."

* * *

We pick up Ralph before Dad drives us home. For a while, we're all there, the family that we used to be. Then he disappears in a flurry of phone calls about marina things that neither Mom nor I seem to care much about. He presses a bristly kiss to my head before he disappears, leaving us alone.

Mom takes my phone the second he leaves—a standard punishment since I got it freshman year. I don't fight her on it like I usually do. Her hollow eyes and soft steps scare me. I don't want to fight her on anything. Not until she comes out of this.

We hover around each other like ghosts in the living room. On the outside, I'm silent as the grave, but just under the skin, I'm screaming. I pluck lint off the couch cushion, pick the split ends out of my hair. Mom leaves the tea I made untouched and stares, glassy-eyed, at the wall until there's nothing left in the room but guilt and regret. And both are eating me alive.

I push myself off the couch and step over my horse of a dog. The floor is cold under my feet. Cold and dirty. I could almost cry with relief over that.

I start in the kitchen, mopping the floor, scrubbing the baseboards. When every inch is gleaming, I move to the dining room, cleaning every dish in the china cabinet. I save my two favorites for last: the owl mug Landon made me in the fifth grade and Grandma's silver butter plate. I swiped it from the big house one of the only times we were there. I was too little to remember, but every time I asked about that dish, my mom and dad would laugh.

I put it back beside the mug and close the doors. The silver glints against the kitchen light. Just like Perry's ridiculous new watch.

I snort. Love to know how he afforded that on a police salary.

My body goes still at once, my grip going slack on the dusting rag. Pieces start clicking neatly together. The new watch. Perry's insistence on Deacon's guilt. The new fishing boat. A cold lump forms in the pit of my stomach. I press my hand against it.

*Is Perry getting paid off?*

My eyes dart around the kitchen, the house phone on the wall tempting me closer. I could call the station to talk to Nelson. He listened to me before, and he looked sorry about Perry. Maybe he was on to something. Maybe the sheriff shut him down because he was actually getting close to the truth.

I could call the state police. The FBI.

Mom shifts on the couch, and reality presses down on my chest. I'm not going anywhere, and I'm not calling anyone. Not while my mom's still awake.

I rub my eyes and check the time. Ten o'clock. Tomorrow, we'll be meeting with Joel. Maybe he'll already know the answers to all the questions I'm asking. At the very least, he'll know what to do.

I put my rags in the laundry room and head through the living room to say good night. I stop, surprised to find her watching me.

"You off to bed?" she asks, her voice startling because it's normal.

I cross my arms over my middle. "Yes. If that's all right with you."

"Why don't you come sit with me for a bit?"

I edge around the couch, Ralph grumbling when I move his

feet out of the way. Everything feels strange. I'm sitting up too straight, smiling too brightly.

Mom is calm, but her eyes are focused and clear now. "Quite the day we've had."

I drop my gaze to my lap. "Mom, I'm sorry. You have every right to be angry."

"Disappointed," she corrects.

Definitely worse than angry in my book. I look up. "You have every right to be disappointed. I'm sorry if it seems like I want to save people. Maybe I'm wrong sometimes, but with my brother…I just feel like both of you have given up on him."

Her eyes flutter, her gaze settling on me. "Oh, sugar, it was the other way around, I can assure you of that."

"I don't think so," I say, because the scab is picked and now I can't stop the bleeding. "I realized what you've been saying for so long. You gave him this opportunity and he walked away, not just from college but from all of us. But he could come back. Maybe if we were less angry. Maybe if you didn't expect—"

Mom's voice goes low. "It was bigger than that, baby."

I pick at the edges of the couch, and she reaches for my hand, smoothing her fingers over mine. "It started with a fake ID," she says. "He was still in high school then."

"He went drinking?"

"Gambling actually. On his senior trip. That was when we first met Joel really."

Joel helped my brother? My lips part in shock. "He never said anything."

"Lawyers never do."

I wrinkle my nose, slouching back into the couch. "I didn't know he was into gambling."

"Well, Landon likes to win. No matter the game." Her smile is a flash of teeth before her frown returns. "He didn't win at college. The studying, the hard sciences. They were difficult. We encouraged tutoring, but he wanted to switch majors. Your father thought we should support the choice and I didn't, but in the end, they wore me down for a program at Virginia Tech."

"Wait...I thought he dropped out of Duke. He went to another college?"

"Two others actually," she says, and this time, her smile doesn't appear. "Of course, he told us there were five, and we both kept sending out those checks, hoping he was serious this time. Hoping to see that same all-star student he'd always been here in Beaufort."

I turn sideways on the couch, my eyes and throat hot and thick. "What do you mean he told you there were five?"

"Landon took tuition money that he never intended to use for tuition. Eighteen thousand dollars' worth to be precise. He stole from us."

My stomach drops out. "Mom..."

Her smile is back, and it's almost normal. She tucks my hair behind my ear. Moves a pillow. Fusses. "It's no matter. I've got you. Now you've made your mistakes for this boy—"

"Mom—"

She ignores me, pressing on. "—but Joel seems confident we'll be able to move past that, so it'll be fine. It will *all* be fine."

I flinch, because it won't be fine. All this time, all these years, I believed my brother was lost, but I was wrong. He was a thief. He used them. I should have pushed harder for the truth, but I missed it.

Just like I missed it with Chelsea and Deacon.

How many times have I fallen for smoke and mirrors like this? How many times have I been so determined to see the best in things that I didn't face the reality right in front of me?

I swallow hard because it won't be fine. I won't forget how wrong I was about Landon, but I also won't keep living my life to fill the hole he left. I can't be that person anymore.

And I can't be the person who walks away from Deacon to make her happy either.

I take a breath and square my shoulders. "Mom, I'm so sorry about Landon. I am. And I promise not to follow in his foot-steps… But I stand behind my choice to defend Deacon. Time will tell on this, and it will tell you he is *innocent*."

Her face blanches, lips thinning. "How can you sit here and say this to me?"

I lean forward, clutching her hands. "Because I *know* this guy, Mom. I've seen him save cats and cook for his sister. I saw him spend three hours picking flowers off of a boat because his mom didn't like lilies. I've seen his temper and his attitude and, yes, Mom, his refusal to live up to his potential, but I still care about him. I can't change that. I don't *want* to change that."

Mom stands up then, wringing her hands. Shaking her head

with a reedy, desperate laugh. "Has it ever occurred to you that he might be lying to you?"

"Yes, it has. But he's not. I know him, Mom."

"You're seventeen years old, Emmie. You don't know anyone. Not even yourself." Her face shutters off, but she hands me my phone. "I'm tracking every text and every call. Make better choices."

I open the phone and see the parent tracker icon on the screen. The same one my parents deactivated on my sixteenth birthday because they said I deserved privacy and they trusted me. And now they don't.

Mom picks up the remote and the cup of tea that must be stone cold by now, and it's back to life as usual. That's what she expects us to pretend at least.

I scratch Ralph's soft head and slip into my bedroom. I close my eyes and lean my head against the door, Mom's words ringing in my ears. *Make better choices.*

I do need to make better choices. But I'm pretty sure Mom won't be crazy about what *better* means to me.

Mom turns off the TV, and the stairs creak under her feet. The thump of her bedroom door drifts down from my ceiling, carrying the weight of the ugliness between us with it.

It's eleven o'clock when I get a text from an unfamiliar number. Hey, it's Chelsea. Are you around?

A thrill runs through my chest at her name, but I chew my lip, because I don't know this number. I don't even know the area code. I ponder over my text before replying.
Hey, whose phone is this?

Aunt Jane's. I'm stuck in Charleston and they took my phone.

My pulse is moving a little faster. It sounds like her. So why the paranoia?

I text again. Are you okay?

I lean forward, willing her to be fast with her reply. A few seconds later, it appears.

Sort of. Can't text long. I need you to call Joel. Weird stuff is going on.

Relief and fear are pushing against each other. It's Chelsea. I'm sure of it. I send another message.

Why did they take your phone?

Too much to text. The sheriff is looking for you and Deke. I'm freaked! Call Joel!

My heart breaks at the text, and I type a reply quick. Joel is already trying to get to you! Are you in danger?

One minute passes. Then another. Terror is swelling in my chest, pushing into my throat until I'm choking on it.

Chelsea?

I sit on the side of my bed, staring holes into the screen of my phone. No typing indicator. Nothing. She's just gone. I try Joel, but his phone goes straight to voice mail, so I stand up and pace a lap around my bed, my stomach pitching like the sea in a storm.

Something taps at my window, and I jump half a mile off the ground. I pad quietly to the window and push back the curtain. My bedroom light illuminates his sharp cheekbones and all-the-colors eyes. His smile pulls at my stomach, dragging me closer. He's still just like gravity. Even now.

# CHAPTER SIXTEEN

· · · · · · · · · · · · · · · · · · · · · · · · · · · · ·

My hands are cold and shaking as I push the window open. Deacon starts to say my name, but I lift a finger to his lips and step into my flip-flops, waving him back so I can come out.

He shakes his head, frowns.

I kneel down until I can smell the salty sea air coming off his clothes.

"Everyone's looking for you," I whisper. "You shouldn't be here."

"I know. I worried when you didn't come."

My heart clenches. "I couldn't, Deke. There's a warrant out for you."

Fear flashes over his face, but he tucks it back fast. "Not surprising, I guess."

I hear the ticking of toenails on a wood floor and a thump upstairs. Ralph changing places in Mom's room. I grab a sweatshirt from the end of my bed and return to the window.

When I start climbing out, Deacon's hand brushes my knee, trying to stop me. "Too dangerous," he counters.

"Don't care," I say. "And it's my choice."

There's one long beat while I wait for him to tell me all the reasons I shouldn't come with him. Deke isn't really one for *shouldn'ts* though. He takes my wrists and helps me out.

We don't go far. I lead him to the shed at the back of my yard, my eyes darting to the dark windows at the top of the house. Mom's room overlooks the front yard, but if she goes to the bathroom or slips into the hallway—

*Stop it. She won't see.*

My flip-flops do nothing to keep the cool, wet grass from tickling my feet, and my grip on Deacon's hand does nothing to keep my legs steady. We wedge into the narrow space between our shed wall and the neighbor's privacy hedge. There's an uneasy feeling in the air, a sharpness to the night sounds.

The last time I was with him, we were kissing like it was a medal-worthy competition. My mind flashes through images of my hands in his hair, his fingers at my waist. Thinking of it fills my belly with hunger and heat.

I rub the goose bumps rising on my arms and press my back against the shed. Deacon stands across from me, melting into the shadows.

"Chelsea is with your aunt and uncle. She said Perry is after us."

"Tell me something I don't know."

"Well, she doesn't have her phone. She was texting from her aunt's phone. Joel thinks they hired a PI—I think it might be Vaughn. Do you think he's advising them to keep Chelsea away from us?"

I show him the text messages, and he scowls. "Could be. They might want full custody. Aunt Jane threatened once years ago." He stops, shakes his head. "We need to call Joel."

"I tried. He's not picking up. He said he was looking into it when I saw him earlier."

"Does he know Thorpe and Charlie are prepping a boat? The *Clementine*. I took my skiff over to Carrot Island and spotted it from the bird-watching trails."

I nod. "They are sending a boat out. Joel is back getting ready for a big charter client."

"It wasn't a charter boat. *Clementine* is one of the bigger fishing rigs."

"Maybe Joel made an exception. Mr. Trumbull is a very big deal client. Huge money. And he's really into fishing."

Deacon shakes his head, plunges his hands into his jeans pockets. "He still wouldn't take this boat. We're shut down for the deep-sea fishing runs without it, and those are our biggest moneymakers."

I press my lips together. "You said Thorpe was on the boat tonight?"

"Yeah. Him and Charlie. Which is starting to make me think twice about Thorpe being innocent. Charlie could have covered for him. I didn't think he'd do something like that, but…"

The hair on the back of my neck prickles. "Thorpe being gross I can definitely see, but Charlie too? He's always so nice."

"I wouldn't believe it either if they weren't on the docks. I can't think of a single reason for them to be down there right now. It's shady. I thought maybe we should call the sheriff."

"I don't know what they're doing," I say, "but there's more you should know before we call anyone. Perry took me in for questioning today—"

He steps closer, eyes dark. "Questioning?"

I touch his arm. "I'm okay. But I think Perry's getting paid to keep quiet."

His breath catches. "Like hush money? Are you sure?"

"It's just a guess. I don't have proof. I talked to Deputy Nelson about the coordinates yesterday, and he really listened, but I think the sheriff shut down his investigation. I saw Perry yelling at him today, and I started putting things together. The sheriff has a new fishing boat and a brand-new watch. An expensive one. Plus, he's been on you like white on rice from the start."

"If he's getting paid, then we don't know who *else* is getting paid around here." He looks around, as if there are people watching in the grass. Then he nods. "Chelsea's right. We need to find Joel. Right now."

I nod and stroke his arm. "I know. He's coming by tomorrow, but his phone's going straight to voice mail. We have to hang tight, I guess."

"So we just sit and wait?" He scoffs, his jaw clenching.

"Just a few more hours, and then I think this will all be over. We'll come get you. Go to the FBI or the state police—whatever we have to do. Joel will know."

He steps closer to me, eyes suddenly swimming with worry. "Did the sheriff threaten you? Did you get in trouble over this?"

I tense. "My parents are flipped out, so that's not fun, but I don't think Perry would do much to me. He really wanted to find you. He keeps bugging me because he knows I helped you. And that I have a thing for you."

His smirk should be registered as a weapon. "You have a *thing* for me?"

I roll my eyes. "No, idiot. I make out with all the guys I run into in abandoned houses."

"Terrible habit. Guys can be trouble." His voice is low, and his eyes are hooded.

"Yeah." My insides go hot, a smile creeping onto my lips. "This one's been a real pain in my ass for years."

He laughs softly as he leans in, his hair brushing my forehead. "Yes, he has."

His hands leave scorch trails down the sides of my neck. I take a breath for strength, because we should probably be thinking. Or planning. But when he kisses me, all of that falls away. And I fall with it.

My fingers curl in his belt loops, and his thumbs trace my jawline. This kiss is slower, deeper than the first. His mouth moves over mine until my limbs are heavy and my mind is loose. Deke pulls back to breathe my name, his rough fingers brushing my lips while he kisses my neck. I'm breathless, dizzy—tumbling end over end into nothingness. But his arms cross tight behind my back, holding me steady.

When we finally part, he runs his hands through my hair while we both catch our breath.

"Why'd I wait so long to kiss you anyway?" he asks.

I laugh. "Maybe you needed the danger to make it interesting."

He grabs my chin gently, gives me a dark look. "No. You're interesting all on your own. You always have been."

A chill snakes up my spine, under my hair. Will I stay interesting? Because Deacon moves fast, especially when it comes to girls.

"And when this is all over?" I ask. "When your name is cleared and life goes back to ordinary? What then?"

A car pulls to the curb near the house. We freeze, checking the yard. It wouldn't be easy to see us from the road, but maybe. If someone looked hard enough.

I fist my hand in the front of Deacon's shirt and pull him into the shadow of the shed. Which means pulling him right into me. I press myself harder against the wall, and Deke palms the shed next to my shoulder.

"You should go," I whisper.

"Don't wanna," he says. His smile is a crime.

His hands slide over my hips, and then that smile is at my mouth. It's dangerous kissing Deacon. I thought it would fill some years-long craving, but it only stokes the fire.

I push him back, chuckling. "You have to go. I'll see you tomorrow."

His groan will be my ruin. I'm already pulling him back when I hear a car door. Then footsteps. Inside the house, Ralph bursts into a series of baritone barks, and my grip tightens on Deacon's shirt.

*Someone's here.*

Deacon's hands press into my hips. I swallow hard. Harder. Wince when I hear my front door open and my mom's voice ringing out.

"She's out back. I think he's with her."

\* \* \*

We run for the back fence the second Perry's flashlight beam hits the grass on my backyard.

"Stay where you are so no one gets hurt!" the sheriff calls.

His voice sends an adrenaline burn through every limb. I hit the fence and start climbing. Perry targeted Deacon. Shut down Nelson. People have already been hurt.

I claw my way up the fence and over, moving into a sprint the second my feet hit the ground. The sheriff is swearing behind us. He climbs faster than I would have guessed, but we're desperate. When he lands on the other side, we're already halfway across Mrs. Kalnicki's yard and stretching our lead.

We turn left on Pollack, heading toward Highway 70, but after one block, Deacon tugs me in between two houses. He doesn't slow when we lose the sheriff. Instead, he leads me east to Marsh Street, where he turns south, toward the water again.

"We're going back?" I gasp.

"No. To Joel's office. He might be there. Last thing Perry saw, we were headed for the highway anyway."

We hear sirens blare in the distance, and my spine turns to steel, my sweaty hand clamping on his arm. "Deacon? What are we *doing*? We're running from the police!"

"Just breathe. Try Joel again."

I fumble my phone out of my pocket to call, but Deke keeps us moving too fast for me to dial. We keep to the backyards on Marsh Street. I can already see the office, four houses away. We edge up the yards between the office and the house next door, staying closer to the neighbor's magnolia trees. We're both panting when we come to a stop.

The back door is on a different lock, so we'll have to use the front. A siren winds up nearby, and my heart thunders into my throat. It dwindles, moving north like Deacon expected. His smile says "I told you so," but I'm too tensed to relax.

We start to head toward Joel's office. A flash of blue-and-white lights sprays ice through my veins. No sirens, just the lights this time.

Deacon stops, pulling us back between the trees, pressing me against the neighbor's white wood siding. I stand quaking like I'm half-frozen, and Deacon strokes my arms.

"It's all right," Deke says, pulling the hood of my sweatshirt up over my pale hair.

I try to breathe. Try harder to believe him.

The cruiser slows at the corner of Ann and Marsh. I can hear the faint squeal of brakes, the hum of the engine. My knees don't just shake—they practically vibrate.

"He'll head toward the highway like the others," Deacon whispers.

He doesn't. He turns south, and my stomach rolls. My teeth chatter hard, though I'm not cold at all. Are we hidden? I think we're hidden, but is it good enough? Deacon pulls me into his chest, and we hold our breath as the car rolls closer. Closer. It drives past, dragging to a stop at Front Street.

I don't breathe until it turns right, heading back into town. Away from us.

After the cruiser, neither one of us says a word. We wait another minute, just to be sure, and then we creep up the porch stairs at the front of the office. Deacon uses his key. We open the door enough to slip into the dark front room. Only the lamp in Joel's office is still lit. It's quiet, and I don't see any evidence that Joel's been here.

Did he drive to Charleston to get Chelsea? Is he still with Mr. Trumbull? I try to call, but it still goes straight to voice mail.

We move quietly into Joel's office. Deacon closes the blinds while I settle at the desk and turn on the computer. I force a breath in and squeeze my trembling fingers into fists. I glare at the smudges on Joel's desktop—I did miss cleaning something—and shake my head.

I need to calm down, make a plan. I text Joel a message to call and wait for the computer to boot.

"Want me to keep trying him?" Deacon asks, taking my phone.

"That'd be great. I'm going to see if there are coordinates listed on our charter rentals." I select my profile on the server and sign on. "I also want to see what's coming up on the schedule. Maybe there is an explanation for Thorpe and Charlie being down there tonight. Maybe we'll even get lucky enough to tie one of them to the coordinates from the receipts."

"Thorpe almost always volunteers for the fishing charters that request crew members with the boat, so he'll be tied to everything. But not Charlie. I don't know how he fits in."

"Well, that's why we're looking, right?" I wrinkle my nose. "I thought your dad and Joel tried to keep Thorpe away from customers."

Deacon chuckles. "We keep him away from girls on account of his total douche-baggery. But I'll give it to him—he knows his way around a fishing boat. His dad was a shrimper and his grandpap worked on a tuna rig, I think. Out of South Carolina."

"Maybe he has more criminal records than Joel thinks," I say, clicking through the charter schedule. "See if you can pull up a record for him in South Carolina on my phone."

We both click quietly, me checking the charters and Deacon searching my phone. I spot entry after entry with Thorpe's initials in the crew section. I sigh. "You're right. Thorpe is assigned to practically everything. So how would that work? Is he faking customer calls to order charters that he uses for smuggling?"

"Maybe." Deacon looks up, brow furrowing. "Or maybe they're using the whole business right under our noses. Think about it. Their clients let them know they're setting up a charter to move *whatever*. The customer calls the office, talks to you or Joel. It all looks legit. And then they contact Thorpe or Charlie with the *real* coordinates and details."

"But wouldn't your dad and Joel figure it out?"

Deacon shakes his head. "I don't see how. Dad and Joel agree on the charter price—they take the sales calls. They don't serve as crew, and they don't set them up. It's Thorpe and Charlie every step of the way. Hell, they even clean the boats when they're done."

"They could be hiding anything," I say. My gaze drags back down to my screen. I spot my name on one of the forms, and my throat tightens. I recognize my careful comments about ordered supplies. *Airtight storage bins.* I remember the call now. Charlie, not Thorpe. I rub my hand over my face. It isn't the first time I've taken a supply call from him.

"Deke, I helped them," I say, my voice cracking. "I took a call from Charlie a month ago. I ordered storage bins for them, for a charter. There are notes right here. I've done it other times too. My name is on those receipts because they called me to order stuff. I helped them do this."

"Emmie, you didn't know." He doesn't look up from my phone screen, but he must have found something good, because I can see his fingers go still, his eyes tracking back and forth. He sucks in a deep breath when he's done. "Found a news article from a few years back that mentions Thorpe with a couple of other guys who got arrested, but I can't find anything on the court system. The charges must have been dismissed."

The back of my neck tenses. "What was the charge?"

Deacon's expression is steely. "Trafficking cocaine."

I can feel the panic rise, but I push it back down until it's a burn in the pit of my belly. "They should track that stuff bet—"

I cut myself off midsentence with a gasp. *Tracking.* My phone has tracking. If Mom thinks about it, she'll know how to find me. There's a decent chance she's thought of it already. "Deke, turn off my phone."

"What?"

"Turn my phone off! Power it down!"

"Okay, okay." He's pressing buttons, looking confused, and then his expression clears. "Location tracking," he guesses. "Do you think they'll have checked it yet?"

"No idea. We shouldn't stay too long," I say. Then I move the mouse to tomorrow's date, checking quickly. "Two charters tomorrow, one out of Morehead City. I'll bet that's Mr. Trumbull—it's got Joel's name listed. And then there's the monthly thing too. Mr. Christopher's charter. I'm sorry, I should have thought of it sooner."

Deacon's head jerks up. "Mr. Christopher?"

"Yes, he charters a boat the last weekend of every month."

"I should have figured it out." Deacon's eyes go flinty. "*Christopher* is Thorpe's son's name. They call him CJ, but his name is Christopher—shit." His face goes slack and pale.

"What? What is it?"

"It really is them. I didn't want to believe it, but there it is. And I think I know why they hurt my dad," he says. "That day it all went down, Dad was in a shit mood. When he found the busted latches on the charter boat, he lost his mind. Blamed Max mostly, who'd brought the boat back, but then he reamed Thorpe and Charlie too. He told them they were all off the charter drop-offs for a while. I thought Dad was being a tool, taking their overtime like that…"

My cheeks feel numb, tingly. "But they were losing a whole lot more than a few hours of extra pay," I say. "If they couldn't deliver goods, they'd have real motive to get your dad out of the way. And now even Joel's out of the way because of Mr. Trumbull."

Deacon's laugh is as bitter as they come. "That's why the whole fight with Dad started. Seeing him using was what sent me over the edge, but I was so mad before that, because he took his mood out on our guys. I actually *apologized* to them." He looks sick over it. I get the feeling.

"You didn't know either," I say. "Do the coordinates back this up?"

"If they were meeting another boat? Sure. Most of them are

within a few hours of here if you're moving fast. Except that Caribbean set you found. That one makes no sense at all."

I push my hands through my hair. "We're sure about the attack though? Because I thought I was wrong about Thorpe. His right hand was bruised, but he's actually left-handed."

Deacon shakes his head. "Thorpe's not left-handed. He's ambidextrous. He brags all the time about how he can drag in fish from any position on the boat."

My stomach flutters. "If he's ambidextrous, he wouldn't have *any* alibi except cleaning those boats."

"And Charlie cleans the boats with him," Deacon says. "It was Charlie too, who told us all about his *hand injury*."

They could have lied. A thrill runs through me, and I lean forward over Joel's desk. "Are there cameras in Morehead City? Like traffic cameras?"

"A few, I think." Deacon sags against the wall. "At the stoplights. But there are ways to get to the boats without hitting those intersections. I doubt it would hold up."

"Try Joel," I say. We use the office phone, but it goes straight to voice mail, so I leave a message.

"Joel, it's Emmie. I'm with Deacon, and we think Thorpe and Charlie are using the charter boats to smuggle. We'll try to call soon."

As soon as I hang up, Deacon heads toward the door of the office.

"Where are you going?" I ask. "We should call the state police. Maybe the Coast Guard."

"I'm sorry, Emmie. I can't sit here and wait. I have to check the boat. If they are setting up for a run, all we need is a picture.

Some morsel of proof, and they go down right now. Even Perry won't be able to stop it."

"It's too dangerous. We should go to the police."

"Except they're paying the sheriff off and who knows who else around here," Deacon reminds me. "Thorpe and Charlie could take off, and we'd end up arrested."

"Arrested." The word sits in my stomach like a greasy rock. I imagine my mom at the police station again, and my mouth goes dry. God, how did this happen? A week ago, I would have been voted least likely to ever be pursued by the police. And now?

I shudder.

Deke sighs. "I respect whatever you have to do, but I have to try to turn Charlie and Thorpe in first. If I see something on a boat, something legit, I can call the Coast Guard station down in Emerald Isle. I'll never be able to live with myself if they just sail away, free and clear. I have to try."

I close my eyes and let his words run through me. I'm still half-terrified, but I'm not going to walk away again. I'm going to see this through.

"Okay," I say, my voice steadier than I feel. "I'm with you."

* * *

We're hunched in a dark store alcove across the street from the Westfield Charters boats. Deacon tugs his baseball cap low over his forehead, and I pull up the hood on my sweatshirt. I'm edgy as all hell, and he isn't much better. Every car, every tourist voice makes us pause.

The boats are anchored and empty. A sign outside the dockside office invites visitors to return tomorrow for "Tours, Fishing, and More!"

I'm not so sure about this plan anymore. "Can we just go to the Coast Guard now?"

"They'll call the local police if they come, so there's no point if we're not sure there's something to find. We'd end up arrested, remember?"

"I know, I know. I hate this though." I chew my lip while he watches the traffic along the boardwalk.

Deke can't see me, but he must sense it in my body language. "Hey, you don't have to do this. I have to check. If Perry catches up with me, I want to know I did everything I could."

"Don't talk like that," I say, and then I press my phone into his hands. "Just go fast. If you find anything, take pictures and get out before they come back, but keep it in airplane mode and turn it right back off. I don't want Perry showing up before the Coast Guard gets here."

His smile is a faint flash of white teeth in the shadows. "Right."

I cross the street with him, pausing by the live oaks and park benches flanking the boardwalk. Deacon keeps moving across the boardwalk and down the dock toward the larger white boat tied there.

It shifts in the water when Deacon climbs on board. It's inevitable and uninteresting to anyone who doesn't know what's going on, but my throat threatens to close off to air altogether, watching it wobble in the still water. Tiny waves ripple out from the motion, and I hold my breath until I see stars.

When my vision clears, I can make out a dark shadow moving toward the cabin and then a faint blue glow illuminating from within. My cell phone. My heart catches on a breath. Did he find something? The light dies, and I wait, watching the pole clock that's featured on half the postcards from this town.

One minute passes.

Three minutes. *Where is he?*

Six minutes.

My stomach squeezes its way up to my heart. That's too long. He should be out by now. I check the boardwalk and the road, waiting for a pickup truck to pass. There's nothing on that boat. No movement at all.

"Dammit, Deke," I mutter.

I cross the boardwalk in four strides and stick to the shadows as best as I can. My limbs are as limp as cooked noodles as I walk. There's no one around to see me wobble though. I dart onto the dock and stare at the boat, still seeing nothing.

I consider calling his name, but that feels crazier than boarding, so I grab the rope, give the pier one last glance, and then climb the ladder. I land on the boat softly, but it gives under my feet, leaving me to grip the railings to stay steady.

There are holes for fishing poles and long benches under a canopy in the main area. Keeps tourists in the shade when the sun proves to be too much. But I'm interested in the small white cabin at the front of the boat.

I step forward and hear the slightest creak. My body goes stiff.

I see the open cabin door but not Deacon. Then I hear him hiss. He's squatting on the floor near the door, staying under the boat sides and out of sight.

Darn good idea now that I think of it.

I drop immediately and then pause, considering the mix of fish guts, vomit, and other assorted tastiness that's probably all over this deck. Not the time to get squeamish. I crawl on my knees to Deacon, who's still squatting.

"What are you doing?" he asks.

"Wondering what's taking you so long."

He looks like he wants to argue but just shakes his head. "There's nothing in the cabin. I checked the benches on the sides too. Haven't checked the hold, but it seems too obvious."

"How about the bathroom?"

Even in the darkness, I can see the strange look he gives me. "The bathroom?"

I shrug. "I don't know. Dad said his captain friends always tell him to keep anything valuable on a boat in the bathroom, because it's the last place people think to look."

He arches a brow. "Worth a shot."

We slip around the corner of the cabin to the starboard side of the boat. A narrow white door opens into a small bathroom. There's a tiny sink with a cabinet and a pressure-flush toilet. I pop the latch on the cabinet, spotting a bucket with cleaners.

"No dice," I say, glancing through the fairly potent bottles. "Unless we want to scrub toilets or maybe start a fire."

We slip out and hear footsteps and voices ring out on the boardwalk. My eyes widen, but we can't see from this side of the boat.

"Probably nothing," Deke whispers. "Dit-dotters."

He moves to slip past me when I hear the distinct thump of the dock shifting, footsteps thumping down the planks. Deacon's hand touches my arm.

"Deke?"

I can't see anything but his shoulder. He backs us into the bathroom again, this time without a word. I can hear them. Someone's coming closer. Talking.

Deacon slides the bathroom door closed, cutting off the meager light entirely. I hear my heartbeat behind my ears. Deacon breathing. The men outside. The boat shifts with the undeniable motion of someone heavy climbing on board. And then a second someone.

*Thump, thump, thump.*

Every sound feels closer than the last. They're on the boat, moving around. My whole body trembles. Oh God, I might fall. Bump something.

They'd hear that for sure. Find us.

Terror spikes through my chest, blooms bitter on the back of my tongue.

I sway on my feet, reaching forward to grab Deacon. I catch his narrow hips, and he places his hands over mine. He's warm and steady, but I can feel the layer of panic sweat on his palms.

They're in the cabin now. Muttering. I hear heavy thumps,

like they're putting things in storage. Probably whatever they're smuggling. Money? Drugs? Bodies? Oh God, are they leaving now? We can't stay here. I bite back the panic until I taste blood.

*Stay calm. Stay. Calm.*

I push my face between Deacon's shoulder blades. My belly brushes something hard in his back pocket. My phone. We could call the police.

We could try. I inch my hand in that direction, but then they're on the move again, footsteps heading out of the cabin. Right past our door. I hear voices.

"...just head out?"

"No. Our guy just got on shift. Another hour. Let's get our shit."

The footsteps retreat off the boat, up the dock. I'm still clawing into Deacon's jeans hard enough to rip the denim, but he relaxes as the steps grow fainter.

He slips the door open, and it feels like light floods in. I cross my arms over my chest, feeling strangely exposed.

"Stay put," he breathes, easing out of the bathroom. He presses his long body against the cabin wall. "They're in the office on the dock. They left something."

"Let's call," I whisper. "Let's call now."

Deacon shakes his head. "He said his guy just came on shift. Perry's been on all day, so I don't think he's talking about the police."

"So?"

"So he could be talking about someone they've got in the Coast Guard. I don't know." He crouches low again like he's heading up to the cabin. I jerk him back by the hem of his shirt.

"Deke, no!" I whisper.

"They put something in the bins, Emmie. I want a picture of it. I want hard proof to send to every damn contact on your phone so that *no one* can hide this anymore. Then I don't care how fast they track us."

He inches toward the cabin again, and I want to scream, want to grab him, but I can see the edge of the shack from here. If I move any further, they'll see me.

Deacon cracks the door to the cabin, and I flinch at the tiny groan the springs make. He's inside. Shuffling, much more softly than the other two.

I glance down at my feet. The cabin's leaving a bank of deep shadows along the floor. If I stay low, I'll still be in that darkness. I creep into the cabin behind Deke, who's leaned over a black storage box, hinges open.

"We need to get out of here," I say. "Do it quick. What is that anyway?"

Deacon grins, holding up a black, waterproof backpack. I've seen dozens like it—it's a popular brand around here.

"What's in it?"

"Maps, notes. Contact numbers. Passports with Charlie and Thorpe's pictures but different names." He smiles. "This is more than enough."

There's a loud laugh from the boardwalk. Doesn't sound like Thorpe or Charlie, but it tenses me all the same.

"Get a picture and send it now," I say, feeling cold sweat trickle under my arms. "We need to get off this boat."

"I'm working on it," he says, fiddling with my phone. He swears softly, and I see the soft glow of the camera app on my phone screen. The red button for taking the picture. The white flash indicator.

"Deacon, wait!"

But he doesn't. The flash goes off. My heart slams out two more beats, and then I hear the door fly open on the shack.

"—flash in the cabin—" is all I hear. The footsteps are back. On the dock.

*Shit.*

Pounding closer.

They're coming.

# CHAPTER SEVENTEEN

. . . . . . . . . . . . . . . . . . . . . . . . . . . . . . . .

I hear Charlie first, his voice a rasp. "Do you see something up there?"

"Where?" Thorpe this time.

The fear is palpable in Deacon's eyes. I've frozen solid. I
can't move. Can't breathe. Deacon grabs the bag and my arm,
tugging us out the cabin door and immediately across to the
far side of the boat, away from the dock. We stick close to
the shadows.

"Over there!" Thorpe's voice booms, moving down the dock.
"The cabin door is open."

They land heavy on the boat, one and then the other.
Everything's wobbling under my feet, slanting sideways. Deacon
drags me to the rear of the boat, keeping the cabin between us
and Thorpe and Charlie.

Air saws out of me. I can't get more back in.

Deacon swears softly. We're at the back of the boat and well
concealed by the thick shadows, but that doesn't matter. They
know someone's onboard. It's only a matter of time.

He adjusts the strap of the bag over his back and scuttles forward, flinging open a hatch that leads down into the belly of the
boat. Then he's back with me in the darkness.

Thorpe and Charlie are still in the cabin, near the storage bins. One of them curses. Then, "It's gone! It's gone!"

A cluster of tourists comes by on the boardwalk. Thorpe and Charlie look toward the noise. They scan the crowd on the boardwalk as if maybe we got off while they weren't looking.

How *are* we going to get off the boat?

The question sends my stomach swirling down an imaginary drain. Because Thorpe and Charlie are leaving the cabin, and they're more frantic now. They know someone has the bag. Blood is roaring in my ears now, almost deafening.

Deacon climbs over the back of the boat on the ladder, beckoning me closer. I slide under the railing as Thorpe thunders closer, my hands slipping on the top rung, my legs heavy as lead as I let them dangle.

The ladder snags my hair, but I rip myself free. Pain shoots across my scalp. I bite back a yelp. A soft noise tells me Deacon is off the ladder and in the water now. The thump of heavy boots hits the dock again. Charlie or Thorpe? Only one of them. I still hear someone banging around in the hold beneath me. My hands are slipping. I can't hold on.

"Emmie," Deke whispers.

I look to see only his head poking out of the oil-slick water. I don't want to go in. I'm so cold, shaking so hard already. I force myself down the ladder, until the water swallows me up to my knees. It's worse than I thought. Tar black and reeking of fish and petroleum. It's so filthy, I'm not even sure it's still water.

I twist to look at Deacon, who beckons me frantically.

My stomach roils, but Thorpe is coming back up on the boat. I can hear his feet on the metal ladder in the hold. There isn't a choice. There is *no* choice at all.

I let myself go and slip quietly into the water. Cold. Cold enough to steal my breath and cramp my joints. I taste brine and darkness and fear. My legs thrash automatically, scraping razor-sharp barnacles on the side of the boat, but Deacon reaches for me, tugging my arm.

We slip under the shadow of the dock. It's rattling under Charlie's steps. "They're not on the boardwalk. Did they go overboard?"

One breath later, Thorpe leans over, searching the water. He moves to the starboard side, repeating that same hungry look, and I don't know if the shadows hide us well enough or if we stirred the water too much. I hold my breath and clench my teeth, though they want to chatter.

We can't stay in here forever. They'll search every inch. They want that bag.

Deacon moves in front of me, points to a small boat at the end of the dock. One of the Westfield skiffs. Fast, but only good for short distances. It's not much, but it's all we've got.

I pull in a breath, try to look around. Everything is quiet. I don't know where Thorpe is. Where Charlie is. I shiver violently on my way to the boat, my strokes rough and my teeth chattering. The bottom drops away beneath me before my fingers graze the side of the skiff. Deacon joins me, pressing a finger to his lips.

As if I need a reminder to stay quiet.

He helps me over the side of the boat. I land in the bottom with a wet thump. My ears prick. Footsteps at the edge of the dock. Thorpe. Shouting. Cursing.

They heard me.

They're coming back.

Deacon hauls himself into the boat, and I hear the soft snick of a pocketknife. Thorpe says his name like it's a filthy word, but Deacon doesn't answer. He cuts the rope and starts the engine. Thorpe's feet are pounding closer. I'm sure he'll leap from the dock, land right on top of me. But then Deacon opens the throttle wide, and the skiff surges with a whine.

We are flying.

I stay on the floor of the boat for what seems like hours, fixated on the layer of grimy water and God-knows-what-else beneath me. Deacon weaves in and out, heading around boats or little marshy bits. I don't know. I don't care.

Wet as I am, I can still feel the filth on the bottom of the boat. I imagine it soaking through my clothes, right into my skin. I push the thought away and focus on the drone of the engine instead. The motion of the ride and my pumping adrenaline roll through my belly until I'm half sick.

I don't know where Deacon is heading, but at some point, he slows down. The scream of the engine drones to a soft purr, and I open my eyes, willing my stomach to settle.

A star-dotted sky rolls above me. I smell trees and the earthy tang of waveless water. He took us into an inlet. I wouldn't know one from the other, so I don't bother to ask for particulars. The Carolina coast is a maze of shallow shoals and barrier islands. It's not a hard place to stay hidden.

"Can I sit up?" I ask.

"Yes," Deacon says, looking down. "God, I'm sorry. Yes."

He slows the boat even further and helps me. I feel stiff and half-frozen, and the air is twice as cold up here. I ease onto a bench seat, hugging my middle. Deacon finds a couple of towels under the driver's seat, and I do what I can to dry my clothes.

"We're safe for the moment," he says.

He's hatless now, and soaked from head to toe. Though he doesn't have a towel, he's not shivering like me. He finds a sweatshirt down there too. I peel off mine and put the dryer option on. It's still cold but so much better.

Deacon stops the boat in a marshy patch, grass rising four feet high on both sides. We bob gently in the water, but he keeps the engine at an idle, not dropping anchor.

"The phone was in my pocket," he says. He pulls it out, and I can tell it's trashed by his expression alone. "I'm sorry, Emmie."

My shoulders sag, but he touches my wrist, pulls me over to the driver's seat. "It's going to be okay. We've got you, right? You'll have a plan before you know it."

Sure. I'll plan us right out of this. Thing is, Deacon's looking at me like that's exactly what I'll do. I love him so much in this second that it physically hurts. Because I *don't* know what to do, but he still believes in me.

I sniff, trying to find strength. "Where are we? Can we get to Emerald Isle? To that Coast Guard station?"

He shakes his head. "North of Beaufort. Near Harker's Island. Nowhere near enough gas for Emerald Isle. I'm not sure we'd make it to Morehead City."

My laugh is humorless. "Of course we're low on gas. Is there an iceberg nearby? Seems like a fine time to bump into one."

Deacon grins. "We could easily make it back to the old Carmine place. My bike's still there."

My shoulders hunch, the wind blowing like January through my wet hair. "There's no phone."

"I'll admit, I'm not crazy about it anyway," he says. "It's closer to Beaufort than I'd like. I'd rather stay out of the sheriff's jurisdiction until we have help."

I adjust on the vinyl seat. "Could we shoot flares?"

Deacon chews his bottom lip. "I don't know. I'm sure Thorpe's looking for us. Not exactly the guy I want *rescuing* us."

"Agreed." I shudder, looking around. Thinking of Thorpe and Charlie in the cabin. "I'm pretty sure they know you have that bag. Whatever it is, they want it pretty bad."

"That's because it's proof that they're up to something. Falsified passports for ex-cons? I'm thinking that alone would be really serious jail time for both of them."

Deacon adjusts on the seat, pulling the strap over his head. He sets the bag on my lap and unzips it. I flip through it too, looking at the contents under the faint dashboard lights on the boat. Maps and a list of coordinates with dates and ticks lined down the right margin of the page.

"They've got red dots all over this map," he says.

"Pencil lines too. Wonder if they're tracking Coast Guard patrol routes?"

"Makes sense, I guess," I say, feeling over the back of the backpack. There's something hard and rectangular in there. My fingers brush the tag on the inside, but something catches my finger. A tiny zipper head, buried in neoprene folds. I push the folds apart and run my finger along the smooth teeth.

"I found something," I say, working out the head of the zipper and tugging it free. The whole lining unzips, revealing another black vinyl layer behind that.

"Is that the waterproofing?" Deacon asks.

"I don't think so." I peel the Velcro loose on the next layer. Then I pull it back, finding a slim plastic box with two latches. It rattles when I take it out, making me think of my old bead organizer from my bracelet-making phase in junior high school. Sturdy clasps for such a cheap-looking box.

I pull it open. There are close to thirty compartments inside, and every single one has a rock or two. Maybe more. It's hard to count them in the low lighting.

"Deacon, is that…is it crack?"

He frowns, looks confused. "I don't know. I'm not exactly a specialist."

I shift the box closer to the dashboard lights to get a closer look. The rocks vary in size—garden peas to lima beans—and they're all sort of translucent. Glassy.

"I don't think crack is clear like that," I say. "Is it?"

Deacon leans in closer to the box. The rocks are organized by size, smallest to largest. There are numbers etched on the sides, I think.

"I have no clue what the hell we're looking at," he says.

I tilt the box until I can see the numbers better: ¾–1½, 1½–3. It goes on this way up to 5–6, and there are tiny letters on the side, so small I can't make them out.

"What are those letters?" I ask.

Deacon squints and shifts the box this way and that. He shakes his head, carefully handing it back. "Maybe c-f? Or c-t?"

*Ct?*

I bite my lip and try to think. And it hits me like a sledgehammer. *Carat.*

"Diamonds." The word comes out like a sigh. Like I barely believe it's true, and I don't. Because it can't be. But I look again, and it is. "Deacon, these are uncut diamonds. They're smuggling *diamonds.*"

He seems tempted to argue, but then his gaze roves the box again before meeting mine. The fear I see there is undoubtedly a reflection of my own.

He swallows hard, and I can hear the lump that tries to stop him. "Holy shit."

"Yeah."

"Holy shit," Deacon says again. I just nod this time, because I'm trying to do the math. Mom had a two-carat diamond engagement ring when she and Dad were married. She kept it after the separation but commented more than once that she was a sentimental fool for letting fifteen thousand dollars sit in a dish on her dresser.

"Emmie, do you have any idea how much all this might be worth?"

I glance over the box, and my mental calculator goes up in smoke. A guesstimate doesn't matter really. I feel the blood drain out of my face. "A whole, whole lot."

\* \* \*

We're bobbing along in the reeds, trying to figure out what to do. Staying out here is too dangerous. Running out of gas and relying on whoever might be out in these waters at two in the morning sounds like an equally bad idea.

Deacon suggests breaking into an empty rental on Harker's Island, but I don't like it. "We are not adding breaking and entering to the list of crimes we're committing."

"We're not committing a crime. We have proof of a crime."

"We have a box of diamonds that we technically *stole*," I say. "You have an outstanding warrant, and I'm already in trouble for helping you. Now we show up—after running from the sheriff, mind you—with this?"

"It's the truth," Deke says.

I rub my shaking hands over my eyes. "I don't know that the truth is enough this time. People are going to see what they want to see. We need somebody we can trust."

"We need Joel," he says. "Or your parents. Or police who aren't being paid."

Joel would be better. My mom called the sheriff on me tonight. Not sure I'd list her among those I trust to help right now—but desperate times. I glance over at the dark sliver of land dotted with the occasional light. "Are there any pay phones on Harker's Island?"

"Doubtful there are any phones at all," Deacon says with a scoff, only half joking. "Just suspicious Down-Easters and the ferry to Cape Lookout. Perry's family lives on Harker's Island. I mean, the chances are slim…"

"With the way our luck is going, we'll end up in Perry's dad's living room. No thanks." I scan the northeast horizon, where the lighthouse should be. There's nothing for a second. Two seconds. Then the light comes, bright white and whirling toward us. It rotates past as suddenly as it arrived.

"Does the lighthouse have phones?" I ask.

"No. But it will in the morning. Tourist phones." Deacon perks up and leans forward, and the boat shifts. "We can hunker down there until dawn. We'll snag a tourist phone and call Joel. We should still have enough gas to get back to the Carmine place. Worst-case scenario, we can claim an emergency and have the park service that runs the ferries take us back to their office. We can call the state police from there."

"Maybe we could just go there now?" I ask, eager to be done with this backpack.

"They're not staffed overnight, and we could run into the police. It's only a few hours until sunrise."

I shiver, watching the light swirl past again. The wind kicks a wave underneath us, and the boat bobbles. "The lighthouse is outside of Perry's jurisdiction, right? Is it patrolled?"

"Not overnight, I don't think."

"Would Thorpe look for us there?"

"Look for us in a tourist trap?" he asks. "Seems like the last place we'd go. Thorpe will expect us to get help. Or to run."

I hunch over, still hugging myself. "This *is* running, isn't it?"

"This isn't running," Deacon says. "It's hiding."

It feels like both, but I nod anyway, and Deacon puts the boat in gear.

Cape Lookout is a typical barrier island, scrubby trees and sand crowned with a single slender lighthouse. That lighthouse is all I can see at first, black-and-white diamonds trailing up its sides. It hasn't been manned since the fifties. Back then, ships depended on the lighthouse to warn them away from the deceptive shallows of the sound. Now, it's little more than a tourist attraction—a North Carolina icon for key chains and refrigerator magnets.

Still, I feel safe under its watchful eye as Deacon motors us closer. We bring the skiff right up to the beach on the sound side of the island. It's imposing tonight, the diamond pattern too stark against the black sky. It's quiet on this side. You can hear the wind moving through the yaupon and switchgrass.

I glance up at the top of the lighthouse, which is dark, dark, dark. Then *light*. It rotates into view, impossibly bright and strong, casting a beam over our heads and into the water. Then it's gone, rotating around once more. I turn away, trying to tune out the pins and needles rolling up my ribs.

"Tourists will start showing up as soon as the sun rises." Deacon slips from his Southern drawl into a Midwestern twang. "Got to get those shells, don't-cha know?"

I laugh as Deke hops into the water, looking like a modern-day pirate as he hauls out the front anchor. I follow after him—less swashbuckler, more drunk puppy—sloshing through the water in my soggy sweatpants. I wobble, almost losing a flip-flop, plunging my arm into the dark water to retrieve it.

Deke laughs at me from the shore, so I chuck my wayward shoe at him. "Laugh all you want. Next time we're at Clawson's, you can talk about who's clumsy as I wipe the floor with you at the dartboard."

Deacon hauls the rope up the beach, securing it around the trunk of a shrub. "I still say you put a hex on the darts."

"You have crap aim. Stop making excuses."

I collect my shoes in one hand, letting my toes press into the cool, damp sand. Maybe three hundred yards down the beach, there's a dock where the ferries drop off tourists to view the lighthouse. I'm guessing that's where we're headed. Deacon pulls the zippers shut on the backpack and slings it over his shoulder.

"This feels like a horrible idea," I say with a glance at the bag.

"Well, I can't leave it here, can I?"

Probably not, but I still hate it. I force myself to look at the island instead. You can hear the faint roar of the ocean on the other side, but this side is just cicada song, rising and falling in a different kind of wave. I frown at the barren docks.

"When do you think the first boat will come?"

He shrugs, falling into step beside me as we head toward the walkway that cuts across the island. "Seven? There'll be private boats earlier than that. We'll be able to steal a phone before you know it. Try to relax."

"I've got a snowball's chance in hell of relaxing. And we're not stealing a phone."

He shoulders into me. "We can say 'borrowing' if you like that better."

"Let's just keep walking. If we walk, I don't have to think about the black-market diamonds strapped to your back."

"If we stop, I could pick one out for you," Deke offers. At my look, he laughs. "Kidding!"

"I know. It's just…they almost got away with this, Deke," I say, the wind blowing my damn hair across my face. I push it back. "How are you so calm with that?"

"Because they aren't getting away with it now." His mouth hardens, his cheekbones going extra sharp under the moonlight. "They won't leave without this bag, and they won't find us here. They'll get caught. And I won't pay for what they did to my dad."

I stop and look at him, seeing the anger he'd been missing for so long. "You thought you were going to go down for this, didn't you? And you accepted that."

He shrugs. "I wouldn't say I accepted it. I obviously chose to dodge Perry. I've been living on the run or whatever."

I *tsk*, looking up at the lighthouse as we pass. "It's lucky you know me. Joel's going to retire eventually, and you're obviously going to need lawyers in your life."

"I'm still not convinced you're going to be a lawyer."

"Joel thinks I have a good shot at the prelaw program." We're halfway across the island, and you can hear the Atlantic now, waves curling in and out, slave to the moon above.

"You have a shot at anything you want. I just think you'll come to your good senses."

"I seem to be lacking in good sense these days," I say, smirking at him.

"Too true. Running from the law. I didn't think you had it in you."

"Me either." I pause to look up at the lighthouse. It's strange being close to it, seeing the cracked exterior and faded paint. Still, it's an imposing thing, this black-and-white sentry standing guard in the darkness.

The wind is up on the ocean side. It cuts through my wet clothes the second we hit the sand. I cross my arms over my chest and pull up the hood on my sweatshirt.

"You're cold," Deke says, putting an arm around me. "We can go back."

"No, I like it here."

The sea is pretty at night, dark waves lapping at the untouched sand. The sky's just starting to lighten, the coming dawn veiling the stars. God, my mom is probably worried sick, but there's no helping that now. I nod toward a disrupted area on the sand.

"That could be a turtle nest, you know."

He smiles at me. "Then it's a good thing we don't have a flashlight, yeah?"

I squeeze his hand and grin. "What are you going to do when you're free? When this is all just a bad memory?"

Deacon stops, his expression turning somber. "You asked me what would happen after this, and I didn't answer you."

Given his look, I'm not sure I want him to answer now.

His brows pull together, and my stomach tenses. If he busts out any version of a "you'd be better off without me" speech, I *will* smack him.

I start first. "What's going on?"

He shakes his head a little and steps closer. "You do realize this is not a match made in heaven, right? I mean I'm—" Deacon pauses, watching me carefully. "Okay, I can see by your face I'm saying this badly."

"Then say it better." My words come out pointy. "Because this feels like a 'we should be friends' talk, and frankly, Deke, if you wanted to be friends, you shouldn't have kissed me. You should have just left it *alone*."

"Hey." He reaches for my shoulder and sighs when I pull away. "I wanted to kiss you. I told you I wanted to kiss you for a while. But you've wanted to kiss me for a lot longer."

I cross my arms over my chest. "So it's a contest? Who wanted who longer?"

"No, it's…" Deke looks skyward. "Man, I'm so bad at this. I just think you've got me on a pedestal, and I'm not going to live up to the hype."

"Don't flatter yourself." I snort and push my windblown hair behind my ears. "You can spare us both this awkward talk. I get it."

"No, you definitely don't," Deacon says. I start walking, and he growls behind me. "Damn it, Emmie, would you stop and let me get this out?"

I turn back to him, hands up. "Maybe I don't want to hear

what you're saying! Because this? I *knew* to expect this, but that doesn't make it hurt any less."

"I don't want it to hurt." He strides up close to me. "I just want you to think about it. About that pedestal I talked about."

"You're not on a pedestal. I could write a *grocery list* of the things I wish you'd change."

"Exactly. But you think I *will* change all of those things. You think I'll hero up one day, stop driving too fast and go be…hell, I don't know…an accountant or something. The point is, you believe in me *so* much."

My bitter laugh is lost in the crash of a wave. "Gee, Deacon, that sounds terrible."

"Hell no, it doesn't," he says. "The world needs people like you, Emmie, but the world isn't going to repay you for all that belief by living up to your expectations." He tugs on a strand of my hair and smiles. "I like you. You're smart and steady and damn funny when you want to be. You've got a solution for everything. You can save anyone."

"Except you, right?" My mom's words boomerang back, echoing in my ears. "Because you don't want to be saved."

"It doesn't matter what I want. There's no saving me from *this*. You want to march back into town and just, what? Pretend the last week didn't happen?"

"Deke, I'm not that naive. I know it won't be easy. It'll be weird at first."

"It would be weird *permanently*. This doesn't end. I'm probably not going to jail, and that's amazing. That's all you, Emmie.

That's how you *did* save me. But I still have an addict dad and I'm still not going to college and I'm still the guy who's going to spend the rest of his life dragging dit-dotters out on one boat or another."

"There's nothing wrong with that," I say.

"No, there's not." He tips up his chin. "I'm proud as hell of our business, and I know I can keep it going. Make it stronger." He touches my face then, smiles fondly. "But you're a college girl. You're going to join a sorority and get a job in Raleigh or something. You're going to be amazing, and frankly, you might decide you wish you'd done better for yourself."

"For myself." The laugh that comes out of me is brittle. Sharp. Deacon doesn't catch it. "Yeah, for you. You're so loyal and decent, you wouldn't leave me even if you wanted better. I don't want that for you. Or for me."

"So you think you know better than I do about what I'd want?"

Deke sighs. "I just want you to think about it."

"I *have* thought about it. And no, Deacon, you're *not* the wise choice. In so many ways. But then, neither is being a lawyer, because it's not what I really want deep down inside—but hey, working with animals isn't smart either, right? Because I might not have a solid job. Or I might have to move away from my mom, who needs me."

His shoulders pull back with a deep breath. "Hell, Emmie, don't go to law school for your parents. Of course, there's a risk in choosing something else, but you should do what *you* want to do."

"Yes, I should." Saying it feels good. I stand up straighter. "I

252

need to stop making every choice with someone else in mind. My parents. Even you and Chelsea."

"Yes," he says, shoulders dropping like he's relieved. "That's part of what I'm trying to say. I want you to think of yourself."

"Then let me be selfish! I selfishly choose you, Deacon." I watch him take the words in, like he's not quite sure I'm speaking the right language. His face breaks me open, touches all my raw places.

I take a breath. No reason to back down now. "The only real question is, do *you* want this? Because I'm not one of the girls who's going to stroll in and out in a week. I'm going to get on your nerves. Pester you to go to homecoming."

"Now you're talking crazy," he says, but he's smirking.

"Maybe. But what's it going to be? This shouldn't be the hard part, Deke."

"It isn't," he says, hand reaching for my face. "It isn't hard."

I'm afraid to move and shatter this moment. I want to cling to it, to the look on his face that makes me feel like living, breathing magic.

I'm more afraid to give him the space to argue, so I close the space between us, wrapping my fingers around his wrists. Deacon exhales, and his mouth moves to mine, and we're not quite kissing, but in some ways it's better. We're breathing each other in. Holding on tight.

It's almost enough to make me forget that dawn is coming, but when I open my eyes, I see the promise of it. The sky is purpling at the edges. The stars are fading away.

Morning will be here soon. We're not out of the woods. Not yet.

# CHAPTER EIGHTEEN

. . . . . . . . . . . . . . . . . . . . . . . . . . . .

The first tourist pickings are slim. The boat drops off eight passengers, a family with two squalling preschoolers and two other pairs. The parents have phones—phones they're passing back and forth between the kids while they haul more bags of toys and towels and snacks than I can count. Another couple heads straight to the beach, wearing sturdy shoes and expensive-looking cameras around their necks.

"Those two?" I ask, pointing at them.

Deacon shakes his head. "Those phones aren't leaving their pockets." He points at the last couple lumbering out. Two girls. College age from the look of it. They're both carrying giant purses and wearing easy-off knot dresses.

Phones are no longer a problem. Keeping the tourist bunnies off of Deacon might prove interesting though.

"You're right, the girls are perfect." I lie down on the bench, my wet, sandy legs in Deacon's lap. "Pretty sure you can handle the heavy lifting here."

"Huh, I pegged you for the jealous type."

"Well, you pegged wrong." I flop my arm over my eyes to block out the rising sun. "I've seen half the girls from Ohio hit on you on their way through town. I'm used to it."

"I'll just swipe the phone," he says.

"You won't have to," I say in a singsong voice.

When he stands up, my nonchalant exterior cracks. I sit up with a frown, picking the paint peeling on the edge of the bench. I never contemplated what it would be like to be with Deacon. The boy flirts with retirees from Florida when he's in tourist mode. I'm not even sure he knows he's doing it.

His walk changes to a swagger as he gets closer. Scratch that. He knows.

They respond just like I expect, with eager eyes and softly parted lips. I can't tell what he's saying, but they're nodding like bobble-heads, and I don't know whether to laugh or worry about what it's going to be like when Deacon goes back to running tours.

Suddenly, Deacon whips around, pointing at me. The girls look over, and my cheeks go hot and undoubtedly red.

Busted.

I force a smile and a wave, and one of the girl puts her hand to her chest, an obvious "Aw" on her lips. If they're disappointed, they don't show it—but they both line up to hand over their phones.

He takes the one on the right, and they watch him go, their smiles only a touch disappointed.

"So you dropped your phone in the water, and I want you to call your parents so they won't worry about you," he says softly.

"And they bought that?" I arch a brow at him. "One of these days, your charms will fail."

"My charms fail on you all the time."

He hands me the phone, and I take in a breath that smells like hope. "All right, Joel. Pick up this time."

He doesn't answer the first time I call. Or the second. I frown at the phone, and Deacon paces. "Try texting him. He won't recognize the number."

"Good point." I shift on the bench after texting, trying one more time.

Joel picks up on the first ring, and I gesture Deke closer, holding the phone between our ears. "Eddie, thank God! Your parents are worried sick. We've been calling all night. They say you're with Deacon."

"I am," I say. "My phone got wet."

"I'm just leaving Daffy," he says. "I needed to get a power of attorney so I can get those records on Chelsea. Do you know they won't let her call anyone?"

"I know. She texted me last night from her aunt's phone. They took hers."

Deacon interrupts. "We've got bigger problems to deal with. Thorpe and Charlie are smuggling. They were loading up the *Clementine* last night."

"No, no, that's the Christopher charter. He takes one out every month."

"He takes the *Clementine*?" Deacon asks, sounding dubious. "Somehow I think we'd notice our biggest boat missing a couple of days a month."

Joel takes a sharp breath, obviously struck silent.

I speak first. "Joel, it's true. They were loading the *Clementine*.

And we found a backpack with marked maps and lists of coordinates on board."

"We found something else too," Deacon says. "Diamonds. They're still not…they're uncut, but we're pretty sure."

Disbelief seems to balloon in Joel's long silence. Finally, he clears his throat and his voice is small. "Are you sure about this?"

I swallow. "Yes. We think they're setting up fake charter rentals. Like Mr. Christopher. Christopher is Thorpe's son's name."

"No, no, his name is CJ—" Joel cuts himself off with a sharp breath. "My God…"

My heart pulls for him. He believed in people. Gave them a second shot, and this is how they're repaying them.

"I'm so sorry," I say softly.

Joel strangles out a noise, but Deacon continues. "Look, the problem is Thorpe knows we have these diamonds. And since the sheriff was already after us—"

"You're worried about how it will look if you show up with them," he says. "All right, where are you? Are you safe for the time being? Can I pick you up somewhere?"

"We're at Cape Lookout," I say. "We've got a boat, but we're low on gas."

It sounds like Joel is walking. Pacing maybe. "Maybe I could call the police. Send them right to you."

"Joel, we think the sheriff might be in on all of this," Deacon says.

"Eddie, Dink, that is just not—"

"He's telling the truth," I say. "I think he might be getting paid off. It's bad, Joel."

"Now, what on earth—"

"Look, we'll explain it all when we see you," Deacon says. "We just want you to go in with us."

He pauses, hesitates. "All right, then I'll come. I'll meet you. But I'm sending the state police after Thorpe and Charlie right now. There's no changing my mind on that."

"Can you meet us on Lennoxville Point road?" I ask. "It's off of Mulberry. There's a little house at the end of the road. Around the curve, back past the rest."

"I'll find it. I should be there within the hour. If you really think Perry's involved in some way, you best not talk to anyone. He's probably got APBs out for you, so stay out of sight until I can get you guys to some real authorities."

"Okay," I say, heaving a relieved sigh. "That sounds really great."

Joel clears his throat. "Dink, are you still there?"

"Yeah?"

"Daffy said he remembers a mask. Like a…uh, ski mask? He can't be sure, but he thinks it was a bigger guy too. Perhaps Thorpe…well, what's important is that your father knows you didn't hurt him."

Deacon swallows hard. "All right."

"I'm sorry," Joel says, voice cracking. "I shouldn't have said— I'm just truly sorry, Dink. More than you know."

Deacon closes his eyes, and I see his shoulders hitch. Just once. I thank Joel for him and end the call. Then I pull Deke close and hold him steady. I watch the dolphins play over his shoulder, free and happy. He will be too, soon.

By the time we give the phone back and start heading to the skiff, the tide's gone out. The boat's resting in sand, and Deacon's anchor is tangled. He's wrestling with it, and I'm pacing grooves into the beach. I want to go. I want this over with.

Joel's call has me nervous. I feel like anyone could be on Thorpe's payroll at this point, so when I see a familiar white-and-blue boat pulling into the dock, my fingers go numb and tingly.

"Deacon."

He follows my line of vision, eyes narrowing when he sees the vessel and the two men in uniform aboard. I don't know exactly who they work for, but they look official. Important.

"It's all right," he says, but he's tying quicker now. "It's Park Service, not the police. They're just patrolling."

"If Perry put out a missing persons notice, they would get it though, right?"

Deacon's lips thin, and he pauses to watch the boat. "Not sure. I wouldn't panic yet."

He says he wouldn't, but he starts coiling the rope faster. The patrol boat stops at the pier, where the girls we borrowed the phone from are sunbathing. My shoulders hunch as the captain talks to them from the water.

Are they talking about us? Is the brunette pointing our way?

"Let's push her out," Deacon says. "Give me a hand?"

I tear my gaze away from the NPS on the hull of the Park Service boat to push our own out. I don't like that they're here. It's like I can feel eyes on us, following us across the sand.

I adjust my grip on the lip of the bow as we shove into the

water. My feet stumble, and my hand slips. Sharp pain lances through my palm. I swallow my hiss down under a swell of fear. Something warm rolls down my fingers. Drips.

No. No, no, no.

The patrol boat is cutting around the pier, and my ribs are shrinking a size with every breath. I'm bleeding, and they will see. Worse still, when Deacon sees, he will freak out and then they'll feel they have to help me. They'll call for more help. Paramedics.

Perry could hear about that call.

"They might be coming to check on us," he says.

He hasn't seen yet. I glance down, and my stomach rolls. Yeah, it's not good. There's blood dripping. I'm going to need stitches.

Deacon hops in the boat and comes to the bow to help me in. "Let's get you in the…" I tense as he trails off, the color draining from his face.

"Deke, it's okay," I say.

He stumbles back until he slumps onto a seat.

Shit.

Shit. Shit. Shit.

I look around. The NPS boat is moving slow, but it'll be here soon. Only one boat between us, another skiff with a middle-aged man.

"I need a towel," I say. He ignores me, staring blankly into the distance. "Deacon! A towel, a shirt—*something*."

Still no response.

I yank my borrowed sweatshirt off, leaving me in a tank top. I wrap the sweatshirt around my hand and tie it in a knot. Then I splash water over the blood on the hull and wade toward the ladder on the back of the boat. It's bobbing and slick, and I'm climbing one-handed.

I haul myself in awkwardly, hearing the drifted conversation from the other boats. They can't be more than a hundred yards away. My hand throbs like a warning. We have zero time.

Deacon hasn't moved. Hasn't spoken.

"Deacon, don't look at my hand. Look at the boat. They're coming over."

I fumble into the driver's seat and start the motor, leaving it at an idle.

Deacon closes his eyes, shudders. I say his name again. Check the NPS boat. It's drifting away from the other skiff, starting the engine. I grip the steering wheel, and my cut screams.

My whimper gets Deacon's attention. He locks onto my gaze, eyes dark with terror. But we can't do a slow come-down from his panic now. Not with Park Service officers closing in and me probably seconds from bleeding through the sweatshirt.

I take a shaky breath. "Deacon, listen to me."

His face twists, and I can see him trying. He's breathing hard. Pushing for control.

"You need to fake it. Right now. Or they will call for help, and I don't know who that help will be, do you hear me?"

I lift my uninjured hand to wave at the NPS boat. I push a smile I've seen my mom wear a thousand times.

"I need you right now, Deke." I say it low, right through my grin. "Do you hear me?"

"Yes."

His voice is a croak, but it's there. He's looking at me. Shaking and breathing too hard, yes, but he's not lost in that dark place. He's here with me.

The NPS boat cuts the engine, pulling up to our starboard side. Ball cap and a white polo. No badge of any kind, thank God.

I grin wider but keep my injured arm down in the boat. "Morning!"

"Good morning," the officer says, a smile creasing his well-lined face.

My smile has frozen to my lips. I try to take a breath and try to come up with something to say. All I can think about is how long it will take them to see that Deacon is ghost-white and drenched in panic sweat.

Oh God, I have to say something else. I have to say something.

"Morning," Deacon says.

My throat unclenches, and I take a breath.

"Heading out already?" the officer asks. "It's going to be a good day."

"Just stopped by for low tide," Deacon says. "No luck on the sand dollars though. Might check out the horses on Shackleford."

The captain nods, but I can't tell if he's smiling now. At this angle, his face is lost under the shadow of his hat. I feel like it's been too long since anyone spoke, but I don't know what to say. The silence stretches, and my eyes focus on the little black walkie-talkie strapped to the captain's hip.

Has it been five seconds? Or fifty?

Someone crackles over the radio, and my jaw goes tight. The

captain checks it and says something I can't make out into the microphone. Seconds feel like centuries while I wait for him to command us off the boat. Maybe call the police. But he raises another friendly wave and starts his engine.

"Y'all be careful out there," he says.

"Yes, sir," I say, flashing teeth as he turns away.

I put the skiff in gear and start driving. My joints feel like rubber bands and my stomach constricts. I might throw up. Deacon looks like he's *definitely* going to throw up. Or maybe he already did and I didn't notice. I take us out a little way from the island, and then he gestures at the wheel.

I get up without another hint. I have no clue where to go. I could be steering for Bermuda right now. He's still shaky and pale when he settles into the captain's seat, but he takes the wheel and opens the throttle wide.

* * *

We head through a narrow strip of water between Shackleford Banks and Cape Lookout to get back to mainland. Deacon guides the boat on autopilot, and I sit, shivering on the bench, too cold and shell-shocked to form a plan.

Deacon leads us along the edge of Shackleford Island, finding a little inlet where he cuts the engine, leaving us bobbing. Absently, I search for horses, but they're hiding too, I guess.

"What are we doing?" I ask when he doesn't start back up. "We need to get to the house, don't we?"

"Your hand," he says, and his gaze is drifting over me, fixing on the sweatshirt I've got wrapped around it.

"It can wait."

Deacon lurches forward, like he might heave, and then jerks his head away, panting. "Doesn't look like it. You're dripping."

I look down at the drops of blood on my sweatpants. "Okay, I'll clean it up. Is there a first aid kit?"

"Behind my seat."

The water is calm, so Deacon drops anchor and I pull out the kit, unclasping the hinges. I unwrap my hand from the sweatshirt and take my first good look. It's as ugly as it feels, a two-inch gash starting in that webbing between my thumb and forefinger and ending at the bottom of my palm. Definitely needs stitches. But right now, all I've got is a couple of rolls of gauze and a guy who's probably going to puke over the side in the next thirty seconds.

I find first aid wipes. It's slow work, cleaning one-handed, but I manage. There's antibacterial wash, so I squirt some of that all over, clenching my teeth to try to hold in my cry.

Okay.

Almost there.

Just need some gauze and some pressure. Probably a lot of gauze.

I press, and the pain pulses to the rhythm of my heart. I rest my head against the back of Deacon's seat and close my eyes. I'm too woozy. Need to get it together here.

Deacon takes a sharp breath, and I turn my head to the side.

"It's okay," I say. "I just need a second. It's hard one-handed."

I feel the seat shift and the shuffle of his feet. When I open my eyes,

Deacon's crouched in front of me, looking ashy but determined.

"What do you need?" he asks.

I put on a brave smile. "I can do it."

"Please let me help."

"Deacon, I know you can't do this. It's okay."

"Like hell it is." The color's coming back to his face, but it's bringing anguish along with it. "I couldn't help my dad when he needed me. What if it's Chelsea next time? I can't stay like this. Tell me what to do."

I take a breath and reach for him with my good hand, my fingers brushing along the inside of his wrist. "I need the gauze and some tape, please."

"Okay."

It takes him twenty minutes to get the job done. His hands shake, and he has to stop every few seconds. There's at least once when he heads to the side of the boat and I'm sure he'll throw up. But he doesn't. He tapes the final piece of bandage in place and sags in relief.

"See?" I say, grinning. "No problem."

He rolls his eyes, but when I kiss him, his lips go soft, and his hand cradles the back of my head. "You think way too highly of me, Emerson May."

I flex my fingers, feeling the pull of the cut and the tape. "Well, I still wouldn't recommend any future plans as a surgeon."

"Ah, I won't need med school. You'll be a doctor of some sort."

"Maybe," I say. "Maybe I won't decide for a while."

"That sounds like a good plan. I approve." He arches a brow, and the old Deacon shines through.

My shoulders relax as we take off again. Deacon pulls into the dock of the abandoned house fifteen minutes later.

I can't see the driveway from here, but Joel's not waiting in the yard. The morning is bright though, turning the water on the sound into a mirror. I hop out of the boat first, taking the rope he tosses and looping it around the pole. Deacon takes it from there, so I look up at the house, the back of my neck prickling.

It's all quiet. The hammock is swaying just a little. The back door is shut tight. The only thing I can hear is Deke working on the boat and a gull crying somewhere in the distance.

"I'm going to go around the front and see if Joel's car is here," I say.

Deacon ties another rope while I head up the side of the house so I can see the driveway. There's a shadow of a vehicle on the grass. My smile blossoms.

"Joel! We're out back," I call, breaking into a jog.

My feet stutter at the edge of the house as the car comes into view. It isn't Joel's BMW. It's a Beaufort police cruiser.

A voice thunders in the backyard, shouting fast, angry words. I can't make them out, but they turn my heart to stone all the same.

I pivot in place, something heavy dropping through my stomach. I stumble back toward the dock. My vision smears into blurs, leaving glimpses of the scene in the yard. The small, sagging house. The hammock swaying in the sun.

Sheriff Perry with his gun drawn.

And Deacon with his hands in the air.

# CHAPTER NINETEEN

. . . . . . . . . . . . . . . . . . . . . . . . . .

Deacon is face down on the ground, and my insides are grinding to dust. I can't move. Can't breathe. Can't do anything but watch and listen as Perry screams at Deacon to kick his legs and arms apart. Red-faced and panting, the sheriff moves around, patting Deacon's back with one hand, up the sides of his legs. Looking for a weapon.

I flinch when the nose of his gun presses into the back of Deacon's head.

"You have the right to remain silent," Perry says. "Anything you say can and will be used against you in a court of law."

The sheriff perches on Deacon's back, fixing a shiny metal cuff on one wrist and then reaching for the other, all the while droning on about rights to an attorney. When Deacon is cuffed, Perry holsters his gun.

"Do you understand these rights as I have presented them to you?"

"Yes." Deacon's voice is muffled in the grass. How did Perry find us? How is any of this happening?

Perry pulls Deacon up to his knees, and our eyes meet. My soul splinters, comes apart. Deacon says nothing and everything in that look.

"Run," he mouths.

No! I can't run. I need to stall until Joel gets here. Because this isn't ending here. It can't end this way. Not after everything.

Determination pushes strength into me. "Are you going to arrest me too, Sheriff? Because I know why you're after Deacon now. I figured you out."

The sheriff turns, fingers grazing—but not pulling—the gun on his hip. "Emmie, you've put me in a difficult situation here. You've interfered with a police investigation, aided a known suspect. You'd still be on the run right now if your mama hadn't thought to check the tracking log on your phone."

"My mom just reinstalled that program. There wouldn't be a log."

"There's always a log when there's a good parent involved," he says. "Those programs are made to run in the background for a reason."

My cheeks flush. She lied to me, told me she trusted me, but all this time she could have kept tabs if she wanted? Was she that paranoid? Because of Landon? It doesn't matter now.

"What you're doing is *wrong* and you know it," I say.

"Young lady, you need to do a lot less talking and a lot more listening," the sheriff says. "Do you understand that I'd be well within my rights to arrest you here and now?"

He actually sounds like he'd regret that, and the good guy act is pissing me off. He jerks Deacon up, drags him through the yard and toward his cruiser in the driveway.

I run and grab the backpack from the dock, because he must not know what we have in there. Thorpe must not trust him with the details. I find him out front by the car, and my head is buzzing like a hornet's nest.

"Thorpe is hiding things from you. Do you know what he's doing? Do you know how much this is worth to him?" The sheriff ignores me. We're at the edge of the driveway, but it feels like the edge of a cliff.

My anger is white hot, but my voice is quiet. "Why won't you answer me, Sheriff? Is he paying you to ignore me too?"

"Emmie, *don't*," Deacon says.

The sheriff whirls on him with rage on his face. "Don't you start, boy!"

Deacon drops his head and goes still. I set the bag at Perry's feet.

"I already told Joel about what's in this bag," I say. "He's already called the state police for Thorpe and Charlie too. It's over. You ignoring me isn't going to change that."

"The state police?" Perry wipes his brow, a dry laugh sputtering out of him. "Emmie, what on earth are you talking about?"

He should be scared, but he just looks confused. And I'm not so sure it's an act, but it has to be, doesn't it? It *has* to be. "How can you keep acting like you don't know? Everybody says you care about this town, but what did it take to buy you off? A boat? A nice, shiny watch?"

The sheriff frowns, looking suddenly older. Smaller. "That watch was a twenty-five-year anniversary gift from my wife."

Deacon looks up, watching Perry with a crease between his brows.

My ribs go tight. Tighter. Is he telling us the truth? Did we have it wrong?

"Emmie," the sheriff starts again, much more gently. "I don't know what sort of craziness this boy has put into your head, but you've got to face reality here."

We *were* wrong. Unless he's hiding a serious talent as an actor, the sheriff isn't involved in this. He could have helped us.

I lift my chin. Maybe he still can.

"Please just look in the bag. Please, Sheriff. We need help, and I think maybe I was wrong to not come to you."

"You think so, do you?" I don't know if it's the waver in my voice or if he does it just to shut me up. But he heaves a sigh and picks up the bag. I watch him paw through the maps and paperwork. He seems dismissive until he finds the passports. His eyes narrow at the names and then his gaze jerks to Deacon. Then me.

"There's a zipper." I say. "In the back."

I can tell when he finds it, because he frowns. He pulls the lining loose and peels down the second layer until the box is revealed.

"It's diamonds," I say. "They aren't polished. Or cut or whatever."

"Where did you find this bag, Emmie?"

"On the big fishing boat. The *Clementine*." Relief washes over me in heavy waves. I was wrong about the payoff. Wrong about him. He can help us. I let out a sigh. "We think they were smuggled, or are being smuggled, I don't know. We thought if we could just prove—"

"Still trying to do my job for me," he says, but I can tell he's not angry now. He's worried. He opens the latches, runs a finger over a couple of the diamonds, shakes his head.

"Is this your bag?" he asks Deacon, and for the first time since this mess started, it feels like a real question. He wants an answer, not another piece of wood to add to Deke's pyre.

"No, sir," Deacon says. "You're looking for Kevin Thorpe and Charlie Jones."

"I'm not sure I believe you," Perry says, but he pulls the radio off of his belt and calls out something in code. I can't make out much other than "immediate backup."

Deacon catches my eye and shrugs, like he can't quite believe what he's seeing and hearing. That makes two of us.

Perry's shoulders settle after the call. I hear a car turn onto the one-lane road. There are only three houses down here, so traffic is rare, but when it drives past the two houses closer to the main road, my ears prickle.

"That's probably just Joel," I say. "He's supposed to meet us here."

But the car stops with a soft squeal of brakes behind the curve of the road, where it's lost in the trees. Wouldn't Joel pull up to the driveway? My throat tightens.

The sheriff picks up his radio again. "What is your ETA, Tom? Over."

"I'm by the bridge. Eight minutes out. Over."

The faint *click-click* of a car door opening follows. We strain to see, but there are too many trees and shrubs around the house and driveway. Perry's wary eyes move across the shrubs with intent.

"Isn't that backup?" I ask with faint hope, but the sheriff's lips go thin. His eyes narrow to slits as he slowly draws his gun. My whole body clenches tight.

Something rustles in the trees, and the sheriff steps forward, gesturing us further behind the house. He looks left, then right. This isn't the same man who picked at me or bad-mouthed Deacon. This is an officer of the law who thinks he's in danger.

Another rustle. The sheriff follows the sound with his gun, but continues to watch the entire line of trees. Whatever or whoever is out there is getting closer.

"Sheriff?" I breathe, my voice a knot of fear on my lips.

His voice is low and steady as he unhooks a ring of keys from his belt, pressing one into my hands. "Get that boy in the house, Emmie. Get in that house and get down. Right now."

He talks into his radio again, low, quick commands with numbers I don't understand. Deacon's still cuffed when he follows me into the back door. We're across from the kitchen, but there's a window where I can still see Sheriff Perry, gun drawn, glancing left and right.

Deacon shoulders into the door, pushing it softly. It closes with a snick, and I see Deputy Nelson coming out of the trees behind Perry. I slump with relief.

"It's just Nelson. It's fine," I say as I unlock Deacon's hands.

Deacon rubs his raw wrists. Outside, the sheriff starts to turn—to talk to Nelson is my guess—but Nelson stays behind him, like he's sneaking. I'm going to ask Deacon about it when I see something in Nelson's hand. It's boxy and strange, but he's holding it in front of him like a firearm.

Like a gun.

Time grinds to a stop, and my breath goes buoyant in my lungs as Nelson aims right between Perry's shoulder blades. I open my mouth to scream—to warn Perry—but before I can, the sheriff goes unnaturally stiff.

"Emmie, down!" Deacon whispers, curling an arm around my shoulders.

I crouch low beside him, so dizzy that the room is going gray around the edges. Deacon's swearing under his breath, but I'm stunned into silence. Outside, I hear a strange *tap-tap-tap-tap-tap*. What is that? Is that the gun? I glance out to see Perry facedown on the ground, two thin wires trailing from his back to the gun in Nelson's hands.

"What is that? What is he doing?" My whisper is panicky.

Deacon leans in close, his words soft against my neck. "It's a Taser. He's okay."

Another crack as Nelson's elbow comes down on the back of Perry's skull, and I pull in a breath that I'm sure will come out in a scream. I bite it back, swallowing hard. Help will come. Help will come in seven minutes. Maybe six now.

Oh God, please let them get here before Joel. Please don't let Nelson hurt Joel too.

Deacon scoots on his knees across the floor, looking out the front window. I can't rip my eyes off the scene out back, Nelson tilting his head as he looks down on Perry. Like he's checking out a mouse he just found in a trap.

"What do you want to do with him now?" Nelson asks.

I jerk because it's almost like he's talking to us. But then I see someone coming around the side of the yard. Tall and broad shoulders. Unbuttoning his suit jacket.

His gray suit jacket.

Deacon looks back my way, catches sight of the new man too. His face goes ten shades paler in an instant. "What the hell?"

He stole the words from my mouth. Because I can't be seeing what I'm seeing. But I am. It's him.

It's Joel.

# CHAPTER TWENTY

· · · · · · · · · · · · · · · · · · · · · · · · · ·

Joel tugs at the cuffs on his jacket, and Nelson looks
worried. Gone is the aw-shucks officer with the cream cheese
on his moustache. This new Nelson terrifies me. And he's holding up his hands in deference to *Joel*.

My head is fuzzy, and Deacon's body has gone rigid behind me.

"We can still sort this out, Joel," Nelson says, placating. "Perry
didn't see me. Nothing has to change. We'll find the boy, and you
can get back to business."

"Every business has an expiration date." Joel shakes his head. "You
make a lousy dirty cop, Nelson, you know that? Deacon showing
up at the house that night? That was a *gift*. But you wasted it."

Deacon looks like he's been slapped, and I feel like the ground
has disappeared, like I'm flailing for footing in a new, awful world.

"I had Perry convinced," Nelson says, "but that kid was a ghost,
Joel. He was nowhere. You should have had Thorpe at the hospital."

"Thorpe already *did* his job!"

It's not possible. Even looking right at this, I can't make my head
stretch around it. I reach for Deke with a trembling hand and
squeeze his shoulder. He's the only thing that feels real anymore.

"You talked a big talk, Nelson," Joel says. "Deacon would take
the fall. Emmie's evidence would disappear. Everything would be

in hand for this run. Isn't that what you said? I sent that girl to your damn *doorstep* with the coordinates!"

Nelson and I both jerk at Joel's volume.

A scuffle on the ground tells me Perry is coming to. He lifts his head with a groan. Joel sighs and draws his right leg back. He's aiming for the sheriff's head, but I can't look away. Not even when the kick connects, Perry's head snapping left violently.

The sheriff's face drops to the dirt again.

Unconscious?

*Dead?*

My stomach rolls, saliva gathering fast in my mouth. Deacon must see the scream in my eyes, because he nudges me, shakes his head over and over, willing me to be quiet.

"How long do we have until backup arrives?" Joel says matter-of-factly, heading to collect the backpack.

"I told them I had it. Tom saw some other mess on the waterfront, but they'll send someone sooner or later."

Joel clucks. "That other *mess* is Charlie Jones going down. We're blown, Nelson. You'd better get a move on."

Nelson hesitates, face drawn in panic, and then dawning horror. His shoulders set in a way that makes it clear his mind is made up. Then he runs for the trees. Joel doesn't pay attention, just picks up the backpack and unzips it, checking the contents.

A shadow passes in front of the window, and Deacon pulls me back. A whiff of fish and tobacco filters through the opening, assaulting my already queasy belly.

Thorpe.

I gag and force a slow, deep breath, trying not to think about Joel's shiny shoe connecting with the sheriff's head.

"The kids aren't in the woods," Thorpe says.

Joel shrugs, slinging the bag over one shoulder. "I have what I came for. I've got a client waiting and a palm tree with my name on it. I don't give a shit what you do with them."

He tosses Thorpe a passport. "Charlie got nailed earlier. So, don't have too much fun before you head out." He pulls out a thick bank envelope and chucks it at Thorpe too.

"What's this?" Thorpe asks, holding up the envelope.

"Did a little last-minute banking. A power of attorney is a beautiful thing." Joel smirks. "Consider it a retirement gift. Or a retainer for your next lawyer. Next time you get strung up for trafficking, I'll be sipping rum out of a coconut."

Joel's laugh crawls up my back like a scorpion. I cringe, waiting for the sting, but it never comes. I watch him turn to slink down the dock. Thorpe stomps through the yard and into the trees. They're going to go. It's going to end, just like that.

I hear the clack of Joel's footsteps on the wooden dock, and Deke grits his teeth so hard I can hear it. Joel was like family to him. The thought of what he must be going through hits like a hammer to my ribs.

Deacon looks at me and then looks at the door.

"Just a few more minutes," I whisper. "Until we're sure they're gone."

"He's going to get away with it," Deke says.

I cringe because he's not as quiet as he should be, and then I see his face. The rage carves the hollows under his cheekbones into something dangerous.

*He's going to do something.*

I reach, but he's too quick, wrenching the door open so hard it slams into the inside wall.

He's going after Joel.

\* \* \*

It's like one of those dreams where you can't run. Your legs are too heavy, and the air feels honey-thick. It takes me hours to get through the door. Crossing the yard will take a century. I scream for Deacon, who's halfway down the lawn, his eyes on the boat and the white-haired man who was supposed to save us.

"How could you do this?" Deacon screams. "How?"

Joel startles, shoulders jerking as he turns to see Deacon barreling down the yard. Deacon reaches the dock, but Joel's already untied the skiff. Joel climbs aboard and pushes the boat back into the water, and Deacon stalls out, hands fisted.

"You lied to us!" he shouts. "Used us!"

"I did what I had to do," Joel says, one hand on the steering wheel. I see the glint of his diamond ring and my stomach twists like Deacon's expression.

For a minute, I think Deacon might run to the end of the dock, maybe jump in after him. But instead, his shoulders droop.

"Why us?" he asks.

Joel's answering laugh is cruel. "Because you were *easy*. It's just business, Dink. Nothing personal."

His words ignite the rage all over again. Deacon storms down the dock, spewing an endless streak of curses. He's going to jump for the boat. I stumble after him.

"Deacon, no!" I shout.

A dark blur moves in from the woods on the left. Thorpe plows into Deacon's back, takes him down hard halfway down the dock. I scream as Deacon hits face-first, Thorpe's knee grinding between his shoulder blades to keep him down.

"Much obliged, Kevin," Joel says.

"Obliged enough to give me the keys to your car? Looks like you're heading out early." Thorpe bumps his chin toward the water pointedly.

Joel laughs. "Good guess. Might want to look into a paint job quick," he says with a wink, then he flings the keys overhead, like he's pitching a baseball.

When Thorpe snatches them from the air, Deacon squirms, earning a punch to the kidney for the effort. I cry out, but Joel barely gives us a perfunctory glance. Then he puts the boat in gear and he's gone.

The roar of the engine fades, leaving Deacon's groans in the air. Thorpe's fist is at his side. His other hand is knotted in Deacon's hair, pulling his face off the dock. I curl my fingers in, fury burning up my middle.

"You won't be so pretty when I'm done with you, you little shit," Thorpe says.

I fly. No plan at all, just my body sprinting down the yard and leaping onto Thorpe's back. I sling my arm around his meaty neck. The slick feel and rancid smell sends the sting of bile into my throat. Thorpe curses, releasing Deacon long enough to shake me off. I come loose like I weigh nothing, thudding painfully into the ground behind him.

I scramble to my feet, and there he is, red-faced and breathing hard as he reaches for me. Deacon attacks him from the back, kicking at his leg, punching his torso.

"Run, Emmie!" Deacon says between hits. "Get help!"

I lunge again, but I'm clumsy this time, my foot going wide. Thorpe dodges me, swinging a heavy fist around at Deacon's temple. Then another to his solar plexus. And another to his eye. It's so fast the punches blur together.

Deacon crumples, throwing an elbow into Thorpe's leg while groaning at me. "Run! Run!"

Another hit from Thorpe and Deacon goes down without a sound. Thorpe doesn't waste a breath. He comes for me.

Adrenaline fires through me like liquid lightning. I knock over the grill in Thorpe's path. Topple one of the rusty chairs. Fling the glass jar of shells at his head. It connects with his shoulder, shatters.

"You little bitch!" he howls.

Nothing left to throw, so I run. Past the house, through the yard, pumping my legs for everything they've got. I'm almost to the trees. I have to get help. Have to.

I start shouting in the woods, underbrush scraping at my bare arms. No one answers, and I can't see the road. I fall silent, because it hits me. I can't hear Thorpe, but he's in here somewhere. Hunting me.

My stomach wrenches, warning me that it might revolt. Something's moving. Rustling in the trees. Footsteps. Not an animal either—the tread is all wrong.

It's him.

I think I hear an engine, but I can't be sure. Is it the police? I'm sprinting now, dodging around underbrush and through the older, thick-trunked trees. I pause to turn and hear Thorpe's feet thudding, cracking twigs and dry leaves as he moves. He's closer.

Too close.

I stop at the edge of the trees, listening. Where is the engine I heard? Is the backup here?

"Going somewhere, blondie?"

Thorpe is right behind me. I break through the trees I'm in and risk bolting across the neighbor's yard. I see a flash of shiny silver fender on the road. *Please.*

I scream for help over and over, until my ears burn and my throat hurts. I'm pushing for the road, for that car. He's behind me, but I don't stop. I fall once, but I'm right back up. Still screaming. I can make it. I can do this.

I'm two steps from the road when a thick arm hooks me around the waist. I gasp and the stench of cigarettes and fish assaults me. I shout and claw into Thorpe's arm, my ears ringing.

I squirm and kick. Throw an elbow into something soft. Something fleshy that makes Thorpe curse.

He lifts me off the ground, and I'm trapped, tucked under his arm like a rag doll. I scream again and flail. A sweaty hand slams into my mouth. Blood coats my tongue, mingling with other tastes I can't and don't want to identify.

"Hold still, pretty," he sneers, ducking low into the grass. "You're going to come with me. Find a way to pay for that stunt with the jar."

I flail, elbows and heels in every direction, and finally, finally, his hold breaks. I hit the ground. The pain is lightning-sharp. Can't stay down. I force myself to my knees. Crawl to my feet.

"Get up here!"

Thorpe's hand is in my hair, dragging me up, harder and higher until I'm screaming and on my feet. He pulls the waistline of my pants so hard they cut into my skin, and all around me is his putrid smell. Sweat and sea and cinnamon.

*Cinnamon.* I hear a metal *click-click* that I've never heard in my life.

I'm pretty sure it's a gun. And it's close.

# CHAPTER TWENTY-ONE

• • • • • • • • • • • • • • • • • • • • • • • • • • •

Let her go," someone says.

Thorpe's hand untangles from my hair, and I fall to all fours, palming the grass beneath me while I try to catch my breath. I look over my shoulder, finding Thorpe, hands raised, and the dark metal gleam of a gun at the back of his head.

Vaughn is holding the gun.

"Kevin Thorpe," he says, pulling something from his waistband. "You're under arrest for transportation of stolen goods and for the assault of James Westfield. Now listen good, because I'm only reading you these rights once."

I try to catch my breath, listen as Thorpe's rights continue, a steady stream from the familiar dark man with the nice smile. Vaughn.

When he's done with the rights, Vaughn turns Thorpe around so he can't look at me. Or maybe so I don't have to see him.

There's more noise in the trees, and I'm scuttling backward on the ground when a man and a woman—both wearing bulletproof vests and earpieces—come into view. They take Thorpe from Vaughn, and that's when I realize Vaughn's wearing a vest too, one with FBI printed across the front. My eyes move back toward the road. The shiny bumper isn't a car—it's an unmarked van. Vaughn isn't a PI. He's an FBI agent.

He reaches down to help me up, still smiling. "My name is Special Agent Bennett. Vaughn Bennett. I'm with the FBI, and I've been working undercover."

I grab his arm as soon as I'm steady. "Deputy Nelson got away. And Joel! There's a man—tall with white hair. He left on Deke's boat. You have to—"

"We're pursuing Nelson now. Mr. Carmichael was intercepted. Looks like he was meeting a larger vessel just east of the inlet. The boat might have had enough gas for that, but it wasn't enough to run from the Coast Guard." He smiles. "We'd have been here earlier, but we were finishing up with another suspect on the docks."

*Charlie. That really is why Tom didn't come.*

My head is swimming, and my cut has broken open. I can feel blood seeping into the gauze. I sniff back sudden tears. "Is Deacon all right? The boy my age."

"Mr. Westfield is just fine," he says. "We'll worry about the rest. For now, I want you to breathe, Emmie. Can you do that? The ambulance should be here any minute."

He lays a steady hand on my shoulder, and it's then that a few tears spill down my cheeks. "I heard you talking to Chelsea that day. I found your note too, but the rain smeared it."

"I wanted you to steer clear of Thorpe. We weren't sure who was involved, but my money was on him. I'd hoped the warning would get you to talk to me."

"Why didn't you just call me?"

"Mr. Carmichael's *business* involved lots of people in the community. If I'd been sure of reaching you directly, I would have, but your family plan only had phones listed for Tim, Mary, and Landon May."

Because I took over Landon's phone. One more way I slid neatly into his place.

"Chelsea's on her way home. We know she's safe now," Vaughn says. "I'm sorry if I frightened you that day in the store."

I nod absently. "How did you find us today?"

The smile is back. "Chelsea called this morning from Charleston."

"Joel was going to try to find her in Charleston," I say, feeling a stab of anger. "She could have been in danger."

"The only interest he had in finding Chelsea was figuring out who she was talking to and how much we knew. And we did have her aunt's house under guard. After filling Chelsea in on the truth, it was too dangerous to leave her here."

"So you're the one who took her phone."

He nods. "Yes, ma'am. And her aunt and uncle were under strict instruction to take calls from no one. I didn't count on Perry finding her aunt's cell phone number. Chelsea called after he spoke with her. She gave us the address, said she believed this is where Deacon would hide. She didn't trust Perry enough to tell him."

"She knew. She knew and she didn't sell us out." I feel teary again. "The sheriff isn't involved, he protected us. Is he all right?"

"He's plenty banged up, but he should be just fine."

After all those ugly confrontations, after everything...he was the one who saved us. I swallow thickly and hear new sirens.

Vaughn nods, keeping that hand on my arm to steady me. "That'll be the ambulances."

They both head past us, to the house at the back. Vaughn taps something I'm guessing is an earpiece, but I shake my head.

"I can walk. I want to see Deacon."

After a quick assessing look, Vaughn leads me down the road. I stumble over the grass when I see behind the house. Officers in FBI vests—bulletproof vests—are everywhere. Some help Perry, who's sitting up now, near the hammock. Others cluster on the tiny dock. Three boats bob in the water now—Deke's and two I don't recognize, one with a bar of lights across the top. Police boat. Lots of guys over there. My stomach squeezes. Is Joel one of them? Is Deacon?

Paramedics hop out of the squad, and an agent, another woman in an FBI vest, helps Deacon up and starts walking him toward us. He isn't cuffed. He isn't arrested.

Relief hits me like a wall. My knees go limp, and my arm flails, catching Vaughn's sleeve to steady myself.

"Let's get you to the ambulance," he says, but I pull away from him.

"Deacon." My voice fails, losing his name in a crackle of breath. I try again. "Deacon!"

He whirls, one eye swollen shut and a bruise shadowing his jaw. We stumble across the grass, and I'm sort of expecting Perry or Vaughn or *someone* to stop us. No one does.

He draws short a couple of feet away, eyes darting toward my bandaged hand. Blood seeps through the gauze—a bright red bloom against the white. I think of hiding it but remember what he said about getting better at this. I have to let him try.

He sucks in a breath that shakes. "Emmie—"

"Just close your eyes," I tell him. "Just close them."

As soon as he does, I hurl myself at him. The hug is too hard, so rough we're stumbling a little to stay upright. But Deacon doesn't loosen his arms, so I don't either.

"Did he hurt you?" His words are muffled in my shirt.

"I'm fine." I slide my good hand down his warm back. "Are you all right?"

"Yeah, I…"

He trails off, and I hear the sound of footsteps on the dock, then on the grass. Deacon's fingers bite into my ribs even harder, his arms flexing as he lifts his head and looks that direction.

"You son of a bitch!"

I disentangle myself, turning to see Joel on the dock, looking our way. I keep myself pressed to Deacon, my arms around his waist. I can feel that he wants to lunge.

With at least ten agents with guns, I don't think there's a chance in hell of that happening, and Deacon stills, jaw grinding. He must see them too. Even cuffed and being led to the waiting FBI van, Joel keeps his eyes right on us.

"Did you give Dad the pills too?" Deacon snarls. "You did everything else. Used us, lied to us, *framed me* for this whole damn mess."

Two of the FBI agents start to move in between them, but Vaughn holds up his hand. Shakes his head. Probably best to get all the details he can. I see Joel's blue eyes go soft, and he smiles a smile I've seen a thousand times.

It always seemed genuine until today.

"I can't imagine what you're talking about, Dink. You're like family to me."

Those are my words he's using, and his sweet-as-honey voice sets the hair on the back of my neck on end. Deacon makes a sound between a growl and a sob. I hold him tight but force myself to look hard at Joel's face. He looks like the nicest guy in the world. Even now.

Vaughn flicks his hands, and the FBI agents lead him away, and fury burns up through me, sudden and bright.

"What about your dead family?" I shout after him. He doesn't flinch. "Or the director you know so well at Duke. Was any of it true?" I shout after him.

"It was what you wanted to hear," Joel says. "That's what matters."

There's a bite to his tone that I don't recognize, and I know that's the real Joel. Hiding under all the warm smiles and free coffees lies the heart of a man who sold his soul and made a small fortune for it.

He did tell me what I wanted to hear. Before this, I would have never believed something so awful of him, no matter the proof. Before this, maybe I would have been happier with a lie.

"This will kill Chelsea," Deacon says. "And Dad..." He trails off, shaking his head.

I touch his face and force his chin down until he looks at me. "This isn't going to kill any of us. This is something we're going to survive together."

"Emmie?" It's Vaughn this time, behind my shoulder. "I want

to get that hand looked at, and it's time to call your parents. And Deacon, I'd like you to head to the hospital too. Maybe I can drive you. Ask a few questions on the way?"

Deacon nods and lets me go. I give him a tremulous smile and let the paramedics swarm in to fuss. They hover at my hand, my knees, over all the places where I'm hurting. Then they strap me onto a narrow gurney and load me into the ambulance.

As they pull away, I close my eyes, feeling the tears roll down my temples. They ask me if I'm crying because of the pain, but I don't answer. I don't know why the tears come now. They just do.

\* \* \*

I'm staring at twelve ugly black stitches when the curtain to my emergency room partition is tugged open. I see dark hair and a sharply carved profile, and my chest swells like the chorus of a song.

"Hi, you," I say.

Deacon turns, and I hold in a gasp, taking in his purpling left eye and puffy jaw. It's already worse.

"You look horrible," I say.

His laugh is soft, and his one good eye is still beautiful as he squeezes himself into the bed beside me. "You have a knack for telling it like it is, you know."

"Someone's got to keep you in line," I say.

"There's a line?" he teases, but I can see the apology in his eyes. His smile wavers. "I'm going to try harder, Emmie."

He doesn't have to say anything else. He presses his forehead to mine and laces our fingers together. Then he feathers a soft kiss over my lips, and that doesn't feel like a bad choice at all.

I close my eyes for just a second, but then I'm startled by a familiar soft voice.

"I'm so sorry."

Deacon jerks beside me, looking as groggy as I feel. I blink up at the dark-haired figure sniffling next to my bed. Chelsea.

Deacon flies off of the bed and hugs her off of her feet. I'm crying and she's crying and Deacon's saying he's sorry over and over again into her shoulder. She can't seem to apologize enough either. Eventually, Chelsea nestles in beside me. She curls in to hug me, bumping my bad hand. I hiss, and Deacon's right there on the other side, fingers feathering over my hair.

"You all right?" he asks, and his face is so tender it might break me.

I nod, seeing Chelsea's lips part out of the corner of my eye. First she looks surprised. Then she looks like she might smile.

Two shadows appear in the curtain opening behind her, and my stomach goes tight.

"Mom? Dad?"

For a moment, the room is frozen. Deacon's face shutters, and Chelsea tenses. She plucks at Deacon's shirt, and they both peel themselves off my bed to stand across from my parents. It leaves me stuck in the middle—between the people I love most.

I lick my lips and hope to God it won't always be like this between us.

"I'm going to just take my brother back to his own room," Chelsea says. "Or area. Whatever."

The Westfield siblings cling to each other as they head past my parents. My mom won't look at them. As much as I love her, it stings like a slap. I give them a pleading look, and finally, it's my dad who relents.

"Chelsea, Deacon…" he starts.

They stop and turn, and I feel their wariness like it's my own. I stare hard at my dad's head, willing him to be kind.

"I'm very sorry for all that you two are going through today."

Deacon nods, but his eyes cut away. He's never going to be the one they'll want, but it's not their choice. Not anymore.

"Thank you, Mr. May," Chelsea says, and then they're gone.

My parents rush in then, and I can see tear tracks through my mom's makeup. It's like a knife in the gut. Mom checked her mascara at her own mother's funeral, so she had to be scared to death.

My apology is lost in my suddenly tight throat. Dad hugs me first, pressing a scratchy kiss to the top of my head. That finally spurs her forward. Her heels click against the hospital floor, and her soft hands go to my face. She looks me over, wincing at every cut, every bruise.

And then she hugs me so hard I can barely breathe.

"I thought I lost you," she says, her voice breaking on a sob. "I thought I lost you."

She cries with her lips to my hair, and I stroke her back with my one good hand, trying to ease her back from the edge. "I'm right here. I'm safe."

She sucks in a shaky breath. "You were with *that boy*."

"I still am." Her hands grow stiff, but I just hug her tighter.

"I'm still with Deacon, and I'm still not going anywhere. You won't lose me."

I repeat it until she breathes again, until she loosens her hold, finally pulling back to accept the tissues my father offers.

"Look at me," she says with a watery laugh. "I'm a fine mess. I've got to pull myself together here."

My dad nudges me gently with a smile. "This is going to be front page news, kiddo. I don't know what to think. Black-market diamonds? Joel Carmichael arrested?"

"I can tell you what I know if you want," I offer. I've been patching together pieces from nurses and paramedics since the ride over.

"Oh, sugar, you don't have to do that," Mom says, still sniffling. "Heaven knows you've had too much excitement already."

I hesitate but then sag back into my pillows. No point in keeping secrets anymore. All the closets are wide open, and these skeletons aren't mine, so they're free to dance.

"*Reader's Digest* version?" I offer.

Dad nods, and Mom clutches her tissues.

"Joel is in jail because he's a con artist. He's befriended the Westfields because of the boats. They think he's been moving diamonds for a long time. Paid off people in town too. Two of the boat guys. Even Deputy Nelson. He had Mr. Westfield beaten because he was getting in the way."

Mom's hand flutters to her throat. "Right here in Beaufort under all our noses. My God."

Dad's shock is quiet. I see it ripple over his face like an

earthquake. Finally, he swallows hard. "And the sheriff? What about Martin?"

I think about the gun to Deacon's head, the nasty threats he dangled over me. In the end, all that screaming was nothing more than a trick of the light, hiding a decent man underneath.

"You were right about him." I smile. "He saved our lives."

Mom goes back to kissing my head, stroking my hair. And Dad settles next to me on a doctor's stool, pointing at the stitches running down my hand.

"There's more you're not telling us," he says.

"No," Mom says, touching my face. "She's been through enough. She will tell us when she decides she's ready."

When I decide. I like the sound of that.

# CHAPTER TWENTY-TWO

· · · · · · · · · · · · · · · · · · · · · · · · · · ·

Four days after the arrests, the town is still crawling with news crews and rumors. The media part is annoying, but after three days of our phone and doorbell ringing nonstop, Mom snapped. She's put up no trespassing signs and called lawyers. She's even started a social media campaign to protect victims from so-called media harassment.

It's good. Gives her a mission.

We haven't talked much about things. I gave her the basics about my injuries and told her I would make no more promises on law school but that I would work hard to make her proud with my choices. She wasn't happy, but she's still speaking to me. It's something.

Agent Bennett filled me in a bit more on Joel's con. He'd been transporting and selling illegally obtained diamonds on Westfield boats for years and planting drugs whenever he needed Mr. Westfield a little less attentive. He definitely needed him less attentive for this last run, which is where Thorpe came in with a ski mask and a violent streak, creating a guaranteed leave of absence for poor Mr. Westfield.

Charlie worked as a snitch and a prep guy in town, but Thorpe was Joel's right hand. Joel had gotten Thorpe out of the trafficking charge in South Carolina, and he called for payment. Thorpe beat Mr. Westfield to a pulp so Joel's last run would go off without a hitch.

Joel's lies ran so deep there are only shards of truth in the ruins. He isn't even Joel Carmichael, but I asked Agent Bennett not to tell me his real name. I don't want to know.

I don't want to think of him at all.

The coordinates I found matched up with a known diamond dealer on a small island off the coast of South America. There was no Mr. Trumbull and no Westfield expansion—just a criminal client ready to partner with Joel for a new endeavor on another continent. The Trumbull charter with all the food and supplies I ordered? Bound for the South America coordinates. Joel had every intention of disappearing forever. He'd used the Westfields up, even emptied the company accounts with the power of attorney Mr. Westfield signed.

I remind myself at least once an hour that if they didn't have those coordinates, the FBI might not have caught the full scope of what they had planned. It's a good thing, even if it doesn't make me feel better about the role I unknowingly played.

"Hold still," Chelsea says from my bedroom floor, where she's kneeling. She's leaving glitter on my rug, and she might as well be using a paint roller to spackle on my eyeliner, but I do as I'm told, curling my fingers into my quilt.

"You're getting glitter on everything," I say, wondering if I have time to vacuum.

"You could use a little glitter in your life. Open your eyes."

I do, and Chelsea smiles. She's as gorgeous as ever, but she looks tired. Having your family's dirty laundry draped all over town will do that to you, I guess.

"How are you?" I ask. "Really?"

She moves in with more eyeliner, and I hold up my hands. "Nope. Not until you answer me. No more dodging, right, Chels?"

She sighs. "Right." She worries her lip before she answers. "I'm starting therapy. My counselor called this morning. So that'll be weird."

"It could be good. Did they say anything helpful yet?"

She flips her hair out of her eyes. "Just that they really feel I should go. I didn't want to, tried to get out of it today, but Deacon said if he's going to go to deal with his anger-management issues, then I should go too, so I can deal with my guilt."

"Guilt? Chelsea, why?"

"Because I trusted Joel. I loved him like family. If I had been more careful maybe—"

"Maybe nothing," I say. "There's no way to see something like that coming, but I hate how much it hurts you. I'm sorry."

"I'm the one who's sorry. I turned on my brother." She shakes her head. Looks sick. "On you. I even turned on Sheriff Perry when he called that morning. God, Joel had me tied up in so many knots. I could have killed you both."

"But you didn't. You saved us when you called Bennett," I point out.

She shrugs. "Maybe. I guess."

"Stop arguing it. You need to let this go. We both need to learn to let some things go."

She smirks. "Right. Does that mean you're going to chill with the cleaning obsession?"

"I'm going to try." I grin wide. "Now, enough eyeliner! We have pirate things to do."

Chelsea runs home to put her costume on, and I get dressed and wait for her. I even resist the urge to vacuum. For the first ten minutes at least. I'm just putting the sweeper away when the doorbell rings. I grab my hat and flip my eye patch down.

"Blackbeard better watch his booty," I tell my reflection, then I swish out of my room, pirate skirts trailing behind.

The door is already open, and my mother is playing gatekeeper. There's been a lot of this for the last four days.

I see Deacon's silhouette behind my mother's back. Her shoulders are iron-tight under her pink sweater. Her only contribution to Pirate Invasion is a tasteful silk skull and crossbones scarf knotted at her neck. And her only effort at civility is allowing Deacon to step inside the door, where he stands corralled like a muddy dog on our entry rug.

Ralph is already flopped at his feet, panting, but Mom's welcome is frostier.

"And what time do you propose to bring my daughter home?" she asks, her accent thick the way it only gets when she's irritated.

"Emmie and I haven't had the chance to discuss that, Mrs. May." Deke's voice is chilly too. This respect thing is new for him. I'm pretty sure he'd rather chew rusty nails.

Mom crosses her arms. "Well, my mama always told me proper planning is a sign of a good upbringing."

I slip into the space between them, my hand clamping onto her elbow. "Hi, Deacon," I say with a smile. "Mom, I'll be home by eleven, okay?"

"Well, I really think nine or ten might be late enough for such a—"

"Eleven," I repeat, and then I force a smile. "I mean, my normal weekend curfew is eleven, so that should be fine, right?"

This is hard for her, my new choice-making ways. Her lips are thin, and every inch of her seems poised to snap, but she holds it tight. Strangles that urge.

I hate that she won't accept him. And I love her for trying to accept this new me. In the end, she's the only mom I've got, so I break my tough-girl stance and wrap my arms around her.

I'm covered in layer upon layer of pirate garb, but she returns the embrace, her hands small and shaky around my waist.

"I love you," I say. When I pull back, there are tears in her eyes, but I smile. "Don't worry, we won't take the motorcycle. I know you'd be a nervous wreck with so many tourists around town."

She swallows thickly and squares her shoulders. "I'd appreciate that very much."

"Have a nice evening, Mrs. May," Deacon says.

Somewhere, pigs are flying. Because I never thought I'd see the day where Deacon would utter a sentence like that.

Outside on the porch, I turn to look him over. "You make a hell of a pirate."

And he really does. Knee-high boots and breeches and a hat tipped to carve wicked shadows across his face.

"I credit my black eye," he says.

I smile and tenderly touch the still-healing bruise while he checks me out. "I'm sure I should say something chivalrous," he says, "but you look ridiculously hot in that getup."

I grin. "Deke, you wouldn't be you with too many manners."

"I have manners."

"Well, you don't chew with your mouth open, so I suppose there's that." I lean in to kiss him but pull away quickly when there's a groan on the sidewalk.

"Okay, absolutely not."

I grin down at Chelsea, who's wearing a mermaid costume complete with sequined bra. With her ample chest, it's a dangerous choice, but she looks amazing. Sparkly and coiffed within an inch of her life.

"There will be no kissing," she says, wagging a finger in a way that makes me think of librarians. "We may have all made up, but I'm not going to play lookout while you two grope."

"Oh, there will definitely be kissing," Deke argues, running a thumb down the back of my arm. "But we'll try to keep it behind your back."

"Fine." Chelsea sniffs, but she takes my other arm, and we walk three wide down the sidewalk toward the center of town.

I can already hear the music from the big tents they put up. The streets will be swarmed with tourists and food trucks and temporary stages. The tourist stuff isn't always fun, but this is special. Tradition, I guess.

At the corner of Front Street, a couple of guys from school

see us. Seth is in the back, and from what I can see, he's turning twelve shades of red over Chelsea's outfit.

"You should go talk to him," I say, nudging Chelsea.

"No." She ducks her head, suddenly unsure. "Too many people are talking."

"Who?" Deacon's voice dips to a pirate growl. "I'll run them through with me sword!"

I roll my eyes. "That's plastic, and you have a blood phobia. Chelsea, you can do this."

"I can't," she says, but even if his friends are talking, Seth is still watching. Hopeful.

"Help?" Chelsea pleads. This is my friend of old, the one who clung to my arm and my advice. I'll still be that lifeline. Always. But I know she has to do some of this for herself.

I pull my arm free and give her a smile. "Yes, you can."

"You just hold your head high and walk on," Deacon says.

"One step at a time," I say.

Chelsea takes my still-tender right hand and Deacon takes my left. Across the street, I see a group of incoming seniors. Some duck their heads, pretend not to see. But Seth smiles wide, waving us over. Chelsea's grip on my hand loosens, and I smile.

"One step at a time," she repeats.

The light turns green, and I nod ahead. "Here we go."

# ACKNOWLEDGMENTS

· · · · · · · · · · · · · · · · · · · · · · · · · · · · ·

I keep thinking this section will get shorter, but with every book, there are new, amazing people to thank. Not a terrible problem to have, I suppose.

First and foremost, thanks to God, who plants my ideas and enough stubbornness to see them through.

To my amazing agent, Cori Deyoe, for all the wise input and unfailing support. To my lovely and insightful editor, Aubrey Poole; my genius marketing coordinator, Alex Yeadon; my publicist, Amelia Narigon; and so many others, including Elizabeth Boyer, Sabrina Baskey, Elsie Lyons, Nicole Komasinski, and Kelly Lawler.

A huge thanks goes to the people of beautiful Beaufort, North Carolina, the hometown of my heart. Most especially to Donna Babington of the real Ann Street Inn (time for another visit!), JoAnn Yue, Jim Nolan, and to the area law enforcement officers who are warm and welcoming and *nothing* like some of the officers in my book. My fictional take on Beaufort is a bit different to fit aspects of the story, but I promise there's no substitute for the original.

I'm surrounded by a group of incomparable writing friends who provide wisdom, support, love, and laughter. This is my writing family, and I am richly blessed to know them. To Margaret

Peterson Haddix, Julia Devillers, Lisa Klein, Erin McCahan, Linda Gerber, and my darling AW support friends, Edith Pattou and Jody Casella. To my lovely Doomsdaisies, Pintip Dunn, Meg Kassel, Stephanie Winklehake, Cecily White, and of course, Romily Bernard.

To Sheri and Robin, who often feed me wine and carbs while providing sage advice. And to Margaret, Susan, and Mel, whose kindness and cheerleading is so appreciated.

A huge shout out to the readers, bloggers, teachers, and librarians who have made my journey so lovely. You are rock stars, and I adore you.

*My Secret to Tell* was written during a very tough year for me, and so many people supported me through this project. Thanks to Sharon, Karen, Sheila, Angela, Debi, Debbie, Kathy, Paul, Jon, Melissa, Colin, Cameran, Leigh Anne, Esther, and Christy. You all loved me when I needed it most. Thank you.

No book of mine would ever happen without my endlessly supportive husband, David, and our three babies, who aren't even close to babies anymore. Ian, Adrienne, and Lydia, I'm so amazed by the people you're becoming. Keep being exactly who you are.

In closing, Dad, I miss you so much. I wish you were still here with us, but I'm finding my peace, just like you hoped I would. Your voice is still here, guiding my heart, and for that, I'm truly grateful. I love you. Always.

# GONE TOO FAR

## Natalie D. Richards

### SEND ME A NAME. MAKE SOMEONE PAY.

Piper Woods can't wait to graduate. To leave high school—and all the annoying cliques—behind. But when she finds a mysterious notebook filled with the sins of her fellow students, Piper's suddenly drowning in their secrets.

And she's not the only one watching…

An anonymous text invites Piper to choose: the cheater, the bully, the shoplifter. The popular kids with their dirty little secrets. And with one text, Piper can make them pay.

But the truth can be dangerous…

Read on for an excerpt from

# Six Months Later

by Natalie D. Richards

# CHAPTER ONE

. . . . . . . . . . . . . . . . . . . . . . . . .

I'm sitting next to the fire alarm, and my best friend is going down in flames. Irony or divine intervention? I can practically feel the metal handle under my fingers. It might as well be whispering my name.

Tempting. One strategic arm stretch and I could send this whole school into an evacuation frenzy.

I could end Maggie's nightmare *right* now.

At the front of the classroom, she swallows hard. She is as pale and shaky as the paper in her hands.

"The social p-pressures and isolation encountered b-by male n-n—"

I can't let her suffer like this.

Maggie shakes her head and tries to shrug it off with a sheepish grin. "S-sorry."

"It's all right," Mrs. Corwin says, playing with the cat pendant around her neck. "There's no reason to be scared."

She thinks stuttering is a fear problem? Aren't teachers supposed to know about speech issues and all that crap? Then again, what can I expect from a woman who has professionally framed pictures of her beloved Siamese, Mr. Whiskers, on her desk?

Maggie takes a breath. "The p-pressures and isolation

encountered by male n-nurses in a predominantly f-female occupation is a compelling argument f-f-f—" She trails off, going crimson.

Someone snickers from the front.

"Go on, Maggie," Mrs. Corwin says. Again.

I'm going to do it.

Beside me, Blake Tanner shifts in his chair. I know this partly because I have good peripheral vision, but mostly because I have freakishly sensitive Blake radar. I hesitate, breathing in the clean hint of his cologne, watching him softly drum a thumb on his desktop.

My face goes hot. I can't do this with him sitting here. I'm completely invisible to this guy. And now I'm finally going to get his attention by, what? By pulling a fire alarm? Yes, I'm sure that will send a great message. To the guy who's been on the student council since the eighth grade.

Maggie tosses her hair back, forging on. "It's a compelling argument f-for s-s-sexism against men. In most modern contexts, concerns about s-s-s-s—"

Maggie goes pink and then red. Tyler and Shannon laugh in the back, and my eyes start to well up. Screw it. I can't sit here for one more second of one more minute.

I sink down as far as I can in my chair and start sliding my arm back along the wall. I reach up, but I'm grasping blind. It kind of hurts. I touch something cool and metal. Bingo. Two seconds and this misery is over.

Blake clears his throat and I bite my lip. Is he watching me?

What's wrong with me? Of course he's not watching me.
I'm invisible.

I turn my head because I'm sure I feel someone's eyes on me.
I do.

Adam Reed. He's slouched low in his seat, his dark hair in
desperate need of the business end of a pair of scissors.

Adam arches one of his brows at me. The half smile on his lips
asks me what I'm waiting for. I don't really have an answer, so I
curl my fingers over the alarm handle and pull hard. And then I
kiss my detention-free junior year good-bye.

• • •

Maggie is waiting outside the principal's office. She's got a couple
of notebooks clutched in her arms and a pencil securing her
strawberry blond waves into a bun.

The office door is barely closed when she starts in on me.
"What were you thinking? You c-could have been expelled."

I sling my backpack over my shoulder and offer our school
secretary, Mrs. Love, a wave. Maggie takes the cue and follows
me briskly back into the hallway. Students are slamming locker
doors and texting madly in the few minutes between periods.

Someone whistles, and across the hall, Connor holds two
thumbs up. "Let's hear it for fire safety!"

The hallway bursts into a smattering of applause and wolf calls.
I blush but give a little bow with a flourish of my hand.

We make our way to the stairs, climbing them two at a time.

"So what happened, Chloe? How b-bad is it?"

"I got a week of detention and a lecture about applying my interest in psychology to evaluating my episodes of acting out."

Maggie looks away, and I can tell she's biting her tongue.

I know that look. It means she's working hard to say something in a way that won't offend the hell out of me.

"Spit it out. You're obviously dying to insert commentary."

She sighs. "Look, I know you w-wanted to help me, but you've got to start thinking about yourself, Chloe. Sometimes it's like you're running away from everything you want."

I try not to look as hurt as I feel. "It's not like I'm afraid of being good, Mags."

She just laughs and takes my arm. "You jumped off the Third Street Bridge on a *dare*, which proves you're not afraid of anything. It also proves you're insane."

"Watch it."

I take a breath as we pass the drinking fountains, heading close to the last stretch of lockers in the hall. An otherwise unremarkable place in this building except for the fact that it's the Blake Zone.

As if on cue, he closes his locker door and appears, the tall, popular king of this lonely hallway. He laughs at a joke I don't hear. It's a perfect laugh that matches his perfect teeth and his perfect everything else.

I sigh. "Did Blake seem...disappointed?"

She blows out an impatient breath and rolls her eyes at me. "I didn't really think to dissect Blake's expression in the chaos and p-panic of the fire evacuation."

Blake laughs again, and I turn away, my cheeks burning. "Right. Sorry."

She gives me a sly grin. "Want me to go ask him?"

I slump back against the wall with a sigh. "How is it that I'm not the one who talks to boys? I'm the bridge jumper, the alarm puller—"

"The streaker," Maggie adds.

"That was one time! And technically, I was in my undies, but yes. How is it that you, High Queen of the Honor Roll, are better at this than me?"

"The stutter makes me a wild card," she says, winking. "No one ever sees me coming. And you talk t-to plenty of guys."

My gaze lingers on the stretch of Blake's polo across his shoulders, the ends of his hair curling over his collar. "Yeah, well. Not that one."

"I've got to g-get to class," Maggie says. "Speaking of which, did you remember to pick up your GPA at the office this morning?"

I feign a big, carefree smile. "Gosh, I must have completely forgotten. But I totally signed up for the SAT study group you told me about."

"And somehow forgot t-to ask for your GPA?" she asks, clearly unconvinced.

"Oh, who cares about a GPA anyway?"

She blinks at me, arms crossed. "Uh, every college you'll be applying to."

"Right. Well, finals aren't until next week. I can fix it."

Her eyes go dark. "Fix it? How bad is it?"

"Um, I—" The warning bell rings, saving me from another lie. "Gotta dash. Study hall and all. Yep, that's me. Study, study, study."

I slip inside the door and hear her calling after me. "You're running out of time, Chloe!"

She's got a point. I have exactly six days left of my junior year to turn my GPA into something that won't doom me to serving bad eggs at Trixie's Diner for the rest of my life. The urgency should inspire me to use every minute of my study hall period. It *really* should.

I pick up my biology notes, but it's all *cellular* this and *genetic* that, and my eyelids feel heavy after two lines. Why can't I get my act together?

Everyone around me is in full-force cram mode. Of course they are. Even Alexis, who spent the whole year reading *Vogue* behind her textbooks, is flipping through a stack of note cards. I'm officially the last slacker standing.

Maybe I could make a waitressing gig awesome. Except I don't want a waitressing gig. I only want one gig, and it doesn't involve rushing baskets of fries to hungry truckers.

It involves a doctorate degree in psychology.

How am I going to get through twelve years of college if I can't even stay awake in study hall?

Too bad I can't make a career out of sleeping in class undetected. I could tutor people in *that*. It's all about the posture. Chin in palm says bored. Chin on knuckles says deeply in thought.

And that sunbeam drifting through the window next to my desk? It says, *Go to sleep, Chloe.*

I tilt my head, watching the late May sunshine stroke my arms with soft, golden fingers. I do have all weekend to study. And I've got that stupid study group tonight, so I'm taking steps in the right direction. How much harm could one *teeny* little catnap do?

I give into the warmth and let my eyes slip closed. I'll worry about my lack of self-discipline after the bell rings.

But the bell doesn't ring.

There's no sound at all to wake me, just a cold sinking feeling in my middle. The hair on the back of my neck prickles, and my heart changes rhythm. Skips one beat. Then another.

And I know something is horribly wrong.

# ABOUT THE AUTHOR

. . . . . . . . . . . . . . . . . . . . . . . . . . . . .

The author of *Six Months Later* and *Gone Too Far*, Natalie spent years writing factual, necessary things for financial and legal companies before she decided she's much better suited to making things up. Natalie lives in central Ohio with her husband, children, three antisocial hermit crabs, and an overgrown dust mop named Yeti.